# The Return of Don Quixote

# The Return of Don Quixote

**G. K. Chesterton**

Waking Lion Press

ISBN 978-1-60096-828-0

Published by Waking Lion Press, an imprint of The Editorium

Additions to original text © 2006 by The Editorium. All rights reserved. Printed in the United States of America.

Waking Lion Press™, the Waking Lion Press logo, and The Editorium™ are trademarks of The Editorium, LLC

The Editorium, LLC
West Valley City, UT 84128-3917
wakinglionpress.com
wakinglion@editorium.com

# Contents

# Chapter 1

# A Hole in the Caste

The end of the longest room at Seawood Abbey was full of light; for the walls were almost made of windows and it projected upon a terraced part of the garden above the park on an almost cloudless morning. Murrel, called Monkey for some reason that everybody had forgotten, and Olive Ashley were taking advantage of the light to occupy themselves with painting; though she was painting on a very small scale and he on a very large one. She was laying out peculiar pigments very carefully, in imitation of the flat jewellery of medieval illumination, for which she had a great enthusiasm, as part of a rather vague notion of a historic past. He, on the other hand, was highly modern, and was occupied with several pails full of very crude colours and with brushes which reached the stature of brooms. With these he was laying about him on large sheets of lath and canvas, which were to act as scenery in some private theatricals then in preparation. They could not paint, either of them; nor did they imagine that they could. But she was in some sense trying to do so; and he was not.

"It's all very well for you to talk about discords," he was saying somewhat defensively, for she was a critical lady, "but your style of painting narrows the mind. After all, scene-painting is only illumination seen through a microscope."

"I hate microscopes," she observed briefly.

"Well, you look as if you wanted one, poring over that stuff," replied her companion, "in fact I fancy I have seen people

*1*

screwing a great thing in their eye while they did it. I hope you won't go so far as that: it wouldn't suit your style at all."

This was true enough, no doubt, for she was a small, slight girl, with dark delicate features of the kind called regular; and her dark green dress, which was aesthetic but the reverse of Bohemian, had something akin to the small severities of her task. There was something a shade old maidish about her gestures, although she was very young. It was noticeable that though the room was strewn with papers and dusters and the flamboyant failures of Mr. Murrel's art, her own flat colour-box, with its case and minor accessories, were placed about her with protective neatness. She was not one of those for whom is written the paper of warnings sometimes sold with paint-boxes; and it had never been necessary to adjure her not to put the brush in the mouth.

"What I mean," she said, resuming the subject of micro-scopes, "is that all your science and modern stuff has only made things ugly, and people ugly as well. I don't want to look down a microscope any more than down a drain. You only see a lot of horrid little things crawling about. I don't want to look down at all. That's why I like all this old Gothic painting and building; in Gothic all the lines go upwards, right up to the very spire that points to heaven."

"It's rude to the point," said Murrel, "and I think they might have given us credit for noticing the sky."

"You know perfectly well what I mean," replied the lady, painting placidly, "all the originality of those medieval people was in the way they built their churches. The whole point of them was the pointed arches."

"And the pointed spears," he assented. "When you didn't do what they liked, they just prodded you. Too pointed, I think. Almost amounting to a hint."

"Anyhow the gentlemen then prodded each other with their spears," answered Olive, "they didn't go and sit on plush seats to see an Irishman pummelling a black man. I wouldn't see a modern prize-fight for the world; but I shouldn't mind a bit being a lady at one of the old tournaments."

"You might be a lady, but I shouldn't be a lord," said the scene-painter gloomily. "Not my luck. Even if I were a king, I should only be drowned in a butt of sack and never smile again. But it's more my luck to be born a serf or something. A leper, or some such medieval institution. Yes, that's how it would be— the minute I'd poked my nose into the thirteenth century I'd be appointed Chief Leper to the king or somebody; and have to squint into church through that little window."

"You don't squint into church through any window at present," observed the lady, "nor has it occurred to you even to do so through the door."

"Oh, I leave all that to you," he said, and proceeded to splash away in silence. He was engaged on a modest interior of "The Throne Room of Richard Coeur de Lion," which he treated in a scheme of scarlet, crimson and purple which Miss Ashley strove in vain to arrest; though she really had some rights of protest in the matter, having both selected the medieval subject and even written the play, so far as her more sportive collaborators would allow her. It was all about Blondel, the Troubadour, who serenaded Coeur de Lion and many other people; including the daughter of the house; who was addicted to theatricals and kept him at it. The Hon. Douglas Murrel, or Monkey, cheerfully confronted his ill-success in scene-painting, having succeeded equally ill in many other things. He was a man of wide culture, and had failed in all subjects. He had especially failed in politics; having once been called the future leader of his party, whichever it was. But he had failed at the supreme moment to seize the logical connection between the principle of taxing deer-forests and that of retaining an old pattern of rifle for the Indian Army: and the nephew of an Alsatian pawn-broker, to whose clear brain the connection was more apparent, had slipped into his place. Since then he had shown that taste for low company which has kept so many aristocrats out of mischief and their country out of peril, and shown it incongruously (as they sometimes do) by having something vaguely slangy and horsey about his very dress and appearance, as of an objectless ostler. His hair was very fair and beginning to blanch quite prematurely; for he also was young, though many years older than his companion. His face, which was plain but not common-place, habitually wore a dolorous expression which was almost comic; especially in connection with the sporting colours of his neckties and waistcoats, which were almost as lively as the colours on his brush.

"I've a negro taste," he explained, laying on a giant streak of sanguine colour, "these mongrel greys of the mystics make me as tired as they are. They talk about a Celtic Renaissance; but I'm for an Ethiopian Renaissance. The banjo to be more truly what's-its-name than old Dolmetch's lute. No dances but the deep, heart-weary Break-Down—there's tears in the very name—no historical characters except Toussaint L'Ouverture and Booker Washington, no fictitious characters except Uncle Remus and Uncle Tom. I bet it wouldn't take much to make the Smart Set black their faces as they used to whiten their hair. For my part, I begin to feel a meaning in all my mis-spent life. Something tells me I was intended for a Margate nigger. I *do* think vulgarity is so nice, don't you?"

She did not reply; indeed she seemed a little absent-minded. Her humour had been faintly shrewdish; but when her face fell into seriousness it was entirely young. Her fine profile with parted lips suddenly suggested not only a child, but a lost child.

"I remember an old illumination that had a negro in it," she said at last. "It was one of the Three Kings at Bethlehem, with gold crowns. One of them was quite black; but he had a red dress like flames. So you see, even about a nigger and his bright clothes—there is a way of doing it. But we can't get the exact red they used now; I know people who have really tried. It's one of the lost arts, like the stained glass."

"This red will do very well for our modern purpose," said Murrel equably.

She still looked out abstractedly at the circle of the woods under the morning sky. "I rather wonder sometimes," she said, "what are our modern purposes.

"Painting the town red, I suppose," he answered.

4

"The old gold they used has gone too," she proceeded. "I was looking at an old missal in the library yesterday. You know they always gilt the name of God? I think if they gilt any word now it would be Gold."

The industrious silence which ensued was at length broken by a distant voice down the corridors calling out: "Monkey!" in a boisterous and imperative manner. Murrel did not in the least object to being called a monkey, yet he always felt a slight distaste when Julian Archer called him one. It had nothing to do with jealousy; though Archer had the same vague universality of success as Murrel had of failure. It had to do with a fine shade between familiarity and intimacy, which men like Murrel are never ready to disregard, however ready they may be to black their faces. When he was at Oxford he had often carried ragging to something within measurable distance of murder. But he never threw people out of top windows unless they were his personal friends.

Julian Archer was one of those men who seem to be in a great many places at once; and to be very important for some reason which is difficult to specify. He was not a fool or a fraud: he acquitted himself with credit and moderation in the various examinations or responsibilities which appeared to be forced upon him. But spectators of the subtler sort could never quite understand why these things always were forced upon him, and not upon the man next door. Some magazine would have a symposium, let us say, on "Shall We Eat Meat?" in which answers would be obtained from Bernard Shaw, Dr. Saleeby, Lord Dawson of Penn and Mr. Julian Archer. A committee would be formed for a National Theatre or a Shakespeare Memorial: and speeches would be delivered from the platform by Miss Viola Tree, Sir Arthur Pinero, Mr. Comyns Carr and Mr. Julian Archer. A composite book of essays would be published called "The Hope of a Hereafter," with contributions by Sir Oliver Lodge, Miss Marie Corelli, Mr. Joseph McCabe and Mr. Julian Archer. He was a Member of Parliament and of many other clubs. He had written a historical novel; he was an admirable amateur actor: so that his claims to take the leading part in the play of "Blondel the Troubadour" could not be disputed. In all this there was nothing objectionable or even eccentric. His historical novel about Agincourt was quite good considered as a modern historical novel; that is, considered as the adventures of a modern public schoolboy at a fancy dress ball. He was in favour of moderate indulgence in meat; and moderate indulgence in personal immortality. But his temperate opinions were loudly and positively uttered, as in the deep and resonant voice which was now booming down the passages. He was one of those who can endure that silence which comes after a platitude. His voice went before him everywhere; as did his reputation and his photograph in the society papers; with its dark curls and bold handsome face. Miss Ashley remarked that he looked like a tenor. Mr. Murrel was content to reply that he did not sound like one.

He entered the room in the complete costume of a Troubadour, except for a telegram which he held in his hand. The complete costume of a troubadour compared favourably with that worn by Mr. Snodgrass, in being more becoming and equally historical. He had been rehearsing his part and was flushed with triumph and exertion; but the telegram, apparently, had rather put him out.

"I say," he said, "Braintree won't act."

"Well," said Murrel, painting stolidly, "I never thought he would."

"Rather rot, I know, having to ask a fellow like that: but there was simply nobody else. I told Lord Seawood it was rot to have it at this time of the year when all his friends are away. Braintree's only an acquaintance, of course, and I can't imagine how he even came to be that."

"It was a mistake, I believe," said Murrel, "Seawood called on him because he heard he was standing for Parliament as a Unionist. When he found it meant a Trade Unionist he was a bit put off, of course; but he couldn't make a scene. I fancy it would puzzle him to say what either of the terms mean."

"Don't you know what the term Unionist means?" asked Olive.

"Nobody knows that," replied the scene-painter, "why, I've been one myself."

"Oh, I wouldn't cut a fellow just because he was a Socialist," cried the broad-minded Mr. Archer, "why there was—" and he was silent, lost in social reminiscences.

"He isn't a Socialist," observed Murrel impassively, "He breaks things if you call him a Socialist. He is a Syndicalist."

"But that's worse, isn't it?" said the young lady, innocently.

"Of course we're all for social questions and making things better," said Archer in a general manner, "but nobody can defend a man who sets one class against another as he does; talking about manual labour and all sorts of impossible Utopias. I've always said that Capital has its duties as well as its—."

"Well," interposed Murrel hastily, "I'm prejudiced in the present case. Look at me; you couldn't have anybody more manual than I am."

"Well, he won't act, anyhow," repeated Archer, "and we must find somebody. It's only the Second Troubadour, of course, and anybody can do it. But it must be somebody fairly young; that's the only reason I thought of Braintree."

"Yes, he is quite a young man yet," assented Murrel, "and no end of the young men seem to be with him."

"I detest him and his young men," said Olive, with sudden energy. "In the old days people complained of young people breaking out because they were romantic. But these young men break out because they are sordid; just prosaic and low, and wrangling about machinery and money—materialists. They just want a world of atheists, that would soon be a world of apes."

After a silence, Murrel crossed to the other end of the long room and could be heard calling a number into the telephone. There ensued one of those half conversations that make the hearer feel as if he were literally half-witted: but in this case the subject matter was fairly clear from the context.

"Is that you, Jack?—Yes, I know you did; but I want to talk to you about it—. At Seawood; but I can't get away, because I'm painting myself red like an Indian. Nonsense, it can't matter; you'll only be coming on business—. Yes, of course it's quite understood: what a pragmatical beast you are—there's no question of principle at all, I tell you. I won't eat you. I won't even paint you—all right."

He rang off and returned to his creative labours, whistling.

"Do you know Mr. Braintree?" asked Olive, with some wonder.

"You know I have a taste for low company," answered Murrel.

"Does it extend to Communists?" asked Archer, with some heat. "Jolly close to thieves."

"A taste for low company doesn't make people thieves," said Murrel, "it's generally a taste for high company that does that." And he proceeded to decorate a vivid violet pillar with very large orange stars, in accordance with the well-known style of the ornamentation of throne-rooms in the reign of Richard the First.

Chapter 2

# A Dangerous Man

John Braintree was a long, lean, alert young man with a black beard and a black frown, which he seemed to some extent to wear on principle, like his red tie. For when he smiled, as he did for an instant at the sight of Murrel's scenery, he looked pleasant enough. On being introduced to the lady, he bowed with a politeness that was formal and almost stiff; the style once found in aristocrats but now most common in well-educated artisans; for Braintree had begun life as an engineer.

"I came up here because you asked me, Douglas," he said, "but I tell you it's no good."

"Don't you like my scheme of colour?" asked Murrel. "It is much admired."

"Well," replied the other, "I don't know that I do particularly like your plastering romantic purple over all that old feudal tyranny and superstition; but that isn't my difficulty. Look here, Douglas; I came here on the strict understanding that I might say what I liked; but for all that I don't particularly want to talk against the man in his own house if I can help it. So perhaps the shortest way of putting the difficulty will be to say that the Miners' Union here has declared a strike; and that I am the secretary of the Miners' Union. And as I'm trying to spoil his work by staying out, I think it would be a little low down to spoil his play by coming in."

"What are you striking about?" asked Archer.

"Well, we want more money," replied Braintree coolly. "When two pennies will only buy one penny loaf we want two pennies

9

to buy it with. It is called the complexity of the Industrial System. But what counts for even more with the Union is the demand for recognition."

"Recognition of what?"

"Well, you see, the Trades Union doesn't exist. It is a grinding tyranny, and it threatens to destroy all British trade; but it doesn't exist. The one thing that Lord Seawood and all its most indignant critics are certain about, is that it doesn't exist. So, by way of suggesting that there might possibly be such an entity, we reserve the right to strike."

"And leave the whole wretched public without coal, I suppose," cried Archer heatedly, "if you do, I fancy you'll find public opinion is a bit too strong for you. If you won't get the coal and the Government won't make you, we'll find people who will get it. I, for one, would answer for a hundred fellows from Oxford and Cambridge or the City, who wouldn't mind working in the mine to spoil your conspiracy."

"While you're about it," replied Braintree contemptuously, "you might as well get a hundred coal-miners to finish Miss Ashley's illumination for her. Mining is a very skilled trade, my good sir. A coal-miner isn't a coal-heaver. You might do very well as a coal-heaver."

"I suppose you mean that as an insult," said Archer.

"Oh, no," answered Braintree, "a compliment."

Murrel interposed pacifically. "Why you're all coming round to my idea; first a coal-heaver, I suppose, and then a chimney-sweep and so on to perfect blackness."

"But aren't you a Syndicalist?" asked Olive with extreme severity. Then, after a pause, she added, "What is a Syndicalist?"

"The shortest way of putting it, I should say," said Braintree, with more consideration, "would be to say that, in our view, the mine ought to belong to the miner."

"Mine's mine, in fact," said Murrel, "fine feudal medieval motto."

"I think that motto is very modern," observed Olive a little acidly, "but how would you manage with the miner owning the mine?"

"Ridiculous idea, isn't it?" said the Syndicalist, "One might as well talk about the painter owning the paint-box."

Olive rose and walked to the French windows that stood open on the garden; and looked out, frowning. The frown was partly at the Syndicalist, but partly also at some thoughts of her own. After a few minutes' silence, she stepped out on to the gravel path and walked slowly away. There was a certain restrained rebuke about the action; but Braintree was too hot in his intellectualism to heed it.

"I don't suppose," he went on, "that anybody has ever realised how wild and Utopian it is for a fiddler to own his fiddle."

"Oh, fiddlesticks, you and your fiddle," cried the impetuous Mr. Archer, "how can a lot of low fellows—"

Murrel once more changed the subject to his original frivolities.

"Well, well," he said, "these social problems will never be settled till we fall back on my expedient. All the nobility and culture of France assembled to see Louis XVI put on the red cap. How impressive it will be when all our artists and leaders of thought assemble to see me reverently blacking Lord Seawood's face."

Braintree was still looking at Julian Archer with a darkened face.

"At present," he said, "our artists and leaders have only got so far as blacking his boots."

Archer sprang up as if he had been named as well as looked at.

"When a gentleman is accused of blacking boots," he said, "there is danger of his blacking eyes instead."

Braintree took one bony fist out of his pocket.

"Oh I told you," he said, "that we reserve the right to strike."

"Don't play the goat, either of you," insisted the peace-maker, interposing his large red paint-brush, "don't rampage, Jack. You'll put your foot in it—in King Richard's red curtains."

Archer retired slowly to his seat again; and his antagonist, after an instant's hesitation, turned to go out through the open windows.

"Don't worry," he growled, "I won't make a hole in your canvas. I'm quite content to have made a hole in your caste. What do you want with me? I know you're really a gentleman; but I like you for all that. But what good has your being a real gentleman or sham gentleman ever done to us? You know as well as I do that men like me are asked to houses like this, and they go there to say a word for their mates; and you are decent to them, and all sorts of beautiful women are decent to them, and everybody's decent to them; and the time comes when they become just—well, what do you call a man who has a letter to deliver from his friend and is afraid to deliver it?"

"Yes, but look here," remonstrated Murrel, "you've not only made a hole, but you've put me in it. I really can't get hold of anybody else now. It isn't to come on for a month; but there'll be fewer people still then; and we shall probably want that time to rehearse. Why can't you just do it as a favour? What does it matter what your opinions are? I haven't got any opinions myself; I used them all up at the Union when I was a boy. But I hate disappointing the ladies; and there really aren't any other men in the place."

Braintree looked at him steadily.

"Aren't any other men," he repeated.

"Well there's old Seawood, of course," said Murrel. "He's not a bad old chap in his way; and you mustn't expect me to take as severe a view of him as you do. But I own I can hardly fancy him as a Troubadour. There really and truly aren't any other men at all."

Braintree still looked at him.

"There is a man in the next room," he said, "there is a man in the passage; there is a man in the garden; there is a man at the front door; there is a man in the stables; there is a man in the kitchen; there is a man in the cellar. What sort of palace of lies have you built for yourselves, when you see all these round you every day and do not even know that they are men? Why do we strike? Because you forget our very existence when we do not strike. Tell your servants to serve you; but why should I?"

And he went out into the garden and walked furiously away.

12

"Well," said Archer at last, "I must confess I can't stand your friend at any price."

Murrel stepped back from his canvas and put his head on one side, contemplating it like a connoisseur.

"I think his idea about the servants is first-rate," he observed placidly. "Can't you fancy old Perkins as a Troubadour? You know the butler here, don't you? Or one of those footmen would Troub like anything."

"Don't talk nonsense," said Archer, irritably, "it's a small part, but he has to do all sorts of things. Why, he has to kiss the princess's hand."

"The butler would do it like a Zephyr," replied Murrel, "but perhaps we ought to look lower in the hierarchy. If he won't do it I will ask the footmen, and if they won't I will ask the groom, and if he won't I will ask the stable-boy, and if he won't I will ask the knife-boy, and if he won't I will ask whatever is lower and viler than a knife-boy. And if that fails I will go lower still, and ask the librarian. Why, of course! The very thing! The librarian!"

And with sudden impetuosity he slung his heavy paint-brush to the other side of the room and ran out into the garden, followed by the wondering Mr. Archer.

It was quite early in the morning; for the amateurs had risen some time before breakfast to act or paint; and Braintree always rose early, to write and send off a rigorous, not to say rabid, leading article for a Labour evening paper. The white light still had that pale pink tinge in corners and edges which must have caused the poet, somewhat fantastically, to equip the daybreak with fingers. The house stood high upon a lift of land that sank on two sides towards the Severn. The terraced garden, fringed with knots of tapering trees carrying white clouds of the spring blossom, with large flower-beds flung out in a scheme like heraldry, at once strict and gay, scarcely veiled, and did not confuse, the colossal curve of the landscape. Along its lines the clouds rolled up and lifted like cannon smoke, as if the sun were silently storming the high places of the earth. Wind and sun burnished the slanting grass; and they seemed to stand on the shining shoulder of the world. At a high angle, but as if by accident, stood a pedestal'd grey fragment from the ruins of the old abbey which had once stood on that site. Beyond was the corner of an older wing of the house towards which Murrel was making his way. Archer had the theatrical sort of good looks, as well as the theatrical sort of fine clothes, which is effective in such natural pageantry; and the picturesque illusion was clinched by a figure as quaintly clad which came out into the sunshine a few moments after. It was a young lady with a royal crown and red hair that looked almost as royal, for she habitually carried her head with something of haughtiness as well as health; and seemed to snuff up the breeze like the war-horse in scripture; to rejoice in her robes as they swept with the sweeping wind and land. Julian Archer in his close-fitting suit of three colours made up an excellent picture; beside which the modern colours of Murrel's tweeds and tie looked as common as those of the stablemen among whom he was in the habit of lounging.

Rosamund Severne, Lord Seawood's only daughter, was of the type that throws itself into things; and makes a splash. Her great beauty was of the exuberant sort, like her good-nature and good spirits; and she thoroughly enjoyed being a medieval princess—in a play. But she had none of the reactionary dreaminess of her friend and guest Miss Ashley. On the contrary, she was very up-to-date and exceedingly practical. Though finally frustrated by the conservatism of her father, she had early made an attempt to become a lady doctor; but had settled down into being a lady bountiful, of a boisterous kind. She had once also been very prominent on platforms and in political work; but whether to get women votes, or prevent their getting them, her friends could never remember.

Seeing Archer afar off, she called out in her ringing and resolute fashion: "I was looking for you; don't you think we ought to go through that scene again?"

"And I was looking for you," interrupted Murrel, "still more dramatic developments in the dramatic world. I say, do you know your own librarian by sight, by any chance?"

"What on earth have librarians got to do with it?" asked Rosamund in her matter-of-fact way. "Yes, of course, I know him. I don't think anybody knows him very well."

"Sort of book-worm, I suppose," observed Archer.

"Well, we're all worms," remarked Murrel cheerfully, "I suppose a book-worm shows a rather refined and superior taste in diet. But, look here, I rather want to catch that worm, like the early bird. I say, Rosamund, do be an early bird and catch him for me."

"Well, I am rather an early bird this morning," she replied, "quite a skylark."

"And quite ready for skylarking, I suppose," said Murrel. "But really, I'm quite serious; I mean dost thou despise the earth where cares abound; that is do you know the library where books abound, and can you bring me a real live librarian?"

"I believe he's in there now," said Rosamund with some wonder. "You've only got to go in and speak to him; though I can't imagine what you want."

"You always go to the point," said Murrel, "straight from the shoulder; true to the kindred points of heaven and home; you're the right sort of bird, you are."

"A bird of paradise," said Mr. Archer gracefully.

"I'm afraid you're a mocking bird," she answered laughing, "and we all know that Monkey is a goose."

"I am a worm and a goose and a monkey," assented Murrel. "My evolution never stops; but before I turn into something else let me explain. Archer, with his infernal aristocratic pride, won't allow the knife-boy to act as Troubadour, so I'm falling back on the librarian. I don't know his name, but we simply must get somebody."

"His name is Herne," answered the young lady a little doubtfully. "Don't go and—I mean he's a gentleman and all that; I believe he's quite a learned man."

But Murrel had already darted on in his impetuous fashion and disappeared round a corner of the house towards the glass doors leading into the library. But even as he turned the corner he stopped suddenly and stared at something in the middle distance. On the ridge of the high garden, where it fell away into the lower grounds, dark against the morning sky, stood two figures; the very last he would ever have expected to see standing together. One was John Braintree, that deplorable demagogue. The other was Olive Ashley. Even as he looked, it is true, Olive turned away with what looked like a gesture of anger or repudiation. But it seemed to Murrel much more extraordinary that they should have met than that they should have parted. A rather puzzled look appeared on his melancholy monkey face for a moment; then he turned and stepped lightly into the library.

Chapter 3

# The Ladder in the Library

The librarian at Seawood had once had his name in the papers; though he was probably unaware of the fact. It was during the great Camel Controversy of 1906, when Professor Otto Elk, that devastating Hebrew scholar, was conducting his great and gallant campaign against the Book of Deuteronomy; and had availed himself of the obscure librarian's peculiar intimacy with the Palaeo-Hittites. The learned reader is warned that these were no vulgar Hittites; but a yet more remote race covered by the same name. He really knew a prodigious amount about these Hittites, but only, as he would carefully explain, from the unification of the kingdom by Pan-El-Zaga (popularly and foolishly called Pan-Ul-Zaga) to the disastrous battle of Uli-Zamul, after which the true Palaeo-Hittite civilisation, of course, can hardly be said to have continued. In his case it can be said seriously that nobody knew how much he knew. He had never written a book upon his Hittites; if he had it would have been a library. But nobody could have reviewed it but himself.

In the public controversy his appearance and disappearance were equally isolated and odd. It seems that there existed a system or alphabet of Hittite hieroglyphics, which were different from all other hieroglyphics, which, indeed, to the careless eye of the cold world, did not appear to be hieroglyphics at all, but irregular surfaces of partially decayed stone. But as the Bible said somewhere that somebody drove away forty-seven camels, Professor Elk was able to spread the great and glad news that in the Hittite account of what was evidently the same incident, the researches of the learned Herne had already deciphered a distinct allusion to only forty camels; a discovery which gravely affected the foundations of Christian cosmology and seemed to many to open alarming and promising vistas in the matter of the institution of marriage. The librarian's name became quite current in journalism for a time, and insistence on the persecution or neglect suffered at the hands of the orthodox by Galileo, Bruno, and Herne, became an agreeable variation on the recognised triad of Galileo, Bruno, and Darwin. Neglect, indeed, there may in a manner have been; for the librarian of Seawood continued laboriously to spell out his hieroglyphics without assistance; and had already discovered the words "forty camels" to be followed by the words "and seven." But there was nothing in such a detail to lead an advancing world to turn aside or meddle with the musty occupations of a solitary student.

The librarian was certainly of the sort that is remote from the daylight, and suited to be a shade among the shades of a great library. His figure was long and lithe, but he held one shoulder habitually a little higher than the other; his hair was of a dusty lightness. His face was lean and his lineaments long and straight; but his wan blue eyes were a shade wider apart than other men's; increasing an effect of having one eye off. It was indeed rather a weird effect, as if his eye were somewhere else; not in the mere sense of looking elsewhere, but almost as if it were in some other head than his own. And indeed, in a manner, it was; it was in the head of a Hittite ten thousand years ago.

For there was something in Michael Herne which is perhaps in every specialist, buried under his mountains of material and alone enabling him to support them; something of what, when it gains vent in an upper air, is called poetry. He instinctively made pictures of the things he studied. Even discerning men, appreciative of many corners of history, would have seen in him only a dusty antiquarian, fumbling with pre-historic pots and pans or the everlasting stone hatchet; a hatchet that most of us are very willing to bury. But they would have done him an injustice. Shapeless as they were, these things to him were not idols, but instruments. When he looked at the Hittite hatchet he did imagine it as killing something for the Hittite pot; when he looked at the pot he did see it boiling, to cook something killed with the hatchet. He would not have called it "something," of course; but given the name of some sufficiently edible bird or beast; he was quite capable of making out a Hittite *menu*. From such faint fragments he had indeed erected a visionary and archaic city and state, eclipsing Assyria in its elephantine and unshapely enormity. His soul was afar off, walking under strange skies of turquoise and gold; amid head-dresses like high sepulchres and sepulchres higher than citadels; and beards braided as if into figured tapestries. When he looked out of the open library window at the gardener sweeping the trim garden walks of Seawood, it was not these things that he saw. He saw those huge enthroned brutes and birds that seemed to be hewn out of mountains. He saw those vast, overpowering faces, that seemed to have been planned like cities. There were even hints that he had allowed the Hittites to prey upon his mind to its slight unsettlement. A story was current of an incautious professor who had repeated idle gossip against the moral character of the Hittite princess, Pal-Ul-Gazil, and whom the librarian had belaboured with the long broom used for dusting the books and driven to take refuge on the top of the library steps. But opinion was divided as to whether this story was founded on fact or on Mr. Douglas Murrel.

Anyhow, the anecdote was at least an allegory. Few realise how much of controversial war and tumult can be covered by an obscure hobby. The fighting spirit has almost taken refuge in hobbies as in holes and corners of the earth; and left the larger public fields singularly dull and flat and free from real debate. It might be imagined that the *Daily Wire* was a slashing paper and the *Review of Assyrian Excavation* was a mild and peaceful one. But in truth it is the other way. It is the popular paper that has become cold and conventional, and full of clichés used without any conviction. It is the scholarly paper that is full of fire and fanaticism and rivalry. Mr. Herne could not contain himself when he thought of Professor Poole and his preposterous and monstrous suggestion about the Pre-Hittite sandal. He pursued the Professor, if not with a broom at least with a pen brandished like a weapon; and expended on these unheard-of questions energies of real eloquence, logic and living enthusiasm which the world will never hear of either. And when he discovered fresh facts, exposed accepted fallacies or concentrated on contradictions which he exposed with glaring lucidity, he was not an inch nearer to any public recognition but he was something which public men cannot invariably claim to be. He was happy.

For the rest, he was the son of a poor parson; he was one of the few who have succeeded in being unsociable at Oxford, not from positive dislike of society but from an equally positive love of solitude; and his few but persistent bodily exercises were either solitary like walking and swimming, or rather rare and eccentric, like fencing. He had a very good general knowledge of books and, having to earn his own living, was very glad to earn a salary by looking after the fine old library collected by the previous owners of Seawood Abbey. But the one holiday of his life had been full of hard work, when he went as a minor assistant in the excavations of Hittite cities in Arabia; and all his day-dreams were but repetitions of that holiday.

He was standing at the open French windows by which the library looked on to the lawn, with his hands in his trousers' pockets, and the rather blind look of introspection in his eyes when the green line of the garden was broken by the apparition of three figures, two of whom at least might have been considered striking, not to say startling. They might have been gaily coloured ghosts, come out of the past. Their costume was far from being Hittite, as even a humbler grade of specialism might well have perceived; but it was almost as outlandish. Only the third figure, in a light tweed jacket and trousers was of a reassuring modernity.

"Oh, Mr. Herne," a young lady was saying to him in courteous but rather confident tones; a young lady framed in a marvellous horned head-dress and a tight blue robe with hanging pointed sleeves. "We want to ask you a great favour. We are in no end of a difficulty."

Mr. Herne's eyes seemed to alter their focus, as if fitted with a new lens, to lose the distance and take in the foreground; a foreground that was filled with the magnificent young lady. It seemed to have a curious effect on him, for he was dumb for a moment, and then said with more warmth than might have been expected from the look of him.

"Anything whatever that I can do . . ."

"It's only to take a tiny little part in our play," she pleaded, "it's a shame to give you such a small one, but everybody has fallen through and we don't want to give up the whole thing."

"What play is it?" he asked.

"Oh, it's all nonsense, of course," she said easily, "it's called 'Blondel the Troubadour,' about Richard Coeur de Lion and serenades and princesses and castles and the usual sort of thing. But we want somebody for the Second Troubadour, who has to go about with Blondel and talk to him. Or rather be talked to, for, of course, Blondel does all the talking. It wouldn't take you long to learn your part." "Just twanging the light guitar," said Murrel encouragingly, "sort of medieval variant of playing on the old banjo."

"What we really want," said Archer more seriously, "is a rich romantic background, so to speak. That's what the Second Troubadour stands for; like 'The Forest Lovers,' boyhood's dreams of the past, full of knights errant and hermits and all the rest of it."

"Rather rough to ask anybody to be a rich romantic background at such short notice," admitted Murrel, "but you know the sort of thing. Do be a back-ground, Mr. Herne."

Mr. Herne's long face had assumed an expression of the greatest grief.

"I'm terribly sorry," he said, "I should have loved to help you in any way. But it's not my period."

While the others looked at him in a puzzled way he went on like a man thinking aloud.

"Garton Rogers is the man you want. Floyd is very good; but he's best on the Fourth Crusade. I'm sure the best advice I could give you is to go to Rogers of Balliol."

"I know him a bit," said Murrel, looking at the other with a rather twisted smile. "He was my tutor."

"Excellent!" said the librarian, "You couldn't do better."

"Yes, I know him," said Murrel gravely, "he's not quite seventy-three and entirely bald; and so fat he can hardly walk."

The girl exploded with something not much more dignified than a giggle; "Goodness!" she said. "Think of bringing him all the way from Oxford and dressing him up like that," and she pointed with irrepressible mirth at Mr. Archer's legs, which were of somewhat dubious date.

"He's the one man who could interpret the period," said the librarian, shaking his head, "As to bringing him from Oxford, the only other man I can think of you'd have to bring from Paris. There are one or two Frenchmen and a German. But there's no other historian in England to touch him."

"Oh, come," remonstrated Archer, "Bancock's the most famous historical writer since Macaulay; famous all over the world."

"He writes books, doesn't he?" remarked the librarian with a fine shade of distaste. "Garton Rogers is your only man."

The lady in the horned head-dress exploded again. "But Lord bless my soul," she cried, "it only takes about two hours!"

"Long enough for little mistakes to be noticed," said the librarian gloomily. "To reconstruct a past period for two solid hours wants more work than you might fancy. If it were only my own period now . . ."

"Well, if we do want a learned man, who could be better than you?" asked the lady, with bright but illogical triumph.

Herne was looking at her with a sort of sad eagerness; then he looked away at the horizon and sighed.

"You don't understand," he said in a low voice, "a man's period is his life in a way. A man wants to live in medieval pictures and carvings and things before he can walk across a room as a medieval man would do it. I know that in my own period; people tell me the old carvings of the Hittite priests and gods look stiff to them. But I feel as if I knew from those stiff attitudes what sort of dances they had. I sometimes feel as if I could hear the music."

For the first time in that clatter of cross-purposes there was a suspension of speech and an instantaneous silence; and the eyes of the learned librarian, like the eyes of a fool, were in the ends of the earth. Then he went on as with a sort of soliloquy.

"If I tried to act a period I hadn't put my mind into, I should be caught out. I should mix things up. If I had to play the guitar you talk about, it wouldn't be the right sort of guitar. I should play it as if it were the *shenaum* or at least the partly Hellenic *hinopis*. Anybody could see my movement wasn't a late twelfth century movement. Anybody would say at once, 'That's a Hittite gesture.'"

"The very phrase," said Murrel staring at him "that would leap to a hundred lips."

But though he continued to stare at the librarian in frank and admiring mystification, he was gradually convinced of the seriousness of the whole strange situation. For he saw on Herne's face that expression of shrewdness that is the final proof of simplicity.

"But hang it all," burst out Archer, like one throwing off a nightmare of hypnotism, "I tell you it's only a play! I know my part already; and it's a lot longer than yours."

"Anyhow, you've had the start in studying it," insisted Herne, "and in studying the whole thing; you've been thinking about Troubadours; living in the period. Anybody could see I hadn't. There'd always be some tiny little thing," he explained almost with cunning, "some little trick I'd missed, some mistake, something that couldn't be medieval. I don't believe in interfering with people who know their own subject; and you've been studying the period."

He was gazing at the somewhat blank if beautiful countenance of the young woman in front of him; while Archer, in the shadow behind her, seemed finally overcome with a sort of hopeless amusement. Suddenly the librarian lost his meditative immobility and seemed to awaken to life.

"Of course, I might look you up something in the library," he said, turning towards the shelves. "There's a very good French series on all aspects of the period on the top shelf, I think."

The library was a quite unusually high room, with a sloping roof pitched as high as the roof of a church. Indeed it is not impossible that it had been the roof of a church or at least of a chapel for it was part of the old wing that had represented Seawood Abbey when it really was an abbey. Therefore, the top shelf meant something more like the top of a precipice than the top of an ordinary bookcase. It could only be scaled by a very long library ladder, which was at that moment leaning against the library shelves. The librarian, in his new impulse of movement, was at the top of the tall ladder before anybody could stop him; rummaging in a row of dusty volumes diminished by distance and quite indistinguishable. He pulled a big volume from the rank of volumes; and finding it rather awkward to examine while balancing on the top of a ladder, he hoisted himself on to the shelf, in the gap left by the book, and sat there as if he were a new and valuable folio presented to the library. It was rather dark up there under the roof; but an electric light hung there and he calmly turned it on. A silence followed and he continued to sit there on his remote perch, with his long legs dangling in mid-air and his head entirely invisible behind the leather wall of the large volume. "Mad," said Archer in a low voice. "A bit touched, don't you think? He's forgotten all about us already. If we took away the ladder, I don't believe he'd know it. Here's a chance for one of your practical jokes, Monkey."

"No thanks," replied Murrel briefly. "No ragging about this, if you don't mind."

"Why not?" demanded Archer. "Why you yourself took away the ladder when the Prime Minister was unveiling a statue on the top of a column and left him there for three hours."

"That was different," said Murrel gruffly; but he did not say why it was different. Perhaps he did not clearly know why it was different, except that the Prime Minister was his first cousin and had deliberately set himself up to be ragged by being a politician. Anyhow, he felt the difference acutely and when the playful Archer laid hands on the ladder to lift it away, told him to chuck it in a tone verging on ferocity.

At that moment, however, it happened that a well-known voice called to him by name from the doorway opening on the garden. He turned and saw the dark figure of Olive Ashley framed in the doorway, with something about her attitude that was expectant and imperative.

"You jolly well leave that ladder alone," he said hastily over his shoulder as he turned away, "or by George . . ."

"Well?" demanded the defiant Archer.

"Or I'll indulge in what we would call a Hittite gesture," said Murrel and walked hastily across to where Olive was standing. The other girl had already stepped out into the garden to speak to her, as she was obviously excited about something; and Archer was left alone with the unconscious librarian and the alluring ladder.

Archer felt like a schoolboy who had been dared to do something. He was no coward; and he was very vain. He unhooked the ladder from the high book-shelf very carefully without disturbing a grain of dust on the dusty shelves or a hair on the head of the unconscious scholar who was reading the large book. He quietly carried the ladder out into the garden and leaned it up against a shed. Then he looked round for the rest of the company; and eventually saw them as a distant group on the lawn, so deep in conversation as to be as unconscious of the crime as the victim himself. They were talking about something else; something that was to be the first step leading to strange consequences; to a strange tale turning on the absence of several persons from their accustomed places, and not least on the absence of a ladder from the library.

Chapter 4

# The First Trial of John Braintree

The gentleman called Monkey made his way rapidly across the
wide and windy sweep of lawn towards the solitary monument
(if it can so be called), or curiosity, or relic, which stood in
the middle of that open space. It was, in fact, a large fragment
fallen from the Gothic gateways of the old Abbey, and here
incongruously poised upon a more modern pedestal, probably
by the rather hazy romanticism of some gentleman a hundred
years ago, who thought that a subsequent accumulation of
moss and moonlight might turn it into a suitable subject for
the ingenious author of "Marmion." On close inspection (which
nobody in particular ever accorded to it) the broken lines of
it could be dimly traced in the shape of a rather repulsive
monster, goggle-eyed and glaring upwards, possibly a dying
dragon, above which something stood up in vertical lines like
broken shafts or columns, possibly the lower part of a human
figure. But it was not out of any antiquarian ardour to note
these details that Mr. Douglas Murrel hastened towards the
spot; but because the very impatient lady who had summoned
him out of the house on urgent business had named this place
for the appointment. From across the garden he could see Olive
Ashley standing by the stone, and see that she was by no means
standing equally still. Even at that distance there seemed to
be something restless and even nervous about her gesture and
carriage. She was the only person, perhaps, who ever did look
at that lump of laboriously graven rock; and even she admitted

that it was ugly and that she did not know what it meant. In any case she was not looking at it now.

"I want you to do me a favour," she said, abruptly, and before he could speak. Then she added, rather inconsequently, "I don't know why it should be any favour to me. I don't care. It's for everybody's sake—society and all that!"

"I see," said Murrel, with gravity, and possibly a little irony.

"Besides, he's your friend; I mean that man Braintree." Then her tone changed again, and she said explosively, "It's all your fault! You would introduce him."

"Well, what's the matter?" asked her companion, patiently.

"Only that I simply detest him," she said. "He was abominably rude and—"

"I say—" cried Murrel, sharply, with a new and unusual note in his voice.

"Oh, no," said Olive, crossly, "I don't mean like that. I don't want somebody to fight him; he wasn't rude in a conventional sense. Simply horribly stuck-up and opinionated, and laying down the law in long words out of his horrid foreign pamphlets—shouting all sorts of nonsense about coordinated syndicalism and proletarian something—"

"Such words are not fit for a lady's lips," said Murrel, shaking his head, "but I'm afraid I don't yet quite understand what it's all about. As I'm not to fight him for saying coordinated syndicalism (which seems to me a jolly good reason for fighting a man), what in the world is it that you want?"

"I want him taken down a peg," observed the young woman, with vindictive gloom. "I want somebody to hammer into his head that he's really quite ignorant. Why, he's never mixed with educated people at all. You can see that from the way he walks and dresses. I feel somehow as if I could stand anything if he wouldn't thrust out that great bristly black beard. He might look quite all right without his beard."

"Do I understand," asked Murrel, "that you wish me to go and forcibly shave the gentleman?"

"Nonsense," she replied, impatiently, "I only mean I want him, just for one little moment, to wish he was shaved. What

I want is to show him what educated people are really like. It's all for his own good. He could be—he could be ever so much improved."

"Is he to go to a continuation class or a night school?" inquired Murrel innocently, "or possibly to a Sunday school."

"Nobody ever learns anything at school," she replied, "I mean the only place where anybody ever does learn anything—the world; the great world. I want him to see there are things much greater than his grumbling little fads—I want him to hear people talking about music and architecture and history, and all the things that really scholarly people know about. Of course, he's got stuck-up by spouting in the streets and laying down the law in low public-houses—bullying people even more ignorant than himself. But if once he gets among really cultivated people, he is quite clever enough to feel stupid."

"And so, wanting a stately scholar, cultured to his finger-tips, you naturally thought of me," remarked Monkey, approvingly. "You want me to tie him to a drawing-room chair and administer tea and Tolstoy, or Tupper, or whoever is the modern favourite. My dear Olive, he wouldn't come."

"I've thought of all that," she said, rather hurriedly, "that's what I meant by calling it a favour—a favour to him and all my fellow creatures, of course. Look here, I want you to persuade Lord Seawood to ask him to some business interview about the strike. That's the only thing he'd come for; and after that we'll introduce him to some people who'll talk right above his head, so that he'll sort of grow—grow up. It's really serious, Douglas. He's got the most terrible power over these workmen. Unless we can make him see the truth they will all—he's an orator in his way."

"I knew you were a bloated aristocrat," he said, contemplating the tense and tenuous little lady, "but I never knew you were such a diplomatist. Well, I suppose I must help in your horrid plot, if you really assure me that it's all for his own good."

"Of course it's for his own good," she replied, confidently. "I should never have thought of it but for that."

"Quite so," replied Murrel, and went back towards the house, walking rather more slowly than when coming away from it. But he did not see the ladder leaning up against the outhouse, or the development of this story might have been disastrously foiled.

Olive's theory about educating the uneducated man by association with educated men seemed to give him considerable food for thought as he went across the grassy plot kicking his heels, with his hands thrust deep in his trousers' pockets. Of course, there was something in it; fellows did find their level sometimes by going to Oxford. They find out in what way their education has been neglected, even if they continue to neglect it. But he had never seen the experiment tried on so dark a social stratum as the black and buried coal-seam for which the Syndicalist stood. He could not imagine anyone quite so rugged and dogged in his demagogy as his friend Jack Braintree gradually learning how to balance a cigarette and a tea-cup and talk about the Roumanian Shakespeare. There was to be a reception of that sort that afternoon, he knew—but Braintree in it! Of course, there was a whole world of things that the sulky tub-thumper out of the slums did not know. He was not so sure whether they could ever be things that he wanted to know.

Having once made up his mind, however, to come to the rescue of Society and Olive Ashley, by thus exhibiting the unlettered coal-miner like a drunken helot, he set gravely about it; and it was highly characteristic of him that his gravity covered his deep and simple joy in a practical joke. Perhaps the question of who was, on whom the joke was being played, was not quite so simple. He made his way towards the wing of the building that contained the study, not often penetrated, of the great Lord Seawood himself. He remained there an hour, and came out smiling.

Thus it came about that through these manoeuvres, of which he was quite unconscious, the bewildered Braintree, his dark beard and hair seeming to bristle in every direction as he looked about him for enlightenment, found himself that afternoon (after a solemn and mysteriously futile interview with the great capitalist) turned loose by another door into the salon of the aristocracy of intellect which was to complete his education. He certainly looked rather incomplete; standing in that room with a stoop and a scowl, which were none the less sullen if they were unconsciously sullen. He was not ugly; but he looked ungainly. Above all, he looked unfriendly; and felt it. It was the other people, to do them justice, who showed the friendliness; sometimes, perhaps, a little heavy with heartiness. There was a large, bland, bald-headed gentleman who was particularly hearty; and never more hearty, one might say never more noisy, than when he was confidential. There was a touch in him of that potentate in the Bab Ballads whose whisper was a horrible yell.

"What we want," he said, softly pulverising something in his hollow palm with his clenched fist, "what we want for industrial peace is industrial instruction. Never listen to the reactionaries. Never you believe the fellows who say popular education is a mistake. Of course, the masses must have education. But above all, economic education. If once we can get into the people's heads some notion of the laws of political economy, we shall hear no more of these disputes that drive trade out of the country and threaten to put a pistol to the head of the public. Whatever our opinions may be, we all want to prevent that. Whatever our party may be, we don't want that. I don't say it in the interests of any party; I say it's something quite above party."

"But if I say," answered Braintree, "that we also want the extension of effective demand, isn't that above party?"

The large man glanced at him quickly and almost covertly. Then he said, "Quite—Oh, quite."

There was a silence and then a few gay remarks about the weather; and then Braintree found that the large man had somehow smoothly and inoffensively passed from him, swimming like some silent leviathan into other seas. The large man's bald head and rather pompously perched pince-nez had somehow given the impression that he was a professor of political economy. His conversation had somehow given the impression that he was not. The first stage of Mr. Braintree's course in culture was, perhaps, unfortunate. For it left that gloomy character with a growing inward impression, right or wrong, to the effect that the partisan of Economic Education for the Masses had not himself the very vaguest idea of what "effective demand" means.

This first fiasco, however, cannot be counted fairly; as the big bald man (who was, in fact, a certain Sir Howard Pryce, the head of a very big soap business) had perhaps put his foot by an accident inside the Syndicalist's own rather narrow province. The salon contained any number of people who were not in the least likely to discuss industrial instruction or economic demand. Among them, it is needless to say, there was Mr. Almeric Wister. It is needless to say it, for there always is Mr. Almeric Wister wherever twenty or thirty are gathered together in that particular sort of social afternoon.

Mr. Almeric Wister was, and is, the one fixed point round which countless slightly differentiated forms of social futility have clustered. He managed to be so omnipresent about teatime in Mayfair that some have held that he was not a man but a syndicate; and a number of Wisters scattered to the different drawing-rooms, all tall and lank and hollow-eyed and carefully dressed, and all with deep voices and hair and beard thin but rather long, with a suggestion of aesthete. But even in the similar parties in country houses there were always a certain number of him; so it would seem that the syndicate sent out provincial touring companies. He had a hazy reputation as an art expert and was great on the duration of pigments. He was the sort of man who remembers Rossetti and has unpublished anecdotes about Whistler. When he was first introduced to Braintree, his eye encountered that demagogue's red tie, from which he correctly deduced that Braintree was not an art expert. The expert therefore felt free to be even more expert than usual. His hollow eyes rolled reproachfully from the tie to a picture on the wall, by Lippi or some Italian primitive; for Seawood Abbey possessed fine pictures as well as fine books. Some association of ideas led Wister to echo unconsciously the complaint of Olive Ashley and remark that the red used for the wings of one of the angels was something of a lost technical secret. When one considered how the Last Supper had faded—

Braintree assented civilly, having no very special knowledge of pictures and no knowledge at all of Pigments. This ignorance, or indifference completed the case founded on the crude necktie. The expert, now fully realising that he was talking to an utter outsider, expanded with radiant condescension. He delivered a sort of lecture.

"Ruskin is very sound upon that point," said Mr. Almeric Wister. "You would be quite safe in reading Ruskin, if only as a sort of introduction to the subject. With the exception of Pater, of course, there has been no critic since having that atmosphere of authority. Democracy, of course, is not favourable to authority. And I very much fear, Mr. Braintree, that democracy is not favourable to art."

"Well, if ever we have any democracy, I suppose we shall find out," said Braintree.

"I fear," said Wister, shaking his head, "that we have quite enough to lead us to neglect all artistic authorities."

At this moment, Rosamund of the red hair and the square, sensible face, came up, steering through the crowd a sturdy young man, who also had a sensible face; but the resemblance ended there, for he was stodgy and even plain, with short bristly hair and a tooth-brush moustache. But he had the clear eyes of a man of courage and his manners were very pleasant and unpretending. He was a squire of the neighbourhood, named Hanbury, with some reputation as a traveller in the tropics. After introducing him and exchanging a few words with the group, she said to Wister, "I'm afraid we interrupted you"; which was indeed the case.

"I was saying," said Wister, airily, but also a little loftily, "that I fear we have descended to democracy and an age of little men. The great Victorians are gone."

"Yes, of course," answered the girl, a little mechanically.

"We have no giants left," he resumed.

"That must have been quite a common complaint in Cornwall," reflected Braintree, "when Jack the Giant-killer had gone his professional rounds."

"When you have read the works of the Victorian giants," said Wister, rather contemptuously, "you will perhaps understand what I mean by a giant."

"You can't really mean, Mr. Braintree," remonstrated the lady, "that you want great men to be killed."

"Well, I think there's something in the idea," said Braintree. "Tennyson deserved to be killed for writing the May-Queen, and Browning deserved to be killed for rhyming 'promise' and 'from mice,' and Carlyle deserved to be killed for being Carlyle; and Herbert Spencer deserved to be killed for writing 'The Man versus the State'; and Dickens deserved to be killed for not killing Little Nell quick enough; and Ruskin deserved to be killed for saying that Man ought to have no more freedom than the sun; and Gladstone deserved to be killed for deserting Parnell; and Disraeli deserved to be killed for talking about a 'shrinking sire,' and Thackeray—"

"Mercy on us!" interrupted the lady, laughing, "you really must stop somewhere. What a lot you seem to have read!"

Wister appeared, for some reason or other, to be very much annoyed; almost waspish. "If you ask me," he said, "it's all part of the mob and its hatred of superiority. Always wants to drag merit down. That's why your infernal trade unions won't have a good workman paid better than a bad one."

"That has been defended economically," said Braintree, with restraint. "One authority has pointed out that the best trades are paid equally already."

"Karl Marx, I suppose," said the expert, testily.

"No, John Ruskin," replied the other. "One of your Victorian giants." Then he added, "But the text and title of the book were not by John Ruskin, but by Jesus Christ; who had not, alas, the privilege of being a Victorian."

The stodgy little man named Hanbury possibly felt that the conversation was becoming too religious to be respectable; anyhow, he interposed pacifically, saying, "You come from the mining area, Mr. Braintree?"

The other assented, rather gloomily.

"I suppose," said Braintree's new interlocutor, "I suppose there will be a good deal of unrest among the miners?"

"On the contrary," replied Braintree, "there will be a good deal of rest among the miners."

The other frowned in momentary doubt, and said very quickly, "You don't mean the strike is off?"

"The strike is very much on," said Braintree, grimly, "so there will be no more unrest."

"Now, what *do* you mean?" cried the very practical young lady, shortly destined to be the Princess of the Troubadours.

"I mean what I say," he replied, shortly. "I say there will be a great deal of rest among the miners. You always talk as if striking meant throwing a bomb or blowing up a house. Striking simply means resting."

"Why, it's quite a paradox," cried his hostess, with a sort of joy, as if it were a new parlour game and her party was now really going to be a success.

"I should have thought it was a platitude, otherwise a plain truth," replied Braintree. "During a strike the workers are resting; and a jolly new experience for some of them, I can tell you."

"May we not say," said Wister, in a deep voice, "that the truest rest is in labour?"

"You may," said Braintree, dryly. "It's a free country—for you anyhow. And while you're about it, you may also say that the truest labour is in rest. And then you will be quite delighted with the notion of a strike."

His hostess was looking at him with a new expression, steady and yet gradually changing; the expression with which people of slow but sincere mental processes recognise something that has to be reckoned with, and possibly even respected. For although, or perhaps because, she had grown up smothered with wealth and luxury, she was quite innocent, and had never felt any shame in looking on the faces of her fellows.

"Don't you think," she said at last, "we are just quarrelling about a word?"

"No, I don't, since you ask me," he said, gruffly. "I think we are arguing on two sides of an abyss, and that one little word is a chasm between two halves of humanity. If you really care to know, may I give you a little piece of advice? When you want to make us think you understand the situation, and still disapprove of the strike, say anything in the world except that. Say there is the devil among the miners; say there is treason and anarchy among the miners; say there is blasphemy and madness among the miners. But don't say there is unrest among the miners. For that one little word betrays the whole thing that is at the back of your mind; it is very old and its name is Slavery."

"This is very extraordinary," said Mr. Wister.

"Isn't it?" said the lady. "Thrilling!"

"No, quite simple," said the Syndicalist. "Suppose there is a man in your coal-cellar instead of your coal-mine. Suppose it is his business to break up coal all day, and you can hear him hammering. We will suppose he is paid for it; we will suppose you honestly think he is paid enough. Still, you can hear him chopping away all day while you are smoking or playing the piano—until a moment when the noise in the coal-cellar stops suddenly. It may be wrong for it to stop—it may be right—it may be all sorts of things. But don't you see—can nothing make you see—what you really mean if you only say, like Hamlet to his old mole, 'Rest, perturbed spirit.'"

"Ha," said Mr. Wister, graciously, "glad to see you have read Shakespeare."

But Braintree went on without noticing the remark.

"The hammering in your coal-hole that always goes on stops for an instant. And what do you say to the man down there in the darkness? You do not say, 'Thank you for doing it well.' You do not even say, 'Damn you for doing it badly.' What you do say is, 'Rest; sleep on. Resume your normal state of repose. Continue in that state of complete quiescence which is normal to you and which nothing should ever have disturbed. Continue that rhythmic and lulling motion that must be to you the same as slumber; which is for you second nature and part of the nature of things. *Continuez,* as God said in Belloc's story. Let there be no unrest.'"

As he talked vehemently, but not violently, he became faintly conscious that many more faces were turned towards him and his group, not staring rudely, but giving a general sense of a crowd heading in that direction. He saw Murrel looking at him with melancholy amusement over a limp cigarette, and Archer glancing at him every now and then over his shoulder as if fearing he would set fire to the house. He saw the eager and half-serious faces of several ladies of a sort always hungry for anything to happen. All those close to him were cloudy and bewildering; but amid them all he could see away in the corner of the room, distant but distinct and even unreasonably distinct, the pale but vivid face of little Miss Ashley of the paint-box, watching—.

"But the man in the coal-cellar is only a stranger out of the street," he went on, "who has gone into your black hole to attack a rock as he might attack a wild beast or any other brute force of nature. To break coal in a coal-cellar is an action. To break it in a coal-mine is an adventure. The wild beast can kill in its own cavern. And fighting with that wild beast is eternal unrest; a war with chaos, as much as that of a man hacking his own way through an African forest."

"Mr. Hanbury," said Rosamund, smiling, "has just come back from an expedition of that sort."

"Yes," said Braintree, "but when he doesn't happen to go on an expedition, you don't say there is Unrest at the Travellers' Club."

"Had me there. Very good," said Hanbury, in his easy-going way.

"Don't you see," went on Braintree, "that when you say that of us, you imply that we are all so much clockwork, and you never even notice the ticking till the clock stops."

"Yes," said Rosamund, "I think I see what you mean and I shan't forget it." And, indeed, though she was not particularly clever, she was one of those rare and rather valuable people who never forget anything they have once learnt.

Chapter 5

# The Second Trial of John Braintree

Douglas Murrel knew the world; he knew his own world, though
that lucky love of low company had saved him from supposing
it was the whole world. And he knew well enough what had
happened. Braintree, brought there to be abashed into silence,
was being encouraged to talk. There was in it perhaps some
element of the interest in a monstrosity or performing animal;
some touch of that longing of all luxurious people for something fresh; but the monstrosity was making a good impression.
He talked a good deal; but he did not have the air of being
conceited; only of being convinced. Murrel knew the world; and
he knew that men who talk a great deal are often not conceited,
because not conscious.

And now he knew what would follow. The silly people had
had their say; the people who cannot help asking an Arctic
explorer whether he enjoyed the North Pole; the people who
would almost ask a nigger what it felt like to be black. It was
inevitable that the old merchant should talk about political
economy to anybody he supposed to be political. It did not
matter if that old ass Wister lectured him about the great
Victorians. The self-educated man had no difficulty in showing
he was better educated than those people were. But now the
next stage was reached; and the other sort of people began
to take notice. The intelligent people in the Smart Set, the
people who do not talk shop, the people who would talk to
the nigger about the weather, began to talk to the Syndicalist

about Syndicalism. In the lull after his more stormy retort, men with quieter voices began to ask him more sensible questions; often conceding many of his claims, often falling back on more fundamental objections. Murrel almost started as he heard the low and guttural drawl of old Eden, in whom so many diplomatic and parliamentary secrets were buttoned up, and who hardly ever talked at all, saying to Braintree: "Don't you think there's something to be said for the Ancients—Aristotle and all that, don't you know? Perhaps there really must be a class of people always working for us in the cellar."

Braintree's black eyes flashed; not with rage, but with joy; because he knew now that he was understood.

"Ah, now you're talking sense," he said. There were some present to whom it seemed almost as much of a liberty to tell Lord Eden he was talking sense as to tell him he was talking nonsense. But he himself was quite subtle enough to understand that he had really been paid a compliment.

"But if you take that line," went on Braintree, "you can't complain of the people you separate in that way, treating themselves as something separate. If there is a class like that, you can hardly wonder at its being class-conscious."

"And the other people, I suppose, have a right to be class-conscious, too," said Eden with a smile.

"Quite so," observed Wister in his more spacious manner. "The aristocrat, the magnanimous man as Aristotle says—"

"Look here," said Braintree rather irritably, "I've only read Aristotle in cheap translations; but I have read them. It seems to me gentlemen like you first learn elaborately how to read things in Greek; and then never do it. Aristotle, so far as I can understand, makes out the magnanimous man to be a pretty conceited fellow. But he never says he must be what you call an aristocrat."

"Quite so," said Eden, "but the most democratic of the Greeks believed in slavery. In my opinion, there's a lot more to be said for slavery than there is for aristocracy."

The Syndicalist assented almost eagerly; and Mr. Almeric Wister looked rather bewildered.

"I say," repeated Braintree, "that if you think there ought to be slaves, you can't prevent the slaves hanging together and having their own notions about things. You can't appeal to their citizenship if they are not citizens. Well, I'm one of the slaves. I come out of the coal-cellar. I represent all those grimy and grubby and unpresentable people; I am one of them. Aristotle himself couldn't complain of my speaking for them."

"You speak for them very well," said Eden.

Murrel smiled grimly. The fashion was in full blast now. He recognised all the signs of that change in the social weather; that altered atmosphere around the Syndicalist. He even heard the familiar sound that put the final touch to it; the murmuring voice of Lady Boole, " . . . any Thursday. We shall be *so* pleased."

Murrel, still smiling grimly, turned on his heel and crossed over to the corner where Olive Ashley was sitting. He noted that she sat watching with compressed lips and that her dark eyes were dangerously bright. He addressed her upon a note of delicate condolence.

"Afraid our practical joke has rather turned bottom up," he said. "We meant him to be a bear and he's going to be a lion."

She looked up and suddenly smiled in a dazzling and highly baffling manner.

"He did knock them about like ninepins, didn't he?" she cried, "and he wasn't a bit afraid of old Eden."

Murrel stared down at her with an entirely new perplexity on his dolorous visage.

"This is very odd," he said. "Why, you seem to be quite proud of your *protégé*."

He continued to stare at her undecipherable smile and at last he said: "Well, I don't understand women; nobody ever will, and it is obviously dangerous to try. But if I may make a mere guess on the subject, my dear Olive, I have a growing suspicion that you are a little humbug."

He departed with his usual gloomy good humour; and the party was already breaking up. As the last of the visitors left, he stood once more for a moment in the gateway leading into the garden and sent a Parthian arrow.

*41*

"I don't understand women," he said, "but I do know a little about men. And now *I'm* going to take charge of your performing bear."

The country seat of Seawood, beautiful as it was and remote as it seemed, was really only five or six miles from one of those black and smoky provincial towns that have sprung up amid beautiful hills and valleys since the map of England presented itself mainly as a patchwork of coal. This particular town, which bore its old name of Milldyke, was already very smoky but still comparatively small. It was not so much directly connected with the coal trade as with the treatment of various by-products such as coal-tar; and contained a number of factories manufacturing various things out of that rich and valuable refuse. John Braintree lived in one of the poorer streets of the town; and found it uncomfortable but not inconvenient. For a great part of his political life was spent in trying to link up the labour organisations directly connected with the coal-field to these other and smaller unisons of men employed on the derivative substances. It was towards his home that he now turned his face, when he turned his back on the great country house to which he had just paid so curious and apparently aimless a visit. As Eden and Wister and the various nobs of the neighbourhood, (as he would put it) slid away in their sumptuous cars, he took a great pride in walking stiffly through the crowd in the direction of the queer and rustic little omnibus that ran in and out between the great house and the town. When he climbed up the omnibus, however, he was rather surprised to find Mr. Douglas Murrel climbing up after him.

"Mind if I share your omnibus?" asked Murrel, sinking on a bench beside the solitary outside passenger; for nobody else seemed to be travelling by the vehicle; they were sitting well forward in the front seats and the full blast of the night air came in their faces as the vehicle began to move. It seemed to wake Braintree out of a trance of abstraction and he assented rather curtly.

"The truth is," said Murrel, "that I feel inclined to go and look at your coal-cellar."

"You wouldn't like to be locked up in the coal-cellar," said the other, still a little gruffly.

"Of course, I should prefer to be locked up in the wine-cellar," admitted Murrel. "A new version of your parable of Labour. The vain and idle revelling above, while the dull persistent sound of popping corks told them that I was still below, toiling, labouring, never at rest. . . . But really, old man, there was a lot in what you said about yourself and your grimy haunts, and I thought I'd have a squint at them."

To Mr. Almeric Wister and others it might have seemed tactless to talk to the poorer man about his grimy environment. But Murrel was not tactless; and he was not wrong when he said he knew something about men. He knew the morbid sensitiveness of the most masculine sort of men. He knew his friend's almost maniacal dread of snobbery; and knew better than to say anything about the successes of the salon. To talk about Braintree as a slave in a coal-cellar was to steady his self-respect.

"Mostly dye-works and that sort of thing, aren't they?" asked Murrel, gazing at the forest of factory-chimneys, that began to show through the haze of the horizon.

"By-products of coal of various kinds," replied his friend, "used for chemical colours, dyes and enamels, and all sorts of things. It seems to me, in capitalist society, the by-product is getting bigger than the big product. They say your friend Seawood's millions come much more from the coal-tar products than from the coal—I've heard that something of the sort was used for the red coat of the soldier."

"And what about the red tie of the Socialist?" asked Murrel reproachfully. "Jack, I cannot believe that red tie of yours is freshly dipped in the blood of aristocrats. Anxious as I am to think well of you, I cannot think you come reeking from the massacre of our old nobility. Besides, I always understood that the blood would be blue. Can it be that you yourself are now a walking advertisement of old What's-his-name's dye-works? Buy Our Red Ties. Syndicalist Gents Suited. Mr. John Braintree, the Well-Known Revolutionist, Writes 'Since Using Your—'"

"Nobody knows where anything comes from nowadays, Douglas," said Braintree quietly. "That's what's called publicity and popular journalism in a capitalist state. My tie may be made by capitalists; so may yours be made by cannibal islanders for all you know."

"Woven out of the whiskers of missionaries," replied Murrel. "A pleasant thought. And I suppose your work is going on the stump for all these workers.

"Their conditions are infamous," said Braintree, "especially the poor chaps working on some of the dyes and paints and things, which are simple damned poisons and pestilences. They've scarcely got any unions worth talking about and their hours are much too long."

"It's long hours that knock a man out most," agreed Murrel. "Nobody gets enough leisure or fun in this world, do they, Bill?"

Braintree was perhaps secretly a little flattered by his friend always calling him Jack; but he was wholly unable to understand why, in an excess of intimacy, he should address him as Bill. He was about to ask a question, when a grunt out of the darkness in front of him suddenly reminded him of somebody whose very existence he was bound to admit he had completely forgotten. It would appear that William was the Christian name of the driver of the omnibus; and that Douglas Murrel was in the habit of addressing him by it. The answering grunt of the person called Bill was sufficient to indicate that he entirely agreed that the hours of proletarian employment were much too long.

"Well, you're all right, Bill," said Murrel. "You're one of the lucky ones, especially to-night. Old Charley comes on at the Dragon, don't he?"

"Why, yes," said the driver in slow and luxuriantly scornful tones. "'E comes on at the Dragon, but . . ." Leaving the matter there, rather as if coming on at the Dragon were something which even the limited faculties of old Charley might be expected to manage, but that beyond that there was very little ground for consolation.

"He comes on at the Dragon and we come off at the Dragon," continued Murrel, "so you can come and have one on me. Show you bear no malice for Golliwog. But I swear I only told you to back him for a place."

"Never mind, Sir. Never you mind about that," observed the benevolent Bill, in a glow of Christian forgiveness. "Never mind having a bit on; and if you lose your bit—why, there you are."

"You are indeed," said Murrel. "And here we are at the Dragon; I suppose somebody's got to go in and fetch old Charley out."

With the worthy object of thus accelerating the service of public vehicles, Murrel appeared suddenly to fall off the top of the omnibus. He fell on his feet, however, having in fact descended by turning a sort of cartwheel in the air on the pivot of a single foothold. He then shouldered his way into the lighted and noisy bar of the Green Dragon, with so resolute a movement that the other two men naturally followed him. The omnibus driver, whose full name was William Pond, followed indeed with no pretence of reluctance. The democratic John Braintree followed with a faint reluctance and some affectation of carelessness. He was neither a prohibitionist nor a prig; and would have drunk beer at any wayside inn on a walking tour naturally enough. But the Green Dragon stood on the outskirts of an industrial town; and the place they entered was not a bar-parlour or a lounge or any of the despicable little cubicles called Private Bars. It was the Public Bar or open and honest place of drinking for the poor. And the moment Braintree stepped across its threshold, he knew he was confronted with some-thing new; with something that he had never touched or tasted or seen or smelt before in all his fifteen years of tub-thumping. There was a good deal to be smelt as well as seen; and much that he did not feel inclined to touch, far less to taste. The place was very hot and densely crowded and full of a deafening clatter of people all talking at once. Many of them did not seem to mind much whether the others were listening or talking at the same time. A great part of the talk was totally unintelligible to him, though evidently full of emphatic expressions; as if a crowd were swearing in Dutch or Portuguese. Every now and then in the stream of rather ugly and unintelligible words one word would occur and an authoritative voice from behind the counter would say: "Now then—now then," and the expression would be tacitly withdrawn. Murrel had gone up to the counter, nodding to various people and rapped on it with a few coppers asking for four of something.

So far as the eddying hubbub had any centre, there seemed to be something like a social circle round one small man who was right up against the counter; and that not so much because he was a talker as because he seemed to be a topic. Everybody was making jokes about him, as if he were the weather or the War Office or any recognised theme for the satiric artist. Much of it was direct, as in the form "Goin' to get married soon, George?" or "What you done with all your money, George?" Other remarks were in the third person, as "Old George 'e's been going out with the girls too much," or "I reckon old George got lost in London," and so on. It was noticeable that this concentrated fire of satire was entirely genial and friendly. It was still more notable that old George himself seemed to feel no sort of annoyance or even surprise at his own mysteriously isolated position as a human target. He was a short, stolid, rather sleepy little man, who stood the whole time with half-closed eyes and a beatific smile, as if this peculiar form of popularity were a never failing pleasure. His name was George Carter, and he was a small green-grocer in those parts. Why he, more than another, should be supposed at any given moment to be in love or lost in London, the visitor could not guess from the talk of two hours, and would probably never have discovered if he had listened to the talk for ten years. The man was simply a magnet; he had some mystical power of attracting to himself all the chaff that might be flying about the room. It was said that he was rather sulky if by any chance he did not get it. Braintree could make nothing of the mystery; but he sometimes thought of it long afterwards, when he heard people talking in Socialistic salons about brutal yokels and savage mobs jeering at anybody defective or eccentric. He wondered whether, perhaps, he had been present at one of these hideous and barbaric scenes.

Meanwhile, Murrel continued to rap at intervals on the counter and exchange badinage with a large young woman who had apparently tried to make her own hair look like a wig. Then he fell into an interminable dispute with the man next him about whether some horse or other could win by some particular number of sections of lengths; the difference being apparently one of degree and not of fundamental principle. The debate did not advance very rapidly to any final conclusion, as it consisted mostly of the repetition of the premises over and over again with ever-increasing firmness. These two disputants were polite as well as firm; but their conversation was somewhat embarrassed by the conduct of an immensely tall and lank and shabby man with drooping moustaches, who leaned across them, talking all the time, in a well-meant effort to refer the point in dispute to the gloomy Braintree.

"I know a gentleman when I see him," repeated the long man at intervals, "and I arsk 'im . . . I jest arsk 'im, as a gentleman; I know a gentleman when I—"

"I'm not a gentleman," said the Syndicalist, with some bitterness.

The long man tried to lean over him with vast fatherly gestures, like one soothing a fretful child.

"Now, don't you say that, sir," said the fatherly person. "Don't say that . . . I know a real toff when I see 'im, and I put it to you—"

Braintree turned away with a jerk and collided with a large navvy covered with white dust, who apologised with admirable amiability and then spat on the sawdust floor.

That night was like a nightmare. To John Braintree it seemed to be as endless as it was meaningless, and yet wildly monotonous. For Murrel took his festive bus-driver on a holiday to bar after bar, not really drinking very much, not drinking half so much as a solitary duke or don might drink out of a decanter of port, but drinking it to the accompaniment of endless gas and noise and smell and incessant interminable argument; argument that might truly be called interminable, in the literal sense that it did not seem even capable of being terminated.

When the sixth public house resounded to booming shouts of "Time," and the crowds were shuffled and shunted out of it and the shutters put up, the indefatigable Murrel began a corresponding tour of coffee-stalls, with the laudable object of ensuring sobriety. Here he ate thick sandwiches and drank pale-brown coffee, still arguing with his fellow-creatures about the points of horses and the prospects of sporting events. Dawn was breaking over the hills and the fringe of factory chimneys, when John Braintree suddenly turned to his friend and spoke in a tone which compelled his attention.

"Douglas," he said, "you needn't act your allegory any more. I always knew you were a clever fellow, and I begin to have some notion of how your sort have continued to manage a whole nation for so long; but I'm not quite a fool myself. I know what you mean. You haven't said it with your own tongue, but you've said it with ten thousand other tongues to-night. You've said, 'Yes, John Braintree, you can get on all right with the nobs. It's the mobs you can't get on with. You've spent an hour in the drawing-room and told them all about Shakespeare and the musical glasses. Now that you've spent a night in the poor streets, tell me—which of us know the people best?"'

Murrel was silent. After a moment the other went on.

"It is the best answer you could make, and I won't trouble you now with answers to it. I might tell you something about why we shrink from these things more than you; about how you can play with them and we have had to fight them. But I'd rather just now show you that I understand and that I don't bear malice."

"I know you don't," answered Murrel. "Our friend in the pub didn't select his terms very tactfully; but there was something in what he said about your being a gentleman. Well, this is, let us hope, the last of my practical jokes."

But he had not done with practical jokes that day; for as he came back through the garden of Seawood he saw something which startled him; the ladder from the library leaning against a tool-shed. He stopped, and his good-humoured face grew almost grim.

Chapter 6

# A Commission as Colourman

As Murrel gazed there gradually grew upon his mind (which
was perhaps clearing itself rather slowly of many festive fumes)
the sense of one result of his nonsensical nocturnal expedition
or experiment in the education of revolutionists. He had been
out all night and had seen nothing of what had lately been
happening to his friends and their theatricals. But he remembered that it was almost exactly at this moment of the morning,
with its long, fine tapering shadows and faint, far-flung flush of
dawn, that he had abandoned his painting of the scenery and
plunged into the library in pursuit of the librarian. He had left
the librarian at the top of the ladder a little more than twenty-
four hours ago. And here was the ladder thrown away like
lumber in the garden, spotted with mildew, a skeleton on which
spiders flung their silvery morning webs. What had happened,
and why was that particular piece of furniture thus thrown out
into the garden? He remembered Julian Archer's jokes, and his
face contracted with a spasm of annoyance as he walked hastily
towards the library and looked in.

His first impression was that the long and lofty room, entirely
lined with books, was empty. The next moment he saw that high
up in the dark corner, where the librarian had found his French
text-books of medieval history, there hung a queer sort of
luminous blue cloud or mist. Then he saw that the electric light
was still burning, and that the veil of vapour through which
it shone was the result of somebody having been smoking on

that remote perch, and smoking for a considerable stretch of hours, possibly (as it began to dawn on the mind of the strayed reveller) all night and a great part of the day before. Then for the first time he clearly visualised the two long legs of Mr. Michael Herne still hanging from his lofty ledge; where it seemed that he had been reading steadily from sunrise to sunrise. Luckily, it would appear that he had something to smoke. But he could not possibly have had anything to eat. "Lord bless us," muttered Murrel, to himself, "the man must be famished! And what about sleep? If he'd slept on that ledge I suppose he'd have fallen off."

He called out cautiously to the man above, rather as one does to a child playing on the edge of a precipice. He said to him, almost reassuringly, "It's all right; I've got the ladder."

The librarian looked up mildly over the top of his large book. "Do you want me to come down?" he asked.

And then Murrel saw the last of the prodigies of his preposterous twenty-four hours. For without waiting for the ladder at all the librarian let himself swiftly down the face of the bookcase, finding footholds in the shelves, with a little difficulty and some danger, falling at last on his feet. It is true that when he reached the ground he gave a stagger.

"Have you asked Garton Rogers?" he asked. "What an interesting period!"

Murrel was not easily startled but for the moment he also almost staggered. He could only reply with a blank stare and the repetition of the word "Period! What period?"

"Well," replied Mr. Herne, the librarian, half closing his eyes. "I suppose we might put the most interesting period say from 1080 to 1260. What do you think?"

"I think it's a long time to wait for a meal," answered Murrel. "Man alive, you must be starving. Have you really been perched up there for—for two hundred years, so to speak?"

"I do feel a little funny," replied, Herne.

"I don't approve of your taste in fun," answered the other. "Look here, I'm going to get you some food. The servants aren't up yet; but a knife-boy who was a friend of mine once showed me the way to the pantry."

He hurried out of the room and returned in about five minutes bearing a tray loaded with incongruous things, among which beer bottles seemed to predominate.

"Ancient British cheese," he said, setting down the several objects on the top of a revolving bookcase. "Cold chicken, probably not earlier than 1390. Beer, as drunk by Richard Coeur de Lion; or all of it that he left. *Jambon froid à la mode Troubadour.* Do start it at once. I assure you that eating and drinking were practised in the best period."

"I really can't drink all that beer," said the librarian. "It's very early."

"On the contrary, it's very late," said Murrel. "I don't mind joining you, for I'm just finishing off a sort of a feast myself. Another little drink won't do us any harm, as it says in the old Troubadour song of Provence."

"Really," said Herne, "I don't quite understand what all this means."

"Nor do I," replied Murrel, "but the truth is I've been out of bed all night too. Engaged on researches. Not exactly researches into your period, but another period; a systematic, organised sort of period, full of sociology and all that. You will forgive me if I am a little dazed myself. I'm wondering whether there was really such a damned lot of difference between one period and another."

"Why, you see," cried Herne eagerly, "in a way that's just how I feel. It's extraordinary the parallels you find between this medieval period and my own subject. How interesting all that change is, that turning of the old imperial official into a hereditary noble! Wouldn't you think you were reading about the transformation of the Nal after the Zamul invasion?"

"Wouldn't I just!" said Murrel with feeble fervour. "Well, I hope you'll be able to let us know all about Troubadours."

"Well, of course you and your friends know what you're about," said the librarian. "You looked it all up long before; but I rather wonder you concentrated so much on the Troubadours. I should have thought the Trouvères would have fitted into your plan better."

"It's a matter of convention, I suppose," answered Murrel. "It's quite a regular thing to be serenaded by a Troubadour; but if they found a Trouvère hanging about the garden, it would not be very respectable and he might be pinched by the police for loitering with intent to commit a felony."

The librarian looked a little puzzled. Then he said: "At first I thought the Trouvère was something like the Zel or lute player; but I have come to the conclusion that he was only a sort of Pani."

"I always suspected it," said Murrel, darkly, "but I should very much like to have Julian Archer's opinion on the matter."

"Yes," replied the librarian humbly, "I suppose Mr. Archer is a great authority on the subject."

"I've always found him a great authority on all subjects," said Murrel in a controlled manner. "But then you see I'm ignorant of all subjects—with the exception perhaps of beer, of which I seem to be taking more than my fair share. Come, Mr. Herne, troll the brown bowl in a more festive manner, do. Perhaps you would oblige the company with a song—an ancient Hittite drinking song."

"No, really," said the librarian earnestly, "I couldn't possibly sing it; singing is not among my accomplishments."

"Falling off the tops of bookcases seems to be among your accomplishments," returned the companion. "I often fall off omnibuses and things; but I couldn't have done it better myself. It seems to me, my dear sir, that you are something of a mystery. Now that you are perhaps a little restored by food and drink, especially drink, perhaps you will explain. If you could have got down at any time during the last twenty-four hours, may I ask why it never occurred to you that there is something to be said for going to bed and even getting up for breakfast?"

"I confess I should have preferred the latter," said Mr. Herne, modestly. "Perhaps I was a little dizzy and nervous of the drop, till you startled me into making it. I don't usually climb up walls in that way."

"What I want to know is, if you are such an Alpine climber, why did you remain on that ledge of the precipice all night, waiting for the dawn. I had no idea librarians were such light-footed mountaineers. But why? Why not come down? Come down, for love is of the valley; and it is quite useless to await the coming of love perched on the top of a bookcase? Why did you do it?"

"I ought to be ashamed of myself, I know," replied the scholar sadly. "You talk about love, and really it's a kind of unfaithfulness. I feel just as if I'd fallen in love with somebody else's wife. A man ought to stick to his own subject."

"You think the Princess Pal-Ul—what's-her-name?—will be jealous of Berengaria of Navarre?" suggested Murrel. "Devilish good magazine story—you being haunted by her mummy, trailing and bumping about all the passages at night. No wonder you were afraid to come down. But I suppose you mean you were interested in the books up there."

"I was enthralled," said the librarian, with a sort of groan. "I had no idea that the rebuilding of civilisation after the barbarian wars and the Dark Ages was so fascinating and many-sided a matter. That question of the Serf Regardant alone. . . . I'm afraid if I'd come on it all when I was younger . . ."

"You'd have done something desperate about it, I suppose," said Murrel. "Hurled yourself madly into the study of Perpendicular Gothic or wasted your substance on riotous old brasses and stained glass. Well, it isn't too late, I suppose."

A minute or two later Murrel looked up sharply in answer to a silence, as men look up in answer to a speech. There was something arresting in the way in which the Librarian had stopped talking; something still more arresting in the way in which he was looking out between the open glass doors across the spaces of the garden which were gradually warmed with the growing sunlight. He looked down the long avenue, with strips of flat but glowing flower-beds on either side, a little like the borders of a medieval illumination, and at the end of that long perspective stood the fragment of medieval masonry poised upon its eighteenth century pedestal above the great sweep of the garden, and the fall of the whole countryside.

"I wonder," he said, "how much there is in that term we hear so often 'Too late.' Sometimes it seems to me as if it were either quite true or quite false. Either everything is too late or nothing is too late. It seems somehow to be right on the border of illusion and reality. Every man makes mistakes; they say a man who never makes mistakes never makes anything else. But do you think a man might make a mistake and not make anything else? Do you think he could die having missed the chance to live?"

"Well, as I told you," said Murrel, "I'm inclined to think one subject is pretty much like another. They'd all be interesting to a man like you and very bewildering to a man like me."

"Yes," replied Herne with an unexpected note of decision. "But suppose one of the subjects really is the subject of men like you and me. Suppose we had forgotten the face of our own father in order to dig up the bones of somebody else's great-great-grandfather? Suppose I should be haunted by somebody who is not a mummy, or by a mummy who is not dead?"

Murrel continued to gaze curiously at Herne and Herne continued to gaze fixedly at the distant monument on the lawn.

Olive Ashley was in some ways a singular person; being described by her friends in their various dialects as an odd girl, a strange bird and a queer fish; and in nothing more queer, when they came to think of it, than in that simple action with which her story starts; the fact that she was still "illuminating" when everyone felt that the play was the thing. She was bent, we might almost say crouched, over her microscopic medieval hobby in the very heart or hollow centre of the whirlwind of the absurd theatricals. It seemed like somebody picking daisies on Epsom Downs with his back to the Derby. And yet she had been the author of the play and the original enthusiast for the subject.

"And then," as Rosamund Severne observed with a large gesture as of despair, "when Olive had got what she wanted, she didn't seem to want it. Gave her her old medieval play and then it was she that got sick of it! Went back to pottering about with her potty little gold paints, and let us do the rest of the work."

"Well, well," Murrel had said, for he was a universal peace-maker, "perhaps it's as well the work is left to you. You are so practical. You are a Man of Action."

And Rosamund was somewhat soothed and admitted she had often wished she were a man.

Her friend Olive's wishes remained something of a mystery; but it may be conjectured that this was not one of them. Indeed it was not quite true to say, as Rosamund said, that they had given her her old medieval play. It would be truer to say that they had taken it away from her. They had improved it immensely; they seemed to be quite confident of that, and no doubt they ought to know. They paid every possible tribute to it, as a thing that could be worked up most successfully for the stage. A little adapted, it afforded some admirable entrances and exits for Mr. Julian Archer. Only she began to have a deep and deplorable feeling, touching that gentleman, that she preferred the exits to the entrances. She did not say anything about it, least of all to him. She was a certain sort of lady; who can quarrel with those she loves, but cannot quarrel with those she despises. So she curled up in her shell; in that shell in which gold paint was quaintly preserved in the old paint-boxes.

If she chose to colour a conventional tree silver, she would not hear over her shoulder the loud voice of Mr. Archer saying it would look shabby not to have gold. If she painted a quaint decorative fish a bright red, she would not be confronted with the exasperated stare of her best friend, saying, "My dear, you *know* I can't wear red." Douglas could not play practical jokes with the little towers and pavilions in her pictures, even if they looked as queer and top-heavy as pantomime palaces. If those houses were jokes, they were her own jokes; and they were not at all practical. The camel could not pass through the eye of the needle; and the pantomime elephant could not pass through the key-hole of the door that guarded her chamber of imagery. That divine dolls'-house in which she played with pigmy saints and pigmy angels was too small for these people, like big clumsy brothers and sisters, to come blundering into it. So she fell back on her own old amusement, amid general wonder. Nevertheless on this particular morning she was a little less mildly monomaniac than usual. After working for about ten minutes, she rose to her feet, staring out on to the garden. Then she passed out almost like an automaton, the paint-brush still in her hand. She stood looking for a little time at the great Gothic fragment on the pedestal, in the shadow of which she and Murrel had debated the terrible problem of John Braintree. Then she looked across at the doors and windows in the opposite wing of the house; and saw that in the doorway of the library the librarian was standing, with Douglas Murrel beside him.

The sight of these two early birds seemed to awaken the third early bird to a more practical contact with the waking world. It seemed as if she suddenly took a resolution, or became aware of a resolution she had already taken. She walked a little more quickly and in an altered direction, towards the library; and when she reached it, almost disregarding the breezy surprise of Murrel's greeting, she said to the librarian with a curious seriousness: "Mr. Herne, I wish you would let me look at a book in the library."

Herne started as from a trance and said, "I beg your pardon."

"I wanted to speak to you about it," said Olive Ashley, "I was looking at a book in the library the other day, an illuminated book about St. Louis, I think; and there was a wonderful red used; a red vivid as if it were red-hot, and yet as delicate in its tint as a clear space in the sunset. Now I can't get a colour like that anywhere."

"Oh, I don't know about that," said Murrel in his easy-going way. "I reckon you can get pretty well anything nowadays if you know where to go."

"You mean," said Olive somewhat bitterly, "that you can get anything nowadays if you know how to pay for it."

"I wonder," said the librarian musing, "if I were to offer to pay for a Palaeo-Hittite *palumon,* now, I wonder whether it would be easy to obtain."

"I don't say that Selfridge actually puts it in the shop-window," said Murrel, "but you'd probably find some other American millionaire somewhere, willing to do what he would call a trade with it."

"Now look here, Douglas," cried Olive with a certain fire, "I know you're fond of bets and wagers and that sort of thing. I'll show you the red colour I mean in the book, and you shall compare it yourself with the colours in my paint-box. And then you shall go out yourself and see whether you can buy me a cake of it."

Chapter 7

# "Blondel the Troubadour"

"Oh," said Murrel rather blankly. "Oh, yes. . . . Anything to oblige."

In her eagerness Olive Ashley had darted past him into the library, without waiting for the assistance of the librarian, who continued to stare into the depths of the distance with blind but shining eyes. She lugged down a lumbering volume from one of the lower shelves and laid it open at a blazoned page on which the letters seemed to have come to life and to be crawling about like gilded dragons. In one corner was the image of the many-headed monster of the Apocalypse; and even to the careless eye of her companion, its tint glowed across the ages with a red that had the purity of flame.

"Do you mean," he asked, "that I am to go hunting that particular animal through the streets of London?"

"I mean you are to go hunting that particular paint," she said, "and as you say you can get anything in the streets of London, you oughtn't to hunt far, I suppose. There was a man called Hendry, in the Haymarket, who used to sell it when I was a child; but I can't get that sort of fine fourteenth century red at any artist's colourmen's round here."

"Well, I've been painting the town red myself in a quiet way, for the last few hours," said Murrel modestly, "but I suppose it wasn't a fine fourteenth century red. It was only a twentieth century red, like Braintree's tie. I told him at the time that the tie might begin to ignite the town."

"Braintree!" said Olive rather sharply. "Was Mr. Braintree with you when you—when you painted it red?"

59

"I can't say he was what you call an uproariously festive boon companion," said Murrel apologetically. "These red revolutionists seem to have had awfully little practice in looking on the wine when it is red. By the way, couldn't I go hunting for that, don't you think? Suppose I brought you back a dozen of port, a few dozens of burgundy, some of claret, flasks of Chianti, casks of curious Spanish wines, and so on—don't you think you could get the right colour? Mixing your drinks, like mixing your paints, might perhaps—"

"But what was Mr. Braintree doing there?" asked Olive with some severity.

"He was being educated," replied Murrel virtuously. "He was taking a course; following out that course of instruction which your own educational enthusiasm marked out for him. You said he wanted to be introduced to a larger world and hear discussions about things he had never heard of. I'm sure that discussion we had at the Pig and Whistle was one that he'd never heard before in his life."

"You know perfectly well," she retorted a little crossly, "that I never wanted him to go to those horrid places. I meant him to have real discussions with intellectual people about important things."

"My dear girl," replied Murrel quietly, "don't you see yet what that means? Braintree can knock all your heads off at *that* sort of discussion. He's got ten times more idea of why he thinks what he does think than most of what you call cultured people. He's read quite as much and remembers much more of what he's read. And he has got some tests of whether it's true or not, which he can instantly apply. The tests may be quite wrong, but he can apply them and produce the result at once. Don't you ever feel how vague we all are?"

"Yes," she replied in a less tart accent, "he does know his own mind."

"It's true he doesn't know enough about some sorts of people's minds," went on Murrel, "but he knows our sort better than some; and did you really expect him to be prostrated before the mind of old Wister? No, no, my dear Olive, if you really want to see him prostrated, or anybody prostrated, you must come with me this evening to the Pig and Whistle—"

"I don't want to see anybody prostrated," she replied, "and I think it was very wrong of you to take him to such low places."

"And what about me?" asked the gentleman plaintively, "What about my morals? Is my moral training of no importance? Is my immortal soul of no value? Why this levity and indifference to my spiritual prospects at the Pig and Whistle?"

"Oh," she replied with elaborate indifference "everybody knows you don't mind that sort of thing."

"I raise against the Red Tie the more truly democratic blazon of the Red Nose; and appeal from the Marseillaise to the Music Hall," he said, smiling. "Don't you think now that if I went hunting for the Red Nose through London, rejecting the pink, the purple, the merely russet, the too dusky crimson, and so on, I might find at last a nose of that delicate fourteenth century tint which—"

"If you can find the paint," retorted Olive, "I don't care whose nose you paint with it. But I'd prefer Mr. Archer's."

It is necessary that the long-suffering reader should know something of the central incident in the play called "Blondel the Troubadour," as that alone could have rendered possible or credible the central incident in the story called, "The Return of Don Quixote." In this drama, Blondel leaves his lady-love in a somewhat unnecessary state of mystification and jealousy, supposing that he is touring the Continent serenading ladies of all nationalities and types of beauty; whereas in fact he is only serenading a large and muscular gentleman for purely political reasons. The large and muscular gentleman, otherwise Richard Coeur de Lion, was to be acted on this occasion by a modern gentleman answering to that description as far as externals went; a certain Major Trelawney, a distant cousin of Miss Ashley. He was one of those men, sometimes to be found in the fashionable world, who seem in some mysterious way to be able to act, when they are hardly able to read, and apparently quite unable to think. But though he was a good-natured fellow and excellent in theatricals, he was also an exceedingly casual fellow and had hitherto been very remiss in the matter of rehearsals. Anyhow, the political motives which were supposed to move Blondel to search everywhere for this large and muscular gentleman were of course of the loftiest kind. His motives throughout the play were of an almost irritating disinterestedness; a purity that amounted to perversity. Murrel could never conceal his amusement at hearing these suicidally unselfish sentiments breathed from the lips of Mr. Julian Archer. Blondel, in short, overflowed with loyalty to his king and love of his country and a desire to restore the former to the latter. He wished to bring the king back to restore order to his kingdom and defeat the intrigues of John, that universal and useful, not to say overworked, villain of many crusading tales.

The climax was not a bad piece of amateur drama. When Blondel the Troubadour has at last discovered the castle that contains his master, and has collected (somewhat improbably) a company of courtiers, court ladies, heralds and the like in the depths of the Austrian forest outside the doors of that dungeon, to receive the royal captive with loyal acclamations, King Richard comes out with a flourish of trumpets, takes the centre of the stage, and there before all his peripatetic court, with exceedingly royal gestures, abdicates his royal throne. He declares that he will be a king no longer, but only a knight errant. He had indeed been sufficiently errant in every sense, when his misfortune fell upon him; but it has not cured him of his own version of the view that it is human to err. He had been wandering in those Central European forests, falling into various adventures by the way, when he finally fell into the misadventure of the Austrian captivity. He now declared that these nameless meanderings, despite their conclusion, had been the happiest hours of his life. He delivers a withering denunciation of the wickedness of the other kings and princes of his time and the disgusting condition of political affairs generally. Miss Olive Ashley had quite a pretty talent for imitating the more turgid Elizabethan blank verse. He expresses a preference for the personal society of snakes to that of Phillip Augustus, the King of France; compares the wild boar of the forests favourably with statesmen managing public affairs at the moment; and makes a speech of a hearty and hospitable sort, addressed chiefly to the wolves and winter winds, begging them to make themselves comfortable at his expense, so long as he is not required to meet any of his relatives or recent political advisers. With a peroration ending with a rhymed couplet, in the Shakespearean manner, he renounces his crown, draws his sword, and is proceeding to Exit R., to the not unnatural annoyance of Blondel, who has sacrificed his private romance to his public duty, only to find his public duty doing a bolt off the stage in pursuit of a private romance. The opportune and exceedingly improbable arrival of Berengaria of Navarre, in the depths of the same forests, at length induces him to return to his allegiance to himself. And the reader must be indeed ill acquainted with the laws of romantic drama if he needs to be told that the appearance of the queen, and her reconciliation to the king, are the signal for an exceedingly hasty but equally satisfactory reconciliation between Blondel and his own young lady. Already an atmosphere fills the Austrian forest, accompanied by faint music and evening light, which corresponds to the grouping of figures near the foot-lights and the hasty diving for hats and umbrellas in the pit.

Such was the play of "Blondel the Troubadour," not altogether a bad specimen of the sentimental and old-fashioned romance, popular before the war, but now only remembered because of the romantic results which it afterwards produced in real life. While the rest were occupied in their respective ways with acting or scenery, two other figures in that human drama remained loyal to other enthusiasms, not without effect on their future. Olive Ashley continued to potter about impenitently with paints and pictured missals from the library. And Michael Herne continued to devour volume after volume about the history, philosophy, theology, ethics and economics of the four medieval centuries, in the hope of fitting himself to deliver the fifteen lines of blank verse allotted by Miss Ashley to the Second Troubadour.

It is only fair to say, however, that Archer was quite as industrious in his way as Herne in another. As they were the

Two Troubadours they often found themselves studying side by side.

"It seems to me," said Julian Archer one day, flinging down the manuscript with which he had refreshed his memory, "that this fellow Blondel as a lover is a bit of a fraud. I like to put a bit more passion into it myself."

"Certainly there was something curiously abstract, and at first sight artificial, about all that Provençal etiquette," assented the Second Troubadour, otherwise Mr. Herne. "The Courts of Love seem to have been pedantic, almost pettifogging. Sometimes it did not seem to matter whether the lover had seen the lady at all; as with Rudel and the Princess of Tripoli. Sometimes it was a courtly bow to the wife of your liege lord, a worship open and tolerated. But I suppose there was often real passion as well."

"There seems damned little of it in Miss Ashley and her Troubadour," said the disappointed amateur. "All spiritual notions and nonsense. I don't believe he wanted to get married at all."

"You think he was affected by the Albigensian doctrines?" inquired the librarian, earnestly and almost eagerly. "It is true, of course, that the seat of the heresy was in the south and a great many of the troubadours seemed to have been in that or similar philosophical movements."

"His movements are philosophical all right," said Archer. "I like my movements to be a little less philosophical when I'm making love to a girl on the stage. It's almost as if she really meant him to be shilly-shallying instead of popping the question."

"The question of avoiding marriage seems to have been essential in the heresy," said Herne. "I notice that in the records of men returning to orthodoxy after the Crusade of Montford and Dominic, there is the repeated entry *iit in matrimonium*. It would certainly be interesting to play the part as that of some such semi-oriental pessimist and idealist; a man who feels the flesh to be dishonour to the spirit, even in its most lovable and lawful form. Nothing of that comes out very clearly in the lines

Miss Ashley has given me to say; but perhaps your part makes the point a little clearer."

"I think he's a long time coming to the point," replied Archer. "Gives a romantic actor no scope at all."

"I'm afraid I don't know anything about any sort of acting," said the librarian, sadly. "It's lucky you've only given me a few lines in the play."

He paused a moment, and Julian Archer looked at him with an almost absent-minded pity, as he murmured that it would be all right on the night. For Archer, with all his highly practical *savoir faire,* was not the man to feel the most subtle changes in the social climate; and he still regarded the librarian more or less as a sort of odd footman or stable-boy brought in by sheer necessity, merely to say, "My lord, the carriage waits." Preoccupied always by his own practical energies, he took no notice of the man's maunderings about his own hobby of old books, and was only faintly conscious that the man was maundering still.

"But I can't help thinking," the librarian was continuing, in his low meditative voice, "that it might give rather an interesting scope for a romantic actor to act exactly that sort of high and yet hollow romance. There is a kind of dance that expresses contempt for the body. You can see it running like a pattern through any number of Asiatic traceries and arabesques. That dance was the dance of the Albigensian troubadours; and it was a dance of death. For that spirit can scorn the body in either of two ways; mutilating it like a fakir or pampering it like a sultan; but never doing it honour. Surely it will be rather interesting for you to interpret bitter hedonism, the high and wild cries, the horns and hootings of the old heathen revel, along with the underlying pessimism."

"I feel the underlying pessimism all right," answered Archer, "when Trelawney won't come to rehearsals and Olive Ashley will only fidget about with her potty little paints."

He lowered his voice a little hastily with the last words, for he realised for the first time that the lady in question was sitting at the other end of the library, with her back to him, bent over books and fidgeting away as described. She had not apparently heard him; in any case she did not turn round, and Julian Archer continued in the same tone of cheerful grumbling.

"I don't suppose you have much experience of what really grips an audience," he said. "Of course, nobody supposes it won't go off all right in one sense. Nobody's likely to give us the bird—"

"Give us what bird?" asked Mr. Herne, with mild interest.

"Nobody's likely to howl at us and hiss us, or throw rotten eggs at us in Lord Seawood's drawing-room, of course," continued Archer, "but you can always tell whether an audience is gripped or not. At least, you can always tell when you've had as much experience as I have. Now unless she can put a little more pep into the dialogue, I'm not sure I can grip my audience."

Herne was trying to listen politely with one half of his mind, but for the other half the garden beyond was taking on, as it so often did, the vague quality of a pageant in a vision. Far away at the end of an avenue of shining grass, among delicate trees, twinkling in the sunlight, he saw the figure of the Princess of the play. Rosamund was clad in her magnificent blue robes with her almost fantastic blue head-dress, and as she came round the curve of the path she made an outward gesture at once of freedom and fatigue, thrusting out her arms or throwing out her hands as if stretching herself. The long pointed sleeves she wore gave it somewhat the appearance of a bird flapping its wings; a bird of paradise, as the actor had said.

A half-thought formed itself in the librarian's mind as to whether it was that sort of bird that nobody would ever give him in Lord Seawood's drawing-room.

As the figure in blue drew nearer down the green avenues, however, even the dreamy librarian began to think that there might be another reason for that outward gesture. Something in her face suggested that the movement had been one of impatience or even of dismay since it cannot help looking like a mask of tragedy over quite trivial irritations. It might be questioned whether she regarded her present irritation as trivial. But she unconsciously carried about with her such a glow of good health and such a confidence of manner, that there was a second incongruity even in the fullness and firmness of her voice. There was something boisterous about it, that made even bad news sound as if it were good.

"And here's a nice state of things," she said indignantly, flapping open a telegram and staring round her in impersonal anger. "Hugh Trelawney says he can't act the King after all."

On some matters Julian Archer's mind worked very swiftly indeed. He was as much annoyed in a sense as she was; but before she had spoken again he had considered the possibility of taking a new part himself, and finding time to learn the lines appropriated to the King. It would be a fag; but he had never minded hard work when it was worth his while. The great difficulty he saw was the difficulty of imagining anybody in his part as the Troubadour.

The rest had not yet begun to look ahead, and the lady was still reeling, so to speak, under the blow of the treacherous Trelawney. "I suppose we must chuck the whole thing," she said.

"Oh, come now," said Archer more tolerantly, "I shouldn't do that if I were you. It seems rather rotten, when we've all taken such a lot of trouble." His eye wandered inconsequently to the other end of the room, where the dark head and rigid back of Miss Ashley were obstinately fixed in concentrated interest on the illuminations. It was a long time since she had been apparently concentrated on anything else; save for long disappearances, supposed to be country walks, which had remained something of a mystery.

"Why, I've sometimes got up at six three days running," said Mr. Archer, merely in illustration of the industry of the company.

"But how can we go on with it?" asked Rosamund in exasperation. "Who else is there who could take the King? We had trouble enough in getting hold of an assistant Troubadour, till Mr. Herne was kind enough to help us."

"The trouble is," said Archer, "that if I took the King, you'd have nobody who could take Blondel."

"Well then," said Rosamund rather crossly, "in that case it ought to be dropped."

There was a silence and they stood looking at each other. Then they all simultaneously turned their heads and looked towards the other end of the long room, from which a new voice had spoken.

For Olive Ashley had risen suddenly from her occupation and faced round to speak. They were a little startled, for they had no idea she had even been listening.

"It ought to be dropped," she said, "unless you can get Mr. Herne to act the King himself. He is the only person who knows or cares what it's all about."

"God bless my soul," was the helpful comment of Mr. Herne.

"I don't know what you people imagine it's all about," went on Olive with some bitterness. "You seem to have turned it all into a sort of opera—a comic opera. Well, I don't know anything about it, in the way he does; but I did mean something by it, for all that. Oh, I don't imagine I can express it properly—not half so well as any old song like the one that says 'Will ye no come back again?' or 'When the King enjoys his own again.'"

"That's Jacobite," Archer explained kindly. "Mixing up the periods a bit, eh?"

"I don't know what King it is who ought to come back, any more than anybody else does," answered Olive steadily. "King Arthur or King Richard or King Charles or somebody. But Mr. Herne does know something about what those men meant by a king. I rather wish Mr. Herne really were King of England."

Julian Archer threw back his head and hooted with delighted laughter. There was something exaggerated and almost unnatural about his laughter; like the shrill mockery with which men have received prophecies.

"But look here," protested the more practical Rosamund, "even supposing Mr. Herne could act the King, then who is going to take his own part, that we had such a bother about before?"

Olive Ashley turned her back once more and appeared to resume tidying up her paints.

"Oh," she said, rather abruptly, "I could arrange that. A friend of mine will take it on if you like."

The others stared at her in some wonder; and then Rosamund said: "Hadn't we better consult Monkey about this? He knows such a lot of people."

"I'm sorry," returned Olive, still tidying up, "I'm afraid I've sent him off on a job of my own. He very kindly offered to get one of my paints for me."

And indeed it was true that, while the social circle was settling down (to the bewilderment of Mr. Archer) into a sort of acceptance of the idea of Mr. Herne's coronation, their friend Douglas Murrel was in the very act of setting out upon an expedition which was to have a curious effect upon all their fortunes. Olive Ashley had asked him to discover whether a particular pigment was still procurable at the artist's colour-men's. But he had all the cheerful bachelor's exaggerated love of adventure, and especially of preparations for adventure. Just as he had started on his nocturnal round with Mr. Braintree with a general sense that the night would last for ever, so he set out on his little commission for Miss Ashley with a general assumption that it would lead him to the end of the world. And indeed it did perhaps in some sense lead him to the end of the world; or perhaps to the beginning of another one. He took out a considerable sum of money from the bank; he stuffed his pockets with tobacco and flasks and pocket-knives as if he were going to the North Pole. Most intelligent men play this childish game with themselves in one form or another; but he was certainly carrying it rather far and acting as if he expected to meet ogres and dragons when he walked up the street.

And, sure enough, no sooner had he stepped outside the old Gothic gateway of Seawood than he came face to face with a prodigy. He might almost have said a monster. A figure was entering the house as he was leaving it; a figure at once fearfully unfamiliar. He struggled with some confusion of identity; as in a nightmare. Then he sank into a stupefied certainty; for the figure was that of Mr. John Braintree; and he had shaved off his beard.

Chapter 8

# The Misadventures of Monkey

Murrel stood staring in the porch at the figure which appeared dark against the outer landscape; and all the fanciful part of him, which was largely subconscious, was stirred by half serious fancies. No black cat or white crow or piebald horse or any such proverbial prodigy could have been so inscrutable an omen at the beginning of his journey as this strange appearance of the Shaven Syndicalist. Meanwhile Braintree stared back at him with a hardihood almost amounting to hostility, despite their mutual affection; he could no longer thrust out his beard, but he thrust out his chin so as to make it seem equally big and aggressive.

But Murrel only said genially, "You are coming to help us, I hope." He was a tactful person and he did not say, "You are coming to help us, after all." But he understood in a flash all that had happened; he understood Olive Ashley's country walks and her abstraction and the way in which her curious social experiment had come to a crisis. Poor Braintree had been caught on the rebound, in the reaction after his depressing experiment as a drunken reveller. He might have easily gone on bullying her along with all the other nobs, so long as he had the sensation of marching into their palace with the populace behind him. But since the night when Murrel himself had sown the seed of doubt about his friend's democratic status, the latter had become merely an intensely sensitive and rather introspective individual; and one on whom graciousness and a delicate sympathy were certainly not altogether thrown away. Murrel understood all about it, except perhaps the end of it, which remained rather cloudy; but he did not allow the faintest trace of intelligence to appear in his tone of voice.

"Yes," replied Braintree stolidly, "Miss Ashley told me somebody had to come in and help. I wonder you don't do it yourself."

"Not much," replied Murrel. "I said at the beginning that if they would insult me by calling me a stage-manager, at least I wasn't wicked enough to be an actor-manager. Since then Julian Archer has taken over all the managing there is lying about. Besides, Miss Ashley has another sort of commission in my case."

"Indeed?" inquired Braintree. "Now I come to look at you, you look as if you were going out to seek your fortunes in the goldfields or somewhere." And he eyed with some wonder the equipment of his friend, who carried a knapsack, a resolute looking walking-stick and a leather belt apparently supporting a sheath-knife.

"Yes," said Murrel, "I am armed to the teeth. I am going on active service—going to the Front." Then after a pause he added, "The truth is I'm going shopping."

"Oh," said the wondering Braintree.

"Say good-bye to my friends, old fellow," said Murrel with some emotion. "If I fall in the first charge at the Bargain Counter, say that my last thought was fixed firmly on Julian Archer. Put up a little stone on the spot where I fell, and when the Spring Sales come back with all their birds and flowers, remember me. Farewell. I wish you luck."

And waving his resolute walking-stick in the air with gestures of benediction, he betook himself briskly along the path through the park, leaving the dark figure in the porch looking rather doubtfully after him.

The birds of spring, which he had just invoked so pathetically, were indeed singing in the bright plantation of little trees through which he went; the light green tufts of leafage had themselves something of the look of sprouting feathers. It was one of those moments in the year when the world seems to be growing wings. The trees seemed to stand on tiptoe as if ready to soar into the air, in the wake of the great pink and white cloud that went before him overhead like a cherubic herald in the sky. Something childish in his memories awoke; and he could almost have fancied that he was a fairy prince and his clumsy walking-stick was a sword. Then he remembered that his enterprise was not to take him into forests and valleys but into the labyrinth of commonplace and cockney towns; and his plain and pleasant and shrewd face was wrinkled with a laugh of irony.

By various stages he made his way first to the big industrial town in which he had gone on his celebrated round of revelry with John Braintree. But now he was in no mood of nocturnal festivity; but in an almost sternly statistical and commercial attitude of the cold white light of morning. "Business is business," he said severely. "Now I am a business man I must look at things in a hard practical way. I believe all business men say to themselves sharply before breakfast, 'Business is business.' I suppose it's all that can be said for it. Seems a bit tautological."

He approached first the long line of Babylonian buildings that bore the title of "The Imperial Stores" in gold letters rather larger than the windows. He approached it deliberately; but it would have been rather difficult to approach anything else, for it occupied the whole of one side of the High Street and some part of the other. There were crowds of people inside trying to get out and crowds of people outside trying to get in, reinforced by more crowds of people not trying to get in, but standing and staring in at the windows without the least ambition to get anywhere.

At intervals in the crawling crush he came on big bland men who waved him on with beautifully curved motions of the hand; so that he felt a boiling impulse to hit these highly courteous bounders a furious blow on the head with his heavy walking-stick; but he felt that such a prelude to adventure might bring matters to a premature end. With raging restraint he repeated the name of the department he desired to each of these polished persons; and then the polished one also repeated the name of the department and waved him onwards; and he passed on, grinding his teeth. It seemed to be generally believed that somewhere or other in these endless gilded galleries and subterranean halls there was a department devoted to Artists' Materials; but there was no indication of how far away it was or how long it would take, at the present rate of progress, to get there. Every now and then they came on the huge shaft or well of a lift; and the congestion was slightly relieved by some people being swallowed up by the earth and others vanishing into the ceiling. Eventually he himself found he was one of those fated, like Aeneas, to descend into the lower world. Here a new and equally interminable pilgrimage began, with the added exhilaration of knowing that it was sunken far below the street, like an interminable coal-cellar.

"How much more convenient it is," he said to himself cheerfully, "to go to one shop for everything, instead of having to walk nearly seventy yards in the open air from one shop to another!"

The gentleman called Monkey had not come to the encounter (or to the counter) altogether unequipped with instruments more appropriate to the occasion than a cudgel and a large sheath-knife. Indeed, the whole thing was not so much out of his way as his demeanour might indicate. He had gone round before now trying to match ribbons or obtain for somebody an exact shade in neckties. He was one of those people who are always being trusted by other people in small and practical matters; and it was not the first errand he had run for Miss Olive Ashley. He was the sort of man who is discovered taking care of a dog, which is not his dog; in whose rooms are to be found trunks and suit-cases which Bill or Charlie will pick up on the way from Mesopotamia to New York; who is often left to mind the baggage and might quite conceivably be left to mind the baby. Yet it is not enough to say that he did not lose his dignity (which, such as it was, was very deep down in him indeed and very indestructible), but, what is perhaps more interesting, he did not lose his liberty. He did not lose his lounging air of doing the thing because he chose; possibly (the more subtle have suspected) because that was really why he did it. He had the knack of turning any of these things into a sort of absurd adventure; just as he had already turned Miss Ashley's earnest little errand into an absurd adventure. This attitude of the all-round assistant sat easily on him because it suited him; something unassuming in his ugly and pleasant face, in his unattached sociability and very variegated friend-ships, made it come quite natural to anybody to ask him a favour. He gravely took out of his pocket-book a piece of old, stiff paper, rather like parchment and embrowned with age or dust, on which was traced in a faint but finely drawn outline the plumage of one part of the wing of a bird, probably intended as a study for the wings of an angel. For a few of the plumes were picked out in strokes like flames of a rather curious flaming red, which seemed still to glow like something unquenchable even upon that faded design and dusty page.

Nobody could really know how much Murrel was trusted in such matters, who did not know what were Olive Ashley's feelings about that old scrap of paper scratched with that un-finished sketch. For it had been made long ago when she was a child by her father; who was a remarkable man in more ways than anybody ever knew, but especially remarkable as a father. To him was due the fact that all her first thoughts about things had been coloured. All those things that for so many people are called culture and come at the end of education had been there for her before the beginning. Certain pointed shapes, certain shining colours, were things that existed first and set a standard for all this fallen world and it was that which she was clumsily trying to express when she set her thoughts against all the notions of progress and reform. Her nearest and dearest friend would have been amazed to know that she caught her breath at the mere memory of certain wavy bars of silver or escalloped edges of peacock green, as others do at the reminder of a lost love.

Murrel, as he took this precious fragment from his pocket-book, took with it a newer and shinier piece of paper, on which a note was written in the words: "Hendry's Old Illumination

Colours; shop in Haymarket fifteen years ago. *Not* Hendry and
Watson. Used to be sold in small round glass pots. J. A. thinks
more likely in country town than London now."

Armed with these weapons of attack, he was borne up against
the counter stacked with artists' materials, he himself being
wedged between a large mild buffer and an eager and even very
ferocious lady. The old buffer was very slow and the lady was
very rapid, and between them the young woman attempting
to sell at the counter seemed to be somewhat distraught. She
looked wildly over her shoulder at one person while her hands
shot out in all directions to deal with others; and the remarks
shot sideways out of her mouth, which were of an irritated
sort, seemed to be addressed to somebody quite different;
apparently to somebody behind.

"Never the time and the place and the loved one all together,"
murmured Murrel with an air of resignation. "It does not seem
perhaps the perfect moment, the perfect combination of conditions, in which to open one's heart about Olive's early childhood
and her fireside dreams about the flaming cherubim, or even
to go very deep into the influence of her father on her growing
mind. And I don't know how else one is exactly to convey how
important this is, or why any of us should take any particular
trouble about it. It all comes of having an open mind and
sympathising with so many different sorts of people. When I
talk to Olive I know that the right and wrong colour are just as
real to her as the right and wrong of anything else; and a dull
shade in the red is like a shadow on honour or somebody not
quite telling the truth. But when I look at this girl, I feel she has
every reason to congratulate herself, when she says her evening
prayers, if she hasn't sold six easels instead of five sketch books,
or thrown all the Indian ink over the people who asked for
turpentine."

He resolved to reduce his original explanation to the simplest possible terms to start with and expand it afterwards, if
he survived. Gripping his piece of paper firmly in his hand, he
confronted the shop girl with the eye of a lion-tamer, and said:
"Have you got Hendry's Old Illumination Colours?"

The young woman gazed at him for a few seconds; and there was on her face exactly the same expression as if he had spoken to her in Russian or Chinese. She forgot for a moment all that mechanical and merciless civility which accompanied the rapid and recognised exchanges. She did not beg his pardon or go through any such form. She simply said, "Eh?" and her voice rose sharply with that deep, incurable, querulous complaint and protest which is the very soul of the accent that we call Cockney.

The way of the conscientious modern novelist is hard; or rather it is much worse, it is soft. It is like plodding heavily through loose and soft sand, when he himself would be only too delighted to leap from crag to crag or from crisis to crisis. When he would fain take the wings of a dove and fly away and be at rest in some reposeful murder, shipwreck, revolution or universal conflagration, he is condemned for a time to toil along the dusty road which is the way such things happen; and must pass through a purgatory of law and order before entering his paradise of blood and ruin. Realism is dull; that is what is meant by saying that realism alone tells the truth about our intense and intelligent civilisation. Thus, for instance, nothing but a mass of most monotonous detail could convey to the reader any impression of the real conversation between Mr. Douglas Murrel and the young woman selling him, or not selling him, paints. To be true to the psychological effect of that cumulative conversation it would be necessary, to start with, to print Mr. Murrel's question ten times over in exactly the same words, till the page looked like a pattern. Still less can any brief and picturesque selection give any notion of the phases through which the wondering face of the saleswoman passed, or the variation in her artless comments. How should rapid narrative describe how big business dealt with the problem? How she said they had got illumination colours and produced water colours in a shilling box. How she then said they had not got illumination colours and implied that there were no such things in the world; that they were a fevered dream of the customer's fancy. How she pressed pastels upon him, assuring him that they were just the same. How she said, in a disinterested manner, that certain brands of green and purple ink were being sold very much just now. How she asked abruptly if it was for children, and made a faint effort to pass him on to the Toy Department. How she finally relapsed into an acid agnosticism, even assuming a certain dignity, which had the curious effect of appearing to give her a cold in her head, and causing her to answer all further remarks by saying: "Dote know, I'be sure."

All this would have to occupy as much space as it did time, before the effect on the customer could be found excusable, especially to himself. A wild protest against the preposterousness of things in general surged up inside him; a sort of melodrama that found its energy in mockery. He leaned over the counter in a lowering and almost bullying fashion, and said: "Where is Hendry? What have you done with Hendry, that household word? Why all these dark evasions when Hendry is mentioned; this sinister and significant silence on this one subject; this still more sinister and significant changing of the subject? Why do you tear the conversation away towards pastels? Why do you erect a screen or barricade of cheap chalks and tin paint-boxes? Why do you use red ink as a red herring? What happened to Hendry? Where have you hidden him?"

He was about to add, in a low and hissing voice, *"or all that remains of him,"* when he had a revulsion, and his better feelings returned with a rush. A sudden sense of the pathos of this bewildered automaton overwhelmed his good-natured spirit with shame; he stopped in the middle of a sentence, hesitated, and then adopted another method for pursuing his purpose. Putting his hand hastily into his pocket, he pulled out some envelopes and a card-case, and presenting his name, asked with courtesy, and almost humility, if he could see the manager of the department. He gave the girl his card, and the next moment regretted that also.

There was one weak side of the many-sided Mr. Murrel on which he could be abashed and thrown off his balance; perhaps it was the only kind of attack he really feared. It was anything like a gross and obvious appeal to the accident of privilege that belonged to his social position. It would be cant to say that he was always unconscious of his rank. Somewhere deep inside him, perhaps, he was even too conscious of it. But it was deeply embedded in him that the only way to defend it was to ignore it. Moreover, there was a certain complexity and conflict; and some pride in the accident of being born with a few others "in the know" wrestled with the real and deep desire of all masculine men for equality. The one thing that embarrassed him was any such reminder, and he remembered too late that his card and address carried certain indications of such things; a club and a formal title. Worst of all, it was working; it was obviously working like a charm. The girl referred back to the mysterious being behind her, to whom so many of her peevish excuses were addressed; that being in turn studied the card, probably with an eye wiser in the wickedness of this world; and after a good deal more fuss, which only a realistic novelist would bother to describe, Douglas Murrel did really find himself bowed into the private apartment of one evidently in authority.

"Wonderful place you have here," he said cheerfully. "All done by organisation, I suppose. I expect you could pretty well get into touch with all the trade conditions in the world if you put your machinery to work."

The manager, however shrewd, had a vanity in such things, and before the conversation had gone much further had committed himself to very vast and universal claims to knowledge.

"This man Hendry whom I was inquiring about," said Murrel, "was really a rather remarkable man. I never knew him myself, but I understand from my friend, Miss Ashley, that he was a friend of her father and of the old group that worked with William Morris.

"He was a man who understood his subject very thoroughly, on the scientific as well as the artistic side. Indeed, I believe he had originally been a doctor and a chemical expert of some note, when he took up this particular business of producing the right pigments for the reproduction of medieval work.

"He kept a little shop in the Haymarket but I believe that it was always full of his artistic friends, like Miss Ashley's father. He knew nearly all the eminent men of his day, and some of them quite well. Now you would think a shopkeeper of that sort could hardly disappear entirely without leaving any trace at all. Wouldn't you expect to be able to find a man of that sort and his wares turning up somewhere?"

"Yes," said the other slowly, "I should expect to find him employed somewhere, certainly; I should expect to find he'd got a job in our works or in some of the big firms."

"Ah," said Murrel, and relapsed into reflective silence.

Then he said, suddenly: "If you come to that, a lot of our little squires and country gentlemen are pretty hard hit nowadays. But I suppose you could find them all acting as butlers and footmen to some of the dukes."

"Oh, well . . . I suppose that would be a bit different," said the manager awkwardly; not being quite sure whether he ought to laugh. He went into a back office to consult business records and books of reference. He left his visitor under the impression that he was looking up the letter "H" to find the name of Hendry. As a matter of fact, he was looking up the letter "M" to find the name of Murrel. But what he found out in the latter inquiry disposed him more favourably to the former. He plunged into a much more elaborate examination of the books, rang up and questioned all the older heads of various departments and after a great deal of this gratuitous labour actually came on a trace of the forgotten affair in question; which, to do him justice, he pursued when he had got it with something of the disinterested energy of a detective in a sensational novel. After some considerable time, he came back to Murrel, wearing a broad smile and rubbing his hands in triumph.

"Very good of you to have paid a compliment to our little attempts at organisation, Mr. Murrel," said the manager in quite a gay and radiant manner. "There is really something to be said for organisation, you know."

"I hope I haven't caused a lot of disorganisation," said Murrel. "I'm afraid my request was rather an unusual one. I suppose very few of your customers come to order dead pre-Raphaelites over the counter. Somehow it doesn't seem to be the sort of place where one would drop in for a chat, merely to say you had a friend who was a friend of William Morris. It's awfully good of you to bother."

"Only too pleased," replied the affable official, "only too pleased to give you a good impression of our system, I assure you. Well, I think I can give you a little information about this man Hendry. It appears that there was a man of that name at one time employed temporarily in this department. He seems to have applied for work, and appeared to have some knowledge of the business. The end of the experiment was very unsatisfactory. I believe the poor fellow was a little cracked; complained of pains in the head and so on. Anyhow he broke out one day and threw the manager of the department slap through a great picture on an easel. I can't find anything about his being sent to prison or to an asylum, as one would naturally expect. As a matter of fact, I may tell you that we keep a pretty careful record of our employees' mode of life, prosecutions by the police and so on; so I imagine that he simply ran away. Of course, he will never work for us again; no good trying to help people of that sort."

"Do you know where he lives?" asked Murrel gloomily.

"No; I think that was part of the trouble," replied the other. "Most of our people were living in at that time. They say he always lunched round at the Spotted Dog; and that alone looked bad, of course; We much prefer our people to use the regular restaurants provided for the purpose. It was probably drink that was really the matter with him; and that sort of man never comes up again."

"I wonder," said Murrel, "what became of his Illuminating Paints."

"Oh methods have been very much improved, of course, since his time," said the other. "Only too glad to be of any service to you, Mr. Murrel, and I hope you won't think I'm trying to force a card. But as a matter of fact, you couldn't do better than the Empire Illuminator that we always sell. It's practically replaced all the others by now; you must have seen it everywhere. The whole apparatus compact and complete and everything much more convenient than the old process."

He went across to one of the desks and took some printed and coloured leaflets which he handed to Murrel in an almost careless fashion. Murrel looked at them and his eyebrows went up in a mild and momentary surprise. On the prospectus he saw the name of the large and pompous manufacturer with whom Braintree had debated in the drawing-room; but the chief feature of the leaflet was a large photograph of Mr. Almeric Wister, the art expert, with his signature appended to a testimonial declaring that these colours alone could please the true instinct for beauty.

"Why, I know him," said Murrel, "He's the man who talks about the great Victorians. I wonder if he knows what happened to the friends of the great Victorians?"

"We can supply you immediately if you wish," said Mr. Harker.

"Thank you," said Murrel, in a rather dreamy fashion, "but I think I will only have a box of those children's chalks that kind young lady offered me."

And he did indeed go back in a grave and apologetic manner to the original counter and solemnly make his purchase.

"Is there nothing else I can do?" anxiously inquired the manager.

"Nothing," said Murrel in an unusually sombre manner. "I quite recognise that there is nothing you can do. Damn it all, perhaps there is nothing to be done."

"Is anything the matter?" asked Harker.

"I am beginning to have pains in my head," said Murrel. "They are probably hereditary. They come on at intervals and produce frightful results. I shouldn't like any repetition of unfortunate scenes . . . with all these easels standing about . . . thank you. Good-bye."

And he betook himself, not for the first time, to the Spotted Dog. At this ancient house he had a stroke of unusual luck. He had led the talk to the attractive topic of broken glass, vaguely feeling that if a man like Hendry went to a public house often enough he would be sure sooner or later to break something. He was well received.

His commonplace and cheerful appearance soon created a social atmosphere in which memories were encouraged to bloom. The young lady in the bar did remember the gentleman who broke a glass; the publican remembered him in greater detail, having disputed about the payment for the glass. Between them they did shadow forth a hazy portrait; of fuzzy hair and shabby clothes and long, agitated fingers.

"Do you remember," asked Murrel casually, "whether Mr. Hendry talked about where he was going next?"

"Dr. Hendry, he always called himself," said the innkeeper, slowly. "I don't know why, except that there was some chemistry mixed up with his paints and things. But he was no end proud of being a real doctor from the hospitals, though I'm damned if I'd like him to attend on me. Might poison you with his paints, I should think."

"You mean by accident?" asked Murrel, mildly.

"By accident, yes," conceded the publican very slowly, and added in a reasonable voice, "but you don't want to be poisoned by accident any more than on purpose, do you?"

"No; I will frankly admit that I don't," said Murrel. "Wonder where he took all his paints or poisons to."

It was at this point that the barmaid became suddenly communicative and conciliatory, and declared that she had distinctly heard Dr. Hendry mention the name of an extinct watering place on the coast. She had even a notion of the name of the street; and with this the hardy adventurer felt himself ready to act without further delay. He had permitted the conversation to trail away with all the traditional badinage and had then betaken himself to the road running to the coast. Before doing so, however, he paid two or three other visits, one to a bank, another to a business friend and a third to his solicitor; and came out on each occasion looking rather grim.

Chapter 9

# The Mystery of a Hansom Cab

A day later he stood in a seaside town where a steep street shot down to the sea; ridge below ridge of grey slate roofs looking like rings of a whirlpool as if that dreary town were being sucked into the sea. It was the dream of a suicide so a broken man might feel the wave of the world wash him away.

Looking down the descending curve of the dreary street Murrel could only see three distinct or detachable objects that could be said to suggest life. One was quite close to him; it was a milk can left outside the low door in an area. But it looked as if it had been left there for a hundred years. The second was a stray cat; the cat did not look sad so much as simply indifferent; it might have been a wild dog or any such wanderer prowling about a city of the dead. The third was more curious; it was a hansom cab standing outside one of the houses; but a hansom cab that partook of the same almost sinister antiquity. All this happened before the hansom cab had become an extinct creature to be reserved only in museums; but this hansom cab might well have been in a museum side by side with a Sedan chair. In fact it was rather like a Sedan chair. Being of a pattern still to be found here and there in provincial towns; made of brown polished wood and inlaid with other ornamental woods or woods once meant to be ornamental; tilted backwards at an unfamiliar angle and having two folding doors that gave the occupant the sensation of being locked up in an ancient eighteenth century cabinet. Still, with all its oddity, it was unmistakably a hansom cab; that unique vehicle which the alien eyes of a clever Jew saw as the gondola of London. Most of us know by this time that when we are told that the pattern of something has been much improved, it means that all its distinctive characters have disappeared. Everybody has motor cabs; but nobody ever thought of having such a thing as a motor hansom cab. With the old pattern vanished the particular romance of the gondola (to which Disraeli was perhaps referring), the fact that there is only room for two. Worse still there vanished something supremely special and striking and peculiar to England; the dizzy and almost divine elevation of the driver above his fare. Whatever we may say of Capitalism in England, there was at least one wild chariot or equestrian group in which the poor man sat above the rich as upon a throne. No more, and in no other vehicle, will the employer desperately lift a little door in the roof, as if he were imprisoned in a cell, and talk to the invisible proletarian as to an unknown god. In no other combination shall we ever feel again so symbolically and so truly our own dependence upon what we call the lower classes. Nobody could think of the men on those Olympian seats as a lower class. They were the manifest masters of our destiny, driving us from above, like the deities of the sky. There was always something distinctive about any man sitting on such a perch; and there was something quite distinctive even about the very back of the man sitting on the quaint old cab as Murrel approached it. He was a broad-shouldered person with side-whiskers of a sort that seemed to match the provincial remoteness of the whole scene.

Even as Murrel approached, the man, as if weary with waiting for his fare, laboriously descended from his lofty place and stood for a moment staring down the street at the scene. Murrel had by this time pretty well perfected his detective art of pumping the great democracy and he soon fell into a conversation with the cabman. It was the sort of conversation which he considered most suited to his purposes; that is it was a conversation of which the first three quarters had nothing whatever to do with anything that he wanted to know. That, he had long discovered, was so much the quickest way to his end as almost to deserve to be called a short cut.

At last, however, he began to discover things that were not without interest. He had found out that the cab was quite a historical antiquity in another way, and eminently worthy of a museum; for the cab belonged to the cabman. His thoughts went back vaguely to that first conversation, with Braintree and Olive Ashley, about the paint-box belonging to the painter and, by inference, the mine to the miner. He wondered whether the vague pleasure he felt in the present preposterous vehicle was not a tribute to some truth. But he also discovered other things. He found that the cabman was very much bored with his fare; but was also in a hazy way afraid of him. He was bored with that unknown gentleman because he kept him waiting outside one house after another in a tedious and interminable pilgrimage round the whole town. But he was also slightly in awe of him because he seemed to have some sort of official right to visit all these places and talked like somebody connected with the police. Though his progression was so slow it seemed that his manner was very hasty; or what is now called hustling. One felt that he had commandeered rather than called the cab. He was somebody who was in a frightful hurry and yet had a great deal of time to spare for each of his visits. It was therefore evident that he was either an American or a person connected with the Government.

Bit by bit, it came out that he was a doctor, a medical man having some sort of official claim to visit a variety of persons. The cabman, of course, did not know his name; but his name was the least important part of him. What was much more important was another name; a name that the cabman did happen to know. It seemed that the next stoppage of the crawling cab would be a little further down the street, outside the lodgings where lived a man whom the cabman had sometimes met in the neighbouring public house; a curious card by the name of Hendry.

Murrel having, by this circuitous route, at last reached his desire, almost leapt like an unleashed hound. He inquired the number in the street which was honoured by Mr. Hendry's residence; and almost immediately after went striding down the steep street towards it.

Having knocked at the door, he waited; and after a considerable interval he heard the sounds of it being very slowly unlocked behind him.

He faced round and fortunately spoke at once. The door had opened by little more than a crack; and the first fact it revealed was that the chain was still up across it. Within, much more dimly, he began to discern inside that high and dark house the glimmering features and figure of a human being. The figure was slim and the features were both pointed and pallid. But something almost atmospheric told him that the figure was feminine and even young; and when he heard the voice, a moment later, it told him something else that was more of a surprise to him.

At first, however, there was no word but only a very swift and silent action. The young woman within having seen nothing but the shape and outline of Murrel's hat and perceived that it was reasonably respectable, proceeded to shut the door again. She had relations already with people who appeared respectable, and even responsible. And that was, at the period in question, her answer to them. But Murrel had something of the promptitude of a fencer leaping and lunging at the only loophole in what seemed like a labyrinth of parry and defence. He thrust into the aperture the wedge of a word.

It was probably the only word that would have arrested the movement. The young woman, alas, was not acquainted with persons who had occasion in such cases to plant a foot in the doorway. She was not unacquainted with the art of slamming the door on it so as to pinch it or procure its prompt removal. But Murrel remembered things he had heard said in the public house and in the shop at the beginning of his journey; and he used the phrase that had never been heard in that street and had almost been forgotten by that woman. An instinct made him take off his hat and say: "Is Dr. Hendry in?"

Man does not live by bread alone, but mostly by etiquette and above all by consideration. It is by consideration that even the hungry live and by the lack of it that they die. It was a very determining detail that Hendry had once been proud of his doctor's degree; and a yet more determining detail that none of his new neighbours were now in the least likely to give it him. And this was his daughter, who was just old enough to remember when it had been freely given. Her hair was in her eyes in an almost slatternly fashion and her apron was as stained and threadbare as any of the other rags in that street; but when she spoke, the stranger knew at once that she remembered; and that the things she remembered were things of tradition and of the mind.

Douglas Murrel found himself inside a tiny hall with nothing but an ugly umbrella stand devoid even of umbrellas. Soon after he found himself mounting a very steep and narrow flight of stairs in almost total darkness; and soon after that abruptly allowed to fall into a frowsy little room, littered with such articles as were just too worthless to sell or even to pawn; where sat the man for whom he had gone on his erratic journey to search, as Stanley went to search for Livingstone.

Dr. Hendry had a head of hair rather like the grey top of a withering thistle; one almost expected it to wither visibly before one's eyes and the parts of the puff-ball to part and drift away drearily on the wind. But otherwise he was rather neater than might have been expected; though the effect may have been produced by his being very tightly and tidily buttoned up to the throat; as is said to be sometimes the habit of the hungry. After years of abstraction amid squalid surroundings, he was still rather perched than seated on his dusty chair, as if something dainty and disdainful even in his subconsciousness made him sit down on it gingerly. He was one of those men who can be so completely unconscious as to be outrageously rude; but who, the moment they are conscious, become almost painfully polite. The moment he became conscious of Murrel his politeness made him jump up with a jerk, like a very thin marionette hung on wires.

If he was staggered with the compliment of being called a doctor, he was still more intoxicated by the topic which his visitor put before him. Like all old men, and most fallen men, he lived in the past; and it seemed to him for one incredible moment that the past was again present. For that dark room, in which he was sealed up and forgotten like a dead man in a tomb, had heard once more a human voice asking for Hendry's Illumination Colours.

He rose on his thin and wavering legs and went without a word to a shelf on which stood a number of highly incompatible objects, and took down an old tin box which he brought to the table and began rather tremulously to open. It contained two or three round and squat glass bottles covered with dust; and when he saw them it seemed as if his tongue was loosened.

"They should be used with the vehicle in the box," he said. "Many people try to use them with oil or water, or all sorts of things"; though indeed it was at least thirty years since anybody had ever tried to use them with anything.

"I will tell my friend to be careful," said Murrel, with a smile. "I know she wants to work on the old lines."

"Ah, quite so," said the old man, suddenly lifting his head with quite a consequential air. "I shall always be ready to give any advice . . . any advice that can be of any use, I'm sure." He cleared his throat with quite a formidable return of fullness in his voice. "The thing to remember, first of all, of course, is that this type of colouring is in its nature opaque. So many people confuse the fact that it is brilliant with some notion of its being transparent. I myself have always seen that the confusion arose through the parallel of stained glass. Both, of course, were typically medieval crafts, and Morris was very keen on both of them. But I remember how wild he used to be if anybody forgot that glass is transparent. 'If anybody paints a single thing in a window that looks really solid,' he used to say, 'he ought to be made to sit on it.'"

Murrel resumed his enquiry.

"I suppose, Dr. Hendry," he said, "that your old chemical studies helped you a great deal in making these colours?"

The old gentleman shook his head thoughtfully.

"Chemistry alone would hardly have taught me all I know," he said. "It is a question of optics. It is a question of physiology." He suddenly thrust his beard across the table and said rapidly in a hissing voice, "It is even more a question of pathological psychology."

"Oh," said the visitor, and waited for what would happen next.

"Do you know," said Hendry with a sudden sobriety of tone, "do you know why I lost all of my customers? Do you know why I have come down to this?"

"As far as I can make out," said Murrel with a certain surly energy that was a surprise to himself, "You seem to have been damnably badly treated by a lot of people who wanted to sell their own goods."

The expert gently smiled and shook his head.

"It is a matter of science," he said. "It is not very easy for a doctor to explain it all to a layman. This friend of yours, now, I think you said she was the daughter of my old friend Ashley. Now there you have an exceptionally sound stock still surviving. Probably with no trace of the affliction at all."

While these remarks, which were totally unintelligible to him, were being uttered with the same donnish and disdainful benevolence, the attention of the visitor was fixed on something else. He was studying with much more attention the girl in the background.

The face itself was much more interesting than he had supposed from the glimpse in the gloom of the doorway. She had tossed back the black elf-locks that had hung over her eyes like plumes on a hearse. Her profile was what is called aquiline and its thinness made it a little too literally like an eagle. But she did not cease to seem young even when she might almost be said to seem dead or dying. There was a taut and alert quality about her and her eyes were very watchful; especially at that moment. For it seemed clear that she did not like the direction that the talk was taking.

"There are two plain principles of physiology," her father went on in his easy explanatory style, "which I never could get my colleagues to understand. One is that a malady may affect a majority. It may affect a whole generation, as a pestilence affects a whole countryside. The second is that maladies affecting the chief senses are akin to maladies of the mind. Why should colour-blindness be any exception?"

"Oh," said Murrel, sitting up suddenly with a jump, and a half-light breaking on his bewilderment. "Oh. Yes. Colour-blindness. You mean that all this has arisen because nearly everybody is colour-blind."

"Nearly everybody subjected to the peculiar conditions of this period of the earth's history," corrected the doctor in a kindly manner. "As to the duration of the epidemic, or its possible periodicity, that is another matter. If you would care to see a number of notes I have compiled—"

"You mean to say," said Murrel, "that that big shop all the way down the street was built in a sort of passion of colour-blindness; and poor old Wister had his portrait put on ten thousand leaflets to celebrate the occasion of his becoming colour-blind."

"It is obvious that the matter has some traceable scientific origin," said Dr. Hendry, "and it seems to me that my hypothesis holds the field."

"It seems to me that the big shop holds the field," said Murrel, "and I wonder whether that shop girl who offered me chalks and red ink knows about her scientific origin."

"I remember my old friend Potter used to say," observed the other, gazing at the ceiling, "that when you had found the scientific origin, it was always quite a simple origin. In this case, for instance, anybody looking at the surface of the situation would naturally say that the whole of humanity had gone mad. Anybody who says the paints they advertise in that leaflet are better than my paints obviously must be mad. And so, in a sense, most of these people really are mad. What the scientific men of the age have failed altogether to investigate adequately is *why* they are mad. Now by my theory the unmistakable symptom of colour-blindness is connected with—"

"I'm afraid you must excuse my father talking any more," said the young woman in a voice that was at once harsh and refined. "I think he is a little tired."

"Oh, certainly," said Murrel, and got up in a rather dazed fashion. He was moving towards the door, when he was suddenly stopped by an almost startling transformation in the young lady. She still stood in a rather rigid fashion behind her father's chair. But her eyes, which were both dark and bright, shifted and shot, as it were, in a shining obliquity towards the window; and every line in her not ungraceful figure turned into a straight line like a steel rod. In the dead silence a sound could be heard through the half-open window. It was the sound of the large and lumbering wheels of the antiquated hansom cab drawing up at the door.

Murrel, still full of embarrassment, opened the door of the room and went out on to the dark landing. When he turned he found, with a certain surprise, that the girl had followed him.

"Do you know what that means?" she asked. "That brute there has come for father."

A dim premonition of the probable state of affairs began to pass across his mind. He knew that a number of new and rather sweeping laws, which in practice only swept over the poor streets, had given medical and other officials very abrupt and arbitrary powers over people supposed to fall short of the full efficiency of the manager of the stores. He thought it only too likely that the discoverer of the remarkable scientific theory of colour-blindness as a cause of social decay might appear to fall short of that efficiency. Indeed, it would even seem that his own daughter thought so, from her desperate efforts to steer the poor old gentleman away from the topic. In plain words, somebody was going to treat the eccentric as a lunatic. And as he was not an eccentric millionaire or an eccentric squire, or even in these days regarded as an eccentric gentleman, it was probable enough that the new classification could be effected rapidly and without a hitch. Murrel felt what he had never felt fully since he was a boy, a sudden and boiling rage. He opened his mouth to speak, but the girl had already struck in with her voice of steel.

"It's been like that all along," she said. "First they kick him into the gutter and then they blame him for being there. It's as if you hammered a child on the head till he was stunned and stupid and then abused him for being a dunce."

"Your father," observed the visitor doubtfully, "does not strike me as at all stupid."

"Oh, no," she answered, "he's too clever, and that proves he's cracked. If he wasn't cracked, it would prove that he was half-witted. If it isn't one way it's the other. They always know how to have you."

"Who are *they?*" asked Murrel, in a low and (for anyone who knew him) rather menacing voice.

The question was in some sense answered, not by the person to whom it was addressed, but by a deep and rather guttural voice coming up the black well of the staircase, from somebody who was mounting the stairs. The crazy stairs creaked and even shook under him as he mounted, for he was a heavy man, and as he emerged into the half-light from the little window on the landing he seemed to fill up the whole entrance with a bulk of big overcoat and broad shoulders. The face that was thus turned up to the light reminded Murrel for the first moment of something between a walrus and a whale; it was as if some deep-sea monster was rising out of the deeps and turning up its round and pale and fishy face like a moon. When he looked at the man more carefully and less fancifully he saw that the effect came from very fair hair being very closely cropped in contrast with a moustache like a pair of pale tusks, and from the light of the window on the round spectacles.

This was Dr. Gambrel, who spoke perfectly good English, but stumbled on the steep stairs and swore softly in some other speech. Monkey listened intently a moment, and then silently slipped back into the room.

"Why don't you have a light?" asked the doctor sharply.

"I suppose I'm a lunatic, too?" Miss Hendry replied, "I'm quite ready to be anything my father is supposed to be."

"Well, well, it's all very painful," said the doctor recovering his composure and with it something more like a callous benev-olence. "But there's nothing to be gained by shilly-shallying over it. You'd much better let me see your father at once."

"Oh, very well," she replied. "I suppose I shall have to."

She turned abruptly and opened the door which let them both into the little dingy room where Dr. Hendry was sitting. There was nothing very notable about it except its dinginess; the doctor had been in it before, and the young woman had hardly been out of it for the last five years. It is therefore perhaps a rather remarkable fact that even the doctor looked at it with a vague surprise, the cause of which he was at the moment too fiercely flustered to define especially. As for the young woman, she looked at the room with a stare of stony astonishment.

There was no other door to the room; Dr. Hendry was sitting alone at his table, and Mr. Douglas Murrel had totally disappeared.

Before Dr. Gambrel could remark on the fact or even become fully conscious of it, the unfortunate Hendry had hopped up from his seat and seemed thrown into a flutter of mingled surrender and expostulation which stopped any other line of conversation.

"You will understand," he said, "that I protest formally against your interpretation of my case. If I could put the facts fully before the scientific world, I should not have the smallest difficulty in showing that the argument is entirely the other way. I admit that, at this moment, the average of our society has, owing to certain optical diseases which—"

Dr. Gambrel had the power of the modern state, which is perhaps greater than that of any state, at least, so far as the departments over which it ranges are concerned. He had the power to invade this house and break up this family and do what he liked with this member of it; but even he had not the power to stop him talking. In spite of all official efforts, Dr. Hendry's lecture on Colour-Blindness went on for a considerable time. It continued while the more responsible doctor edged him gradually towards the door, while he led him down the stairs, and at least until he managed to drag him out on to the doorstep. But meanwhile other things had been happening, which were not noticed by those who were listening (however unwillingly) to the lecture which had begun in the room upstairs.

. . . . . . . .

The cabman perched upon the ancient cab was a patient character and had need to be. He had been waiting outside the house of the Hendrys for some time, when something happened which was certainly more calculated to entertain his leisure than anything that had happened yet.

It consisted of a gentleman apparently falling out of the sky on to the top of the cab, and righting himself with some difficulty in the act of nearly rolling off it. This unexpected visitor, when eventually he came the right way up, revealed to the astonished cabman the face and form of the gentleman with whom he had had a chat recently a little further down the road. A prolonged stare at the newcomer, followed by a prolonged stare at the window just above revealed to the driver that the former had not actually dropped from heaven, but only from the window-sill. But though the incident was not by definition a miracle, it was certainly something of a marvel. Those privileged to see Murrel fall off the window-sill on to the top of the hansom cab might have formed a theory about why he had originally been called Monkey.

The cabman was still more surprised when his new companion smiled across at him in an agreeable manner and said, like one resuming a conversation: "As I was saying—"

It is unnecessary to go back after all these years, and the adventurous consequences they brought forth, to record what he was saying. But it is of some direct importance to the story to record what he said. After a few friendly flourishes he sat himself down firmly with his legs astraddle on the top of the cab, and took out his pocket book. He leaned across at the considerable peril of pitching over, and said, confidentially: "Look here, old fellow, I want to buy your cab."

Murrel was not entirely unacquainted with the scientific regulation, under which was being enacted the last act of the tragedy of Hendry's Illumination Colours. He remembered having had an argument a long time ago with Julian Archer who was great on the subject. It was a part of that quality in Julian Archer which fitted him so specially and supremely to be a public man. He could become suddenly and quite sincerely hot on any subject, so long as it was the subject filling the newspapers at the moment. If the King of Albania (whose private life, alas, leaves so much to be desired) were at that moment on bad terms with the sixth German princess who had married into his family, Mr. Julian Archer was instantly transformed into a knight-errant ready to cross Europe on her behalf, without any reference to the other five princesses who were not for the moment in the public eye. The type and the individual will be completely misunderstood, however, if we suppose that there was anything obviously unctuous or pharisaical in his way of urging these mutable enthusiasms. In each case in turn, Archer's handsome and heated face had always been thrust across the table with the same air of uncontrollable protest and gushing indignation. And Murrel would sit up opposite him and reflect that this was what made a public man; the power of being excited at the same moment as the public press. He would also reflect that he himself was a hopelessly private man. He always felt like a private man, though his family and friends had considerable power in the state; but he never felt so hopelessly and almost pitiably private as when he thus remained like one small frozen object, still moist and chilly in the blast of a furnace.

"You can't be against it; nobody can be against it," Archer had cried. "It's simply a Bill to introduce a little more humanity into asylums."

"I know it is," his friend had replied, with some gloom. "It introduces a lot more humanity into asylums. That's exactly what it does do. You'll hardly believe it, but there's quite a lot of humanity still that doesn't want to be introduced into asylums." But he recalled the story chiefly because Archer and the newspapers had congratulated each other on another new feature rather relevant to the present case. This was the greater privacy of the proceedings. A special sort of magistrate would settle all such cases in an interview as private as a visit to a physician.

"We're getting more civilized about these things," said Archer. "It's just like public executions. Why we used to hang a man before a huge crowd of people; but now the thing is done more decently."

"All the same," grumbled Murrel. "We should be rather annoyed if our friends and relatives began disappearing quietly; and whenever we'd mislaid a mother or couldn't put our hands on a favourite niece, we heard that our poor relation had been taken away and hanged with perfect delicacy."

Murrel knew that Hendry was being taken to such an interview; and listened grimly to his medical monologue in the cab. Hendry was a hopelessly English lunatic, he reflected, in having thus taken refuge in a hobby and a theory instead of a grievance and a vendetta. He had been ruined as Hendry of the secret of medieval pigments. Yet he was almost happy in being Hendry of the secret of diseased eyesight. Dr. Gambrel, curiously enough, also had a theory. It was called Spinal Repulsion and traced brain trouble in all those who sat on the edges of chairs, as Hendry did. Dr. Gambrel had collected quite a large number of poor people off the edges of chairs; fit symbol of the insecure ledge of their lives. He was quite prepared to explain this theory in the court, but he had no opportunity of explaining it in the cab.

There was something macabre about the progress of the cab crawling up the steep streets of that grey seaside town. From infancy he had felt the phrase "a crawling cab" had a touch of nightmare; as if the cab crept after its fares and swallowed them with its yawning jaws. The horse had an angular outline: the dark woods inlaying the cab the hint of a coffin. The road grew steeper, the street rearing against the cabhorse or the cabhorse against the cab. But they came to a standstill before a porch with two pillars between which they saw the grey-green sea.

# Chapter 10

# When Doctors Disagree

The house with the pillared porch to which the crawling cab eventually crawled, had little to distinguish it from a prosperous private house. For the policy of all recent legislations and customs had been in the direction of conducting public affairs in private. The official was all the more omnipotent because he was always in plain clothes. It was possible to take people to and from such a place without any particular show of violence; merely because everybody knew that violence would be useless. The doctor had grown quite accustomed to taking his mad patients casually in a cab; and they seldom made any difficulty about it. They were not so mad as that.

This particular branch of the new Lunacy Commission had been only recently established in the town; for the distribution of such bureaus through the smaller places had been an afterthought. The attendants who lurked quietly in the vestibule or opened the gates and doors were new, if not to their job, at least to their neighbourhood. And the magistrate who sat in an inner room, to consider the cases as they came, was the newest of all. Unfortunately, while he was new he was also old. He had done the same work in many other places; and so formed into the habit of doing it smoothly and rapidly and dangerously well. But he was beginning to be a little old to do anything. His sight was not what it was; his hearing was not what he thought it was. He was a retired army surgeon of the name of Wotton. He had a carefully trimmed grey moustache, and a rather sleepy expression; he had reached a rather sleepy stage both of that day's work and of his life's work also.

He had a number of papers on his desk, among which was a note of certain appointments that afternoon in connection with the Commission in Lunacy. In his deep and comfortably padded room he naturally did not hear the crazy cab crawl up to the door; still less the rapid and quiet movement by which a gentlemanly person assisted the two occupants to alight and, with many polite phrases, managed to hustle them into the outer room of the building. The person was so very gentlemanly that nobody thought for the moment of questioning his right to act as intermediary; the official attendants accepted him as being obviously a highly polished part of machinery, and even the official doctor permitted himself to be courteously waved into a side room to the left of the magistrate's sanctum. Perhaps if they had looked out of the window a moment before, and seen the gentlemanly person fall off the top of the cab, they might have been more disturbed. As it was, the official doctor began to be very decidedly disturbed when the gentlemanly person (whom he had seen only dimly on a dark staircase and hardly begun vaguely to recognise) not only closed the door behind him with a courtly bow, but suddenly locked it.

Of all this the magistrate heard nothing; since it was carried out with quiet swiftness amid that momentum of routine that sleeps like a spinning top. The first notification he had was a knock at the door and a voice saying "This way doctor." It was the regular practice in such cases for the medical man responsible for the segregation to interview the magistrate first; who then had an interview (generally much briefer) with the victim. On that particular afternoon Mr. Wotton hoped that both interviews would be very brief indeed. He did not look up from his papers, but merely said:—"It is Case No. 9,871, isn't it; a case of conspiracy mania, I think."

Dr. Hendry inclined his head in his most graceful manner. "Conspiracy is, of course, a symptom rather than a cause," he said. "The cause is purely physical . . . purely physical," he coughed in a refined manner. "We don't need to be told at this time of day that the distortion of the sense reacts upon the brain, eh? In this case I have the strongest reason for supposing that the trouble arose originally from a very common malady of the optic nerve. The process by which I reached this conclusion is rather interesting in itself."

At the end of about ten minutes, it became apparent that Mr. Wotton did not think so. His head was still bowed over his papers and consequently did not study directly the figure before him. If he had he might have been moved to some suspicion by Dr. Hendry's remarkably shabby clothes. As it was, he only heard Dr. Hendry's remarkably cultivated voice.

"I don't think we need go into all that," he said at last, after his visitor had gone into a good deal of it, and seemed alarmingly capable of going into a good deal more. "If you're sure it's a case of that sort, a case of really dangerous mania, I suppose it's all right."

"In all my experience," said Dr. Hendry solemnly, and with a full sense of responsibility, "I have never known a clearer one. This optical question is becoming grave, sir. It is becoming menacing. Even at this moment, while I speak, persons unquestionably mad are wandering about the world, and even delivering authoritative opinions on scientific subjects. Only the other day—."

At this moment his melodious and persuasive voice was drowned for an instant in very remarkable sounds from the next room. The noise resembled that of some huge and heavy body being hurled against the door; and in the silence that followed something like guttural imprecations, as if hoarse and faint with fury, could be heard through the thick partition.

"Good heavens!" cried Mr. Wotton, awakening with a start and looking up for the first time. "What on earth was that?"

Dr. Hendry wagged his head with a beautiful sadness, but he continued to smile.

"Ours is a melancholy occupation," he said. "Dealing with the weaker and the wilder aspects of our fallen nature . . . the body of our humiliation, I think it is in the Greek Testament . . . the body of our humiliation. It sounds only too like the struggle of some unfortunate whom society finds it a sad necessity to restrain."

At this moment the body of our humiliation was again thrown crashing against the door; and it seemed to be a body of some weight and momentum and even nobility. The magistrate was not altogether satisfied. Patients or prisoners (or whatever the new social victims ought to be called) were indeed frequently taken into the adjoining room to await examination; but generally under the guardianship of attendants who would prevent them indicating their impatience in so lively a style. The only other hypothesis was that the lunatic next door was so exceedingly lively as to have killed his keeper.

Whatever else the old army surgeon was, he was a man of courage. He got up from his desk and went across to the door that was still shaking and vibrating with the shocks from within. He looked at it for a moment with his head on one side; and then deliberately unlocked it. Though he showed no fear, he had to show a good deal of agility, in leaping back and not being flung flat on the floor by the thing that came out of the room. At that moment he would have called it a thing rather than a man. It had goggle eyes that stood out of its head like horns; and Mr. Wotton had a confused feeling confirming the doctor's theory that the unfortunate creature must have something the matter with its eyes. It had long tawny tufts of moustache and hair standing out in all directions; for it had been ineffectually brushing its hair against the wall for some time past. It was only when it had fallen into the full daylight of the room that the magistrate saw that it was wearing a white waistcoat and a grey pair of trousers, such as are seldom worn by a walrus or even a wild man of the woods.

"Well, anyhow," he muttered, "he is clothed, if not exactly in his right mind."

The huge man who had fallen through the doorway straightened himself and stood up with a rather wild stare; his tawny tusks more aggressive than ever. But it soon became apparent at least that he possessed the power of speech. His first remarks, being curses in a Continental language, might indeed have

been mistaken for inarticulate cries; but the two scientific characters who were listening to him were soon able to recognise
the sound of scientific language disentangling itself from other
foreign languages. In fact, the official doctor was making his
official report; but it did not sound like that.

The situation was rather hard on him; and the trick from
which he had suffered will not be seriously defended, but only
silently enjoyed, by the wise and good. He also had a very
complete theory of the causes of mental breakdown among his
fellow citizens. He also could trace to physiological and organic
causes the mental condition of his captive. He could explain
the nature of Spinal Repulsion quite as sanely and serenely
as Hendry could that of Colour-Blindness. But somehow he
had not had the stage set for him so satisfactorily for its exposition. At the very moment when he should have sailed into
the magistrate's room to make his report, and Hendry should
have been locked up in the waiting room to wait for the result
of it, the unscrupulous Mr. Murrel had rapidly reversed the
positions of the two men of science, with the deplorable results
that we have already seen. The official, finding himself trapped,
had behaved as very full-blooded and confident people often
behave when something happens to them which they never
believe to be possible. For it is the man whose life goes with
a smooth and swift motion, who is normally self-satisfied and
smiling, who has never been made to turn aside for anything,
who comes with a crash into a real obstacle. On the other hand,
the history of poor Hendry had been exactly the opposite. He
had clung pathetically to his polite manners, as the only relic of
his social status, through a hundred humiliations; and he was
used to explaining things elegantly to creditors and assuming
a cultivated and slightly pedantic tone in talking to policemen.
The consequence was that while the official doctor gasped
and snorted and swore in unintelligible manner, the certified
lunatic stood with his head gracefully on one side, making a soft
clucking noise in his throat to indicate sorrow over the downfall
of the human mind. The Army surgeon looked from one to the
other for a moment, and then fixed his eyes upon the cursing

foreigner; as he had fixed them on many homicidal maniacs before. So did these three distinguished medical men meet at last; in a rather informal consultation.

Outside, in the street that struggled crazily to the sea-cliff, Douglas Murrel sat on the top of his cab, with his face upturned to heaven like one whose work has been well and worthily done. He was wearing an exceedingly battered and shabby black top hat, which was not his own; for he had bought the hat along with the cab; though it was the sort of hat which a man might well have been paid to wear, rather than pay for wearing it. It served his particular purpose, however, with great simplicity and success. The hat dominates and defines a figure in inconspicuous and colourless clothes; and so long as he wore it he passed well enough for the driver of such an ancient vehicle. When he took it off and slipped among the officials, with his well-brushed hair and gentlemanly manner, they had no reason to doubt his claims to a different position. On the top of the cab, however, he had resumed the hat; not without pomp, as a conqueror might crown himself with laurel.

He thought he knew what would probably happen and he decided to wait for it. The end of the immediate drama of the captured government expert he did not expect to see at that stage; he promised himself that if it went too far, he would be able to communicate with the authorities later. As it was, he left it almost reverently as a rounded and perfected thing, a poem. But if all went well, one consequence was likely enough to follow; and when he had waited for about ten minutes, he was gratified to find his calculation correct.

Dr. Hendry, once famous in the artistic world, walked out between the dark pillars of the porch that stood out against the sea; as free as the sea-gull that was swerving along the line of the cliff. He had an air of almost aggressive good taste; as if informing the whole street that he would refuse to inform anybody about the delicate professional secrets just confided to him. He made a movement as if pulling on a pair of invisible gloves, and he quite naturally stepped into the hansom cab, before he had thought of it. The conscientious cabman pulled down his top hat over his brows and rapidly drove him away up the steep and stony streets.

For the present at least, the chronicler may well maintain an awful silence about what happened between the magistrate and the doctor. And indeed Murrel's own mind showed a curious and rather indescribable disposition to drop the whole topic and to leave it behind him. He had a reputation for playing practical jokes. But this moment of his life will be somewhat misunderstood if it be supposed that he thought of it first and foremost as a practical joke upon the foreign doctor. A hazier and yet happier feeling was in his mind, as if the real story lay rather in front of him than behind him; as if the unexpected liberation of the poor old crank, with the colour-blind monomania, were but a symbol of the liberation of many things and the opening of a brighter world. Something had snapped; if it was only a bit of red tape; and he did not know yet how much had been set free. As he turned the corner a shaft of sun shot down the steep street, seeming as solid as that from solid clouds in the old Bible pictures, and looking up at the window of the high narrow house he saw Hendry's daughter.

The woman who looked out of the window appeared, after a fashion, for the first time in this story. Hitherto she had been cloaked in shadows, in the shades of the steep stairways and the high dark house. She had been disguised in destitution; and it is necessary to have lived in such a house to know how much destitution can disguise. She had turned pale like a plant in a narrow and shuttered house; a house in which there were no mirrors; least of all those human mirrors that we call faces. She had long ceased to think of her appearance; and she would have been more surprised than anyone else if she could have stood in the street and seen her appearance at the window. And yet, as she looked down into the street, she was something more than surprised. The beauty that unfolded from within, like some magic flower upon the balcony, was not due altogether to the burst of sun that had struck the street. It was the most beautiful thing in the world; perhaps the only really beautiful thing in the world. It was astonishment which was lost in Eden and will return with the Beatific Vision, in astonishment so strong that it will last for ever.

It was indeed only amazement at what she saw in the street; but there was in it the joy that only hails the reversal of all things in the world; what is too good to be true. To understand her astonishment it would be necessary to tell her story; and her story would be of a very different sort from this story, and more like those long scientific and realistic novels which are not stories at all. Since the day when her father had been ruined by a gang of rascals who happened to be too rich to be punished, her life had descended step after step into that world where all the people are assumed to be rascals and punished in a sort of rotation; the police regarding themselves rather as the warders of a large loose prison with the roof off. She had long given up having any sharp reaction to the tendency; it seemed perfectly natural so long as it was a downward tendency. If her father had been taken away and hanged, she would have been miserable and bitter and indignant; but she would not have been surprised.

But when she saw him coming back smiling in a hansom cab, she was completely surprised. Never had she known any living thing escape from the trap into which she thought he had fallen; never had she seen footprints coming out from that dark den of efficiency. It was as if she had seen the sun turn backwards towards the East, or the Thames stop suddenly at Greenwich and begin to go back to Oxford. But there was no doubt that it was her father, leaning back and smiling in the cab. As he had come out with the gesture of pulling on invisible gloves, so he leaned back with the gesture of smoking an invisible cigar. As she stared at him, she became conscious that the cabman had taken off his hat to her, with a remarkably fine flourish for so very deplorable a hat. The removal of the hat gave the last shock to her senses; for it revealed the colourless but carefully brushed hair of Mr. Murrel, the eccentric gentleman who had called at the house a few hours before.

Dr. Hendry leapt from the cab with quite youthful grace, and his hand went with another automatic gesture towards a totally empty pocket. He was living in the brave days of old.

"Don't mention it," said Murrel hastily, replacing the atrocious hat. "This is my own cab and I do it for amusement. Art for art's sake, as your old friends used to say. I am an arrangement, as Whistler said; an arrangement in black and brown. Your friend the mad doctor is, I trust, by this time an arrangement in black and blue."

Hendry recognised the educated voice, for there are some things a man never forgets. He recognised the voice in spite of the hat, even when it was rather obviously talking through the hat.

"My dear sir," he said, "I owe you a great debt of gratitude. Pray come inside."

"Oh, thank you," said Murrel, getting down from his perch. "My Arab steed, who has slept in my tent so often in the desert, will probably keep a faithful watch outside. He does not seem to suffer from any mad impulse to gallop."

He ascended for the second time the dark and steep staircase, up which he had seen the worthy mental specialist mounting like some monster out of the deeps. His thoughts went back to that unfortunate expert in a momentary remorse; but he told himself that there would be little difficulty in putting the matter straight.

"But won't that mean," she said, "that he will come back again for my father?"

Murrel smiled and shook his head. "Not if I know anything about him," he said, "or about old Wotton either. Wotton is a perfectly honest old gentleman; and will see at once that there couldn't be much the matter with your father, not half so much as with the other man. And even the other man won't be exactly anxious to proclaim to the world that he gave such a good imitation of a raving maniac that they locked him up."

"Then you have really saved us," she said. "It is a very wonderful thing."

"Not so wonderful as your requiring to be saved, I should say," said Murrell. "I really don't know what the world is coming to. I suppose they set a lunatic to catch a lunatic on the principle of setting a thief to catch a thief."

"I have known some thieves," said Dr. Hendry, twirling his moustache with a sudden fierceness, "but they are not caught yet."

Murrel looked across at him for a moment, and knew that his spirit had returned to him.

"Perhaps we shall try to catch the thieves after all," he said; and did not know that he was uttering a sort of prophecy of the fate of his home and his friends and many things he knew. For far away in Seawood Abbey things that he would have thought utterly fantastic were taking colour and form and marching towards the climax of this history. Of these things he knew nothing; but, curiously enough, his own imagination was already clouded with new colours more glowing and romantic than Hendry's Illumination Paints. He had a vague sensation of victory; but it had culminated when he looked up and saw the girl's face at the window; he leaned impulsively across and said: "Do you often look out of the window like that. . . . if I should be passing some time . . . ?"

"Yes." She said, "I often look out of the window."

Chapter 11

# The Lunacy of the Librarian

Far away in Seawood Abbey the great performance of "Blondel the Troubadour" was over. It had been not only a success but a sensation. After it had been performed twice on successive afternoons, a sort of special encore performance had been given comparatively early on the following morning, for the gratification of the school-children and others; and Julian Archer was finally putting off his armour with an air of some weariness and relief. Some of the more malicious said his fatigue was partly due to the fact that he himself had not been the sensation.

"So that's over," he said to Michael Herne who was standing beside him, still in the romantic green rags of the Outlaw King. "I'm off to get into some comfortable togs. Thank the Lord we shan't have to wear these again."

"I suppose not," said Herne and looked down at his own long green legs in a sort of daze, rather as if he had never seen his legs before. "I suppose we shall never wear them again."

He remained standing thus for a moment; then as Archer darted back to his own dressing room, the librarian slowly followed him and betook himself to his own apartments adjoining the library.

One other person remained as if stunned with thought, though the performance had long been over. And that was the writer of the play; who did not feel in the least as if she had written it. Olive Ashley felt as if she had merely struck a match at midnight and it had burst and broadened into the unearthly splendours of the midnight sun. She felt as if she had painted one of her gold and crimson angels and the painted face had spoken, and spoken terrible things. For the eccentric librarian, turned for an hour into a pantomime king, might have been possessed of a devil. Only the devil had been a little like the gold and crimson angel. Something seemed to come pouring out of him that nobody had ever thought was in him; and which the poet could not claim to have put in him. He seemed to her to span and take in his stride all the abysses and the heights known to the secret humility of the artist. She did not seem to be hearing the verses she had written. They sounded like the verses she would have liked to have written. She had not only excitement but expectation. For he had the power of making each line seem greater than the last; and yet they were only her own pretty tolerable verses. The moment which glowed in her memory, and in that of many much less sensitive, was that in which the King, who had been captured as an outlaw, refused the offer of his own crown and declared that in a world of wicked princes he preferred the wandering life of the woods.

> Shall I who sing with the high tree-tops at morning
> Sink to be Austria; even as is that brute
> And brigand that entrapped me, or be made
> A slave, a spy, a cheat, a King of France?
> And what crowns other shadow this the earth?
> The evil kings sit easy on their thrones
> Shame healed with habit; but what panic aloft
> What wild white terror if a king were good!
> What staggering of the stars; what prodigy.
> Men easily endure an unjust master
> But a just master no man will endure
> His nobles shall rise up, his knights betray him
> And he go forth, as I go forth, alone.

A shadow fell across her upon the grass; and preoccupied as she was she seemed to know even the shape of the shadow. Braintree reclothed and in his right mind (which some considered a very wrong mind) had joined her in the garden.

Before he could speak, she had said impulsively: "I've discovered something. It's more natural to talk poetry than to talk prose. Just as there's more spontaneity in singing than in stammering. Only, you see, most of us stammer."

"Your librarian certainly didn't stammer," said Braintree. "You might almost say he sang. I'm a pretty prosaic person; but I feel somehow as if I'd been listening to good music. It all seems very mysterious. When a librarian can act a King like that, there seems to be only one possible inference; that he has only been acting a librarian. And excellent as he was as the King, I consider his creation of the part of an embarrassed bookworm in the library was an even more finished performance. Do theatrical stars often come and conceal themselves behind bookcases in this way?"

"You think he was always acting," said Olive, "and I know he was never acting. That is the explanation."

"I fancy you are right," he answered. "But couldn't you have sworn you were in the presence of a great actor?"

"No, no; that is just the point," she cried sharply. "I could have sworn I was in the presence of a great man."

After a pause she went on: "I don't mean a great acting man like Garrick or Irving or somebody. I mean a great *dead* man— most awfully alive. I mean a medieval man: a man risen out of the grave."

"I know what you mean," assented the other, "and of course you are quite right. You mean that he couldn't have taken any other part. Your friend Mr. Archer could have taken any other part; but he is only a good actor."

"It all seems so strange," said Olive. "Why should Mr. Herne out of the library be—like that?"

"I think I know why," said Braintree, and his voice deepened to something like a growl. "In a sense that nobody understands he really does take it seriously. And so do I; I take it damned seriously."

"Do you mean my play?" she asked with a smile.

"I consented to put on those troubadour togs and act," he said, "I couldn't give a greater proof of devotion than that."

"I mean," she said a little hastily, "what do you mean about taking the King's part seriously?

"I don't like Kings," replied Braintree rather roughly. "I don't like Knights and nobles and all that parade of armed aristocracy. But that man likes them. He doesn't only pretend to like them. *He* is not a snob or a silly flunkey of old Seawood. He is the only man I have ever seen who might really defy democracy and the revolution, I know it simply from the way he strode about that silly stage and spoke—"

"And spoke those silly verses, you were going to say," said the poetess, pointing at him with a finger and laughing with a curious indifference rather rare among poetesses. It almost seemed as if she had found something that interested her more than poetry.

But it was one of Braintree's more virile qualities that he was never easily forced into flippancy; and he went on in his quiet pulverising fashion, a man always meditating with a clenched fist.

"I tell you when he was right on top, and seemed to tower over everything, when he said he would chuck away his sceptre and go wandering in the woods again with a spear, I knew—"

"Why here he is," cried Olive hastily and lowering her voice, "and the joke of it is that he is still wandering in the woods with a spear."

For indeed Mr. Herne was still in the theatrical costume of an Outlaw, having apparently forgotten to change his clothes when he drifted to his dressing-room; and the long hunting-spear on which he leaned in his blank verse soliloquies was still grasped unconsciously in his hand.

"I say," exclaimed Braintree, "aren't you going to get into any other clothes before lunch?"

The librarian looked at his legs again and said in a dull voice, "What other clothes?"

"I mean your ordinary clothes," replied Braintree.

"Oh never mind now," said the lady, "you'd better change after lunch now, I should think."

"Yes," replied the abstracted automaton, in the same wooden voice, and took his long green legs and spear away with him.

The lunch was pretty informal anyhow; and though all the others had managed to get out of their theatrical costumes, they had not all thoroughly got back into their conventional ones. Some of them, especially the ladies, were in a transitional state before the full splendours of the afternoon. For there was that afternoon at Seawood Abbey a grand political and social reception eclipsing even that which had attempted the education of Mr. Braintree. Needless to say it contained most of the same unmistakable figures with many more in addition. Sir Howard Pryce was there, wearing if not the white flower of a blameless life at least the white waistcoat of a Victorian merchant, whose life was always assumed to be blameless. He had lately passed equally blamelessly from Soap to Dyes, of which he was a financial pillar and a partner in certain commercial interests of Lord Seawood. Mr. Aubrey Wister was there, wearing his exquisite blend of artistic and fashionable raiment; wearing also his long moustache and melancholy smile. Mr. Hanbury, squire and traveller, was there, wearing nothing that could be noticed in particular and wearing it very well. Lord Eden was there, wearing his single eyeglass and the hair that looked like a yellow wig. Mr. Julian Archer was there, wearing clothes so good that they are hardly ever seen on a living man but only on the ideal beings in tailors' shops. And Mr. Michael Herne was there, still wearing a suit of green rags suitable to a royal outlaw in exile and quite unsuitable to the present occasion.

Braintree was not a conventional person but he was brought up against this walking mystery with an involuntary stare.

"You do seem to be dawdling about," he said. "I thought you'd gone off to dress long ago."

Herne appeared to be rather sulky in his last phase.

"Dress as what," he asked.

"Well, dress as yourself, I suppose," answered the other. "Give your celebrated imitation of Mr. Michael Herne."

Michael Herne lifted his rather hang-dog head with a jerk and stared at the other for a moment with almost blinding concentration; and then moved away towards the house, presumably to perform the belated toilet. And Mr. John Braintree did the only thing he ever did do in these rather uncongenial assemblies; went in search of Miss Olive Ashley.

Their conversation was lengthy and largely theoretical; and it is a remarkable fact that even after the afternoon guests had gone and dinner loomed in the distance, when Olive had retired to dress and then reappeared in a violet and silver vesture of rather unusual richness, they encountered each other again in the garden, by the broken monument where they had their first dispute. But they encountered something else as well.

Mr. Herne, the librarian, was standing beside that scrap of grey sculpture like a green statue; it might have been a bronze statue green with rust, but it was in fact a familiar figure still clad in the forester's fancy dress.

Olive Ashley said almost automatically, with a sort of jerk: "Are you *never* going to change?"

He swung his head slowly round and looked at her with blank blue eyes; then he seemed to recall his voice from the ends of the earth and said rather huskily.

"Am I ever going to change? . . . Or never change?"

She seemed to see something suddenly pictured in his staring eyes that started her trembling a little and she half shrank into the shadow of the man beside her, who struck in with something like a defensive authority: "Are you going to get into ordinary clothes, I mean?"

"What do you mean by ordinary clothes?" asked Herne.

"Well," replied Braintree, with a short laugh, "I suppose I mean the sort of clothes I wear; though I've never been considered exactly a leader of fashion." He smiled a moment in his grim fashion and added, "Nobody here will insist on your wearing a red tie."

Herne suddenly bent his brows upon the other man with a fixed and concentrated but rather puzzling expression and then said, in a soft voice: "And you think yourself revolutionary because you wear a red tie?"

"I have given other indications," answered Braintree, "but the tie has certainly become rather a symbol of them. I assure you some people whom I admire very much regarded it rather as a scarf dipped in gore. In fact, if you go back to the beginning, I think that was the reason why I wore it."

"I dare say," said the librarian thoughtfully, "that was why you wore a red tie. But I want to know why you wore a tie. I want to know why anybody, of all the sacred race of man, ever wore a tie."

Braintree, who was always sincere, was suddenly silent and the other man went on, still gazing at him earnestly, as if he were a specimen or a stranger from a foreign clime: "What do you do?" he said in the same soft accent. "You get up; you wash . . ."

"So far," said Braintree,' "I will confess to conventionality."

"You put on a shirt. Then you take a separate strip of some linen or something and hook it round your neck with a complicated set of knobs or hooks. Then, not content with that, you take another and longer strip of some sort of cloth or something, of some particular colour that you fancy. You wreathe that strip round the other strip in most complicated convolutions of a particular kind of knot. You do this every morning; you do it all your life; you never think of doing anything else; you never are for one moment moved to cry aloud on God and rend your garments, like the prophets of old. You do precisely this or pretty much like it, because a vast number of other people are so mysteriously employed at the same hour of the day; you never think it too much trouble; you never complain because it is always the same. And then you call yourself a revolutionist—and boast because your tie is red!"

"There is something in what you say," said Braintree, "but am I to understand that this is your reason for putting off the evil hour when you must abandon your fantastic attire?"

"Why do you call my attire fantastic?" asked Herne. "It's very much simpler than yours. It just goes over your head and there you are. Besides, it has all sorts of sensible elements you don't discover till you've worn it for a day or so. For instance," he looked up at the sky with a sort of frown, "it may be going to rain or something; it may turn very cold or the wind be very strong. What will you all do then? You will make a bolt for the house and come back with a paraphernalia of things for the lady; perhaps a huge horrible umbrella that will force you to walk about like a Chinese Emperor under a canopy; perhaps a lot of wraps and waterproofs and things. But nine times out of ten a man only wants something to pull over his head in this climate; he simply does this," and he plucked forward the hood that hung between his shoulders, "and for the rest of the time he can belong to the Hatless Brigade. . . . Do you know," he added abruptly and in a lowered voice, "there's something very satisfying about wearing a hood . . . something symbolical; I don't wonder they corrupted the name of the great medieval hero into Robin Hood."

Olive Ashley had been looking away across the undulating slopes of the valley, to where they vanished into a shining haze of evening, as if she were somewhat distrait and detached from the conversation, but she looked round, as if at the sound of a word which could penetrate her dreams.

"What do you mean," she said, "by saying a hood is symbolical?"

"Have you never looked through an archway?" asked Herne, "and seen the landscape beyond as bright as a lost paradise? That is because there is a frame to the picture. . . . You are cut off from something and allowed to look at something. When will people understand that the world is a window and not a blank infinity; a window in a wall of infinite nothing? When I wear this hood I carry my window with me. I say to myself— this is the world that Francis of Assisi saw and loved because it was limited. The hood has the very shape of a Gothic window."

Olive looked over her shoulder at John Braintree and said: "Do you remember what poor Monkey said? . . . No, it was just before you came."

"Before I came?" asked Braintree in a momentary doubt.

"Before you first came here," she answered colouring and looking again at the landscape. "He said he would have to look through a leper's window."

"A very typical medieval window, I should think," said Braintree rather sourly.

The face of the man in medieval masquerade suddenly flamed as at a challenge to battle.

"Will you show me a King," he cried, "a modern reigning King, by the grace of God, who will go and handle lepers in a hospital as St. Louis did?"

"I am not very likely," said Braintree grimly, "to pay such a tribute to reigning Kings."

"Or a popular leader either," insisted the other. "St. Francis was a popular leader. If you saw a leper walking across this lawn, would you rush at him and embrace him?"

"He is as likely to do it as any of the rest of us," said Olive, "Perhaps more."

"You are right," said Herne, with abrupt sobriety "Perhaps none of us would do it. . . . But what if the world needs such despots and such demagogues?"

Braintree slowly raised his head and looked steadily at the other man. "Such despots . . ." he said, and frowned heavily.

Chapter 12

# The Statesman and the Summer-House

At this point of the conversation that particular corner of the garden was filled with the broad and breezy presence of Julian Archer in resplendent evening dress; he entered with a swing and then stopped dead, staring at Michael Herne.

"I say," he cried, "are you *never* going to change."

Perhaps the sixth repetition of this single sentence was what drove the librarian of Seawood mad.

Anyhow he swung round, staring also, and suddenly cried out in a voice that rang down the garden path.

"No. I am never going to change."

After glaring for a moment he went on "You all love change and live by change; but I shall never change. It was by change you fell; it is by this madness of change you go on falling. You had your happy moment, when men were simple and sane and formal and as native to this earth as they can ever be. You lost it; and even when you get it back for a moment, you have not the sense to keep it. I shall never change."

"I don't know what he means," said Archer, rather as if he had been speaking of an animal or at least an infant.

"I know what he means," said Braintree grimly, "and it's not true. Do you really believe yourself, Mr. Herne that all that mysticism is true? What do you mean exactly by saying that this old society of yours was sane?"

"I mean that the old society was truthful and that you are in a tangle of lies," answered Herne. "I don't mean that it was perfect or painless. I mean that it called pain and imperfection by their names. You talk about despots and vassals and all the rest; well, you also have coercion and inequality; but you dare not call anything by its own Christian name. You defend every single thing by saying it is something else. You have a King and then explain that he is not allowed to be a King. You have a House of Lords and say it is the same as a House of Commons. When you do want to flatter a workman or a peasant you say he is a true gentleman; which is like saying he is a veritable Viscount. When you want to flatter the gentleman you say he does not use his own title. You leave a millionaire his millions and then praise him because he is 'simple,' otherwise mean and not magnificent; as if there were any good in gold except to glitter! You excuse priests by saying they are not priestly and assure us eagerly that clergymen can play cricket. You have teachers who refuse doctrine, which only means teaching; and doctors of divinity disavowing anything divine. It is all false and cowardly and shamefully full of shame. Everything is prolonging its existence by denying that it exists."

"What you say may be true of such things or some of them," answered Braintree. "But I do not want to prolong their existence at all. And if it comes to cursing and prophesying, by God, you will see some of them dead before you die."

"Perhaps," said Herne looking at him with his large pale eyes, "you may see them die and then live; which is a very different thing from existing. I am not sure that the King may not be a King once more."

The Syndicalist seemed to see something in the staring eyes of the librarian that changed and almost chilled his mood.

"Do you think this is an age," he asked, "for anybody to play King Richard?"

"I think this is an age," replied the other, "when somebody ought to play . . . Coeur-de-Lion."

"Ah," said Olive, as if she began to see something for the first time. "You mean we lack the only virtue of King Richard."

"The only virtue of King Richard," said Braintree, "was staying out of the country."

"Perhaps," she answered. "He and his virtue might come back."

"When he comes back he will find the country a good deal changed," said the Syndicalist grimly. "No serfs; no vassals; and even the labourers daring to look him in the face. He will find something has broken its chain; something has opened, expanded, been lifted up; something wild and terrible and gigantic that strikes terror even into the heart of a lion."

"Something?" repeated Olive.

"The heart of a man," he replied.

Olive stood looking in a sort of daze or dazzle from one to the other. For on one side stood all the things she had dreamed of, clothed in their right century. And on the other something more deeply thrilling, of which she had never dreamed. Her tangled emotions broke out of her with a rather curious cry.

"Oh I wish Monkey were back again!"

Braintree glanced sharply at her and asked rather gruffly: "Why?"

"Because you are all changing," she said. "Because you are all talking as you did in the play. Because you are both of you fierce and splendid and magnificent and magnanimous and have neither of you a grain of common sense."

"I didn't know you specialised in having common sense," said Braintree.

"I never had any," she replied. "Rosamund always told me I hadn't got any. But any woman would have more than you have."

"Here comes the lady in question," said Braintree rather gloomily. "I hope she will meet your requirements."

"She will say what I say," said Olive calmly. "The madness is infectious. The infection is spreading. None of you can get out . . . of my poor little play."

And indeed when Rosamund Severne came sweeping across the lawn in her resolute way, like a wind, the wind struck something and turned to a storm. The storm raged for an hour or two and we need only record its end; which was that Rosamund did what was very rarely done by her or anyone else; what had not been done since Murrel had presented the petition for the admission of Braintree. She burst into her father's study and faced her father.

Lord Seawood looked up from a pile of letters and said: "What is it?" His tone might have been called apologetic or even nervous; but it was of the sort that makes others feel nervous and apologise.

But Rosamund never felt nervous and did not think of apologising; or indeed even of explaining. She said explosively: "Things out there are getting perfectly awful. The librarian won't take off his clothes."

"Well, I should hope not," said Lord Seawood, and waited patiently.

"I mean," she added hastily, "I mean it's getting past a joke. Don't you understand? He's still dressed in all his green."

"I suppose, strictly speaking, our livery is blue," said Lord Seawood thoughtfully. "That doesn't matter much nowadays; but heraldry was always a hobby of mine.... Well, I don't think it's possible now to insist on the correct colours. And nobody ever sees much of the librarian. Libraries are not very popular resorts. And the fellow himself ... very quiet fellow, if I remember right. Nobody likely to notice him."

"Oh," said Rosamund, with almost ominous quiet and restraint. "You think nobody will ever notice him?"

"Shouldn't think so," said Lord Seawood. "I never noticed him myself."

If Lord Seawood has hitherto remained behind the scenes of the drama of "Blondel the Troubadour," if he has remained behind the curtains and tapestries of Seawood Abbey, it is only because he did so remain during all such superficial social proceedings, and was, in the true sense of the word, conspicuous by his absence. This fact arose from many causes but chiefly from two: first that he had the misfortune to be an invalid and second that he had the misfortune to be a statesman. He was one of those who withdraw into a narrower and narrower world on the pretence of acting in a wider and wider sphere.

He lived in a small world out of a love of large questions. He had, as he had suggested, a sort of hobby of heraldry and the tracing out of the history of his own and other noble families, but he had felt all the more at ease because there were only two or three other experts in England who troubled about such things at all. And as he dealt with heraldry, so he dealt with society; with politics and many other things. He never talked to any people except experts; that is, in trusting the expert, he always trusted the exception. Exceptional people gave him information of exceptional value; but he never knew what was going on in his own house. Now and then he was conscious that the details of his domestic arrangements were not what they had always been; and this was about the extent of his consciousness of the whole business of the Troubadour play and its strange sequel. But if he had noticed the librarian on the top of the ladder, it is doubtful whether he would have asked him why he was there. It is more probable he would have opened communications with a scientific specialist on the use of ladders; but only after he was honestly convinced that he had the very best specialist of the time. He would defend the aristocratic principle by an appeal to the Greek derivation, saying that he insisted on having the best of everything. And, to do him justice, though he was too much of an invalid and perhaps too much of a faddist to drink or smoke, he never had any wine or cigars in his house except the very best. He was, in his personal capacity, a bony and brittle little man, with a high-bridged nose and angles all over him, and a capacity for staring at people suddenly with a look of startled attention, which had an almost stunning effect on those who made the mistake of supposing that he was merely a fool. The whole of his somewhat secretive personality, with its concentration and its bewilderment, its attention and its inattention, must be understood with a sympathy bordering upon subtlety, before the conditions of this drama can be conceived. Probably he was the only man in the world who could have had these things happening in his own house without realizing how far they had gone.

But there comes a point when even the hermit in a cave on the mountains looks forth and sees that the city in the valley is flaming with flags. There comes a point when even the most drugged and dreamy scholar in an attic looks out of the window and sees that the town is illuminated. And at last Lord Seawood began to realize that a revolution had taken place outside the door of his own study, although he had received no official report in connection with it. If it had been a revolution in Guatemala, he would have known all about it as soon as he could have communicated with the Guatemalan Minister in London. If it had been a revolution in Northern Thibet, of course he would have sent for Biggle, who is the only fellow who has ever really *been* to Northern Thibet. But as it was only ramping and roaring all over his own garden and drawing-room, he was cautious about receiving what might be exaggerated accounts. Thus it happened that about a fortnight later he was seated in the summer-house that stood at the end of the garden path opposite the library, engaged in grave consultation with the Prime Minister. He did not notice anything in the whole landscape except the Prime Minister. This was not in the least an indication of snobbishness, for he considered himself, in the social and genealogical sense, more important than any Prime Minister; though the one in question was the Earl of Eden. But he did attach importance to being closetted only with people of importance. He listened with solemn receptivity to all the news that so important a messenger could bring him from the outer world; but he cared for nothing except the outer world. He lived, if not at the end of the earth, at any rate at the end of the telephone. The views of the Prime Minister himself, about this concentrated complacency in his host, might have been worth hearing, for Lord Eden was a man of some humour, of the sort that is counted rather crabbed and cynical, because it faces facts and does not deal very much in catch-words. Lord Eden was a man with a lean and wrinkled face so much in contrast with his yellow hair as to make it look like a yellow wig. He was doing most of the talking, but his host never lost the air of one listening gravely to a report brought to headquarters.

"The trouble is," said the Prime Minister, "that their side has suddenly developed somebody who believes in something. It's not fair, in a way. We knew all about Labour members, of course, and they were damned like all other members. You couldn't insult them; you got at them by degrees; you told them they were admirable parliamentarians and foemen worthy of your steel, and then, of course, you found some sort of a job for them sooner or later; and there you were. But this business of the Coal-Tar people is different. The Unions wouldn't have been much different by themselves, of course. People at a Trade Union meeting don't know what they're voting about—"

"Of course not," said Seawood nodding gravely and graciously, "quite ignorant, I suppose?"

"—any more than we do," went on Lord Eden, "any more than the House of Commons or the House of Lords. Did you ever know a party meeting that knew what it was voting about? They called themselves Socialists or something and we called ourselves Imperialists or something. But, as a matter of fact, things had got quieter and quieter on both sides. But now that this man Braintree has turned up, talking all their nonsense in a new sort of way, we don't seem to have any of our nonsense to call up against him. It used to be the Empire. But something has gone wrong with all that; the damn Colonials would come over and people saw them, and there you are. They won't talk as if they wanted to die for us, and nobody seems to want very much to live with them. But whatever it was, all that sort of picture and poetry of the thing seems to have given out on our side; just at the moment when something picturesque turns up on the other side."

"Is this Mr. Braintree picturesque?" asked Lord Seawood, being entirely unaware that Mr. Braintree had been his guest for a considerable time.

"These fellows seem to think so," replied the Prime Minister. "It's not so much the Coal people themselves; it's much more the affiliated Unions connected with the by-products; all the people he seems to have worked up just round here. That's why I came to ask you about it. We are both interested in Coal-Tar as well as Coal, and I'd be very glad to have your opinion. There seems to be such a devil of a lot of these small Unions mixed up with the business. You must know more about 'em than anybody else—except Braintree himself, of course. And it's no good asking him. I wish to God it were."

"It is quite true that I have considerable interest in this neighbourhood," said Lord Seawood, inclining his head, "as you know, most of us have nowadays to go into trade a little. Would have horrified our ancestors, I suppose, but it's better than losing the estates and so on. Yes, I may tell you in confidence that my interests are even more committed to the by-products than to the original material, so to speak. It is all the more unfortunate that this Mr. Braintree should have chosen that for a field of battle."

"It jolly well looks like a field of battle," replied the politician gloomily. "I don't suppose they'd actually come and kill people but they're pretty well ready for anything short of that. And that's just the worst of it. If they'd only actually rebel, they could be put down easily enough. But what the devil are you to do with rebels who don't rebel? I don't believe Machiavelli ever gave any advice on the problem."

Lord Seawood put his long thin fingers together and cleared his throat.

"I do not profess to be Machiavelli," he said with marked modesty, "but I hope I am not wrong in supposing that, in a certain sense, you are asking my advice. Well, the conditions are such, I admit, as to call for rather special knowledge, and I have given some attention to this problem, and especially to parallel problems in Australia and Alaska. To begin with, the conditions of the production of all the derivatives of coal involves considerations that are commonly understood—."

"My God!" cried Lord Eden and ducked suddenly as if a blow had been aimed at his head. His exclamation was natural enough; though, such was the incredible self-absorption of the other man that he saw the cause at least a second later.

What Lord Seawood saw was a long feathered arrow that stood still quivering in the timber of the summer-house, immediately above Lord Eden's head. But what Lord Eden had seen was the same singular missile come singing through the air out of some remote part of the garden and passing above him with a noise like that of some gigantic insect. Both the noblemen rose to their feet and regarded this object for a moment in silence; before the more practical politician observed that the shaft had fastened to it a flapping fragment of paper, on which something seemed to be written.

Chapter 13

# The Victorian and the Arrow

The arrow that had entered the summer-house with a sound like song awakened the worthy proprietor of the place to a world without which had been entirely transformed. Why it had been transformed, and what was the nature of the transformation, he found it sufficiently bewildering to discover; but it is almost equally bewildering to describe. It began, in a sense, with the isolated insanity of one man; yet it was almost equally due, by a not uncommon paradox, to the equally isolated sanity of one woman.

Mr. Herne, the librarian, had positively and finally refused to change his clothes.

"Well I can't," he cried in despair. "I simply can't. I should feel like a fool, just as if—."

"Well," asked Rosamund regarding him with round eyes.

"I should feel as if I were in fancy dress," he said. Rosamund was less impatient than might have been expected.

"Do you mean," she asked very slowly, as if she were thinking things out, "that you find you feel more natural in those things?"

"Why, of course," he cried with a sort of delight. "Why, they are more natural. Lots of things are really more natural, though I've never had them in my life. It's natural to hold your head up, but I never did it before. I used to put my hands in my trousers' pockets and somehow that seems to mean standing always with a sort of a stoop. Now I put my hands in my belt and it makes me feel ten inches taller. Why, look at this spear."

He had a habit of walking about with the boar-spear which King Richard had carried in his capacity of forester; and he now planted the staff in the grass to bring it to her attention, though it was very literally as plain as a pike-staff.

"The minute you begin to carry a thing of this sort," he cried, "you realise at once why men generally used to carry long poles of one sort or another; spears or pikes or pilgrims' staffs, or pastoral staffs. You can hold them at arm's length and then throw your head back as if it wore a crest. You have to lean down to the little modern walking-sticks in order to lean on them; as if you were leaning on a crutch, and so you are. The whole of this world of ours is leaning on a crutch, because it is a cripple."

Then he stopped abruptly and looked at her with a sort of sudden timidity.

"But you ... I was just thinking you ought to walk about with a sceptre like a spear ... but, of course ... if you really disapprove of it all—."

"I'm not sure," she answered in her slow and slightly perplexed manner, which contrasted occasionally with her usual voluble efficiency, "I'm not perfectly sure I do disapprove of it."

He seemed to experience a silent shock of relief, not perhaps very easy to explain. But indeed this was the element in his demeanour which is least easily explained. For all his lifted head and leonine demeanour in moments of abstraction, for all the fixity of his attitude or antic, he had not any air of impudence or even, in the ordinary sense, of defiance. He was simply embarrassed, or rather paralysed, in the presence of his own old clothes. In short he had precisely the same attitude about getting out of his green costume that he had once had about getting into it.

When Rosamund had swept in her swift way across the lawn to the little group where Herne was arguing with Braintree, everyone in the world, including the two distracted disputants, would have expected her to dash into nothing the whole nonsensical dispute. She might have been expected to tell the librarian to run and change his clothes at once, like a naughty little boy who had fallen in a pond. But the quaint and almost fabulous creatures called human souls do not always, or perhaps even often, do what is expected of them. If any sensible person can be supposed to have foreseen all this crazy tale, he would have had no doubt about which of the two women involved would have been more impatient with its craziness. The sensible man would have said that Olive Ashley, with her hobby of medievalism, would have understood even a rather mad medievalist; whereas anyone so modern as her red-haired friend would not even have stopped to ask whether it was medievalism, in face of the obvious fact that it was madness. But then no sensible man would ever have believed that it would happen at all.

In any case the sensible man would have been wrong, as he often is. Olive always had her own dreams: but Rosamund's heart hungered after two things, simplification and action. Her thinking was slow; so she liked simplicity. Her impulses were swift; so she liked action.

Rosamund Severne in a bodily sense was born worthy of a crown; and even in a biographical sense under the shadow of a coronet. It was her fate to move against a magnificent background of river and terraced hills and the ruins of a historic place, and the medieval masquerade she had assumed seemed altogether fitted to her presence. To the visionary eyes of the librarian, she appeared to be equally a princess in that costume or in a more conventional one. But these accidents of birth and even of beauty are very misleading in psychology. If Mr. Herne had possessed more knowledge of the world, he would have recognised a type to be seen in very different surroundings. The great green valley and the great grey abbey house would have faded from his sight and he would have seen in their place desks and typewriters and rows of very dull works of reference. He would have seen in that square face and those grave and honest eyes a type that is very modern and very variously distributed in the modern world. That young woman is to be found in many places where she is wanted to support the wavering unworldliness of men like Mr. Herne. As Secretary to the Submarine Colonisation Company, she explains firmly to a long procession of inquirers that there is room in the sea for more men that ever went into it. As Lady Manager of the Elastic Pavements Society, she knows the whole case for this essential reform, and can show how it eliminates the necessity for better boots or a country life. The movement for proving that "Paradise Lost" was written by Charles II owes its wide popularity entirely to her energy and efficiency. The arrangement by which the tops of top-hats can be lifted with a string, for purposes of ventilation, would never have reached its present universal success, if there had not been one sane person in the office. In all these positions she has the same powerful simplicity and the same sincerity in following out one idea at a time. In all these positions she is very conscientious and very unscrupulous.

It was characteristic of Rosamund that she had always been not only bewildered but wearied by the broadmindedness, or rather the indiscriminate intellectual hospitality of a man like Douglas Murrel. To her it appeared mere vagueness and emptiness and absence of object. She could never comprehend how he could be at once an intimate friend of Olive and her medievalism and of Braintree and his Bolshevism. She wanted somebody who would do something; and Murrel absolutely refused to do anything. But when somebody was really ready to do something, she was so pleased that she rather neglected to criticise what it was that he was going to do.

Quite suddenly, and perhaps accidentally, there had become clear to her very single eye something like a ray of light that she could follow; something that she could understand. Doubtless she understood it better because it was linked up in a loose fashion with the traditions that she had been taught from childhood to preserve. She had never bothered about her father's taste in heraldry; she had not even seen very much of her father. But just as she was glad that her father was there, she was glad the heraldry was there. People who have that sort of historical support always remember it, if only in their subconsciousness. Anyhow, the obvious inference was incorrect, and people soon began to say that she was actually encouraging the librarian in his capacity of lunatic.

It is almost needless to say that the daughter of Lord Seawood moved about trailing clouds of glory in the form of crowds of young men. She had indeed a threefold claim to that sort of popularity. She was an heiress; but it is due to them to say that many of the more chivalrous admired her not because she was an heiress but because she was beautiful. She was beautiful, but it is due to her to say that many of the more rational admired her not because she was a beauty but because she was a good sort; and more especially what they called a good sport. It followed, therefore that where she led many would follow, even if she led them a dance quite different from the dances then in fashion. Thus there grew up, half in jest and yet more and more in earnest, a new fashionable "medievalism"; a chase in which all the young men followed the lady who followed the librarian. And because there was a certain candour of calf-love about it, of the moon-calf who is not ashamed to cry for the moon, it had something in it of the sincerity of youth and springtime. It was a romance as well as a rag. The young men became in a manner poets, if very minor poets. With the help of Herne as a scholar and Rosamund as a vigorous stage-manager, they filled their lines with emblems and ensigns and processions, even more defiant of modernity than the theatrical dress which they had dropped and Herne had retained. The young men were especially fascinated by the notion of reviving the use of the bow; possibly with a subconscious memory of the arrows of the god of love. Perhaps it was some foolish association of Valentine's that started the game of sending arrows as messengers of welcome or of war.

Archery was a fashion in the Victorian time; and many Victorian ladies and gentlemen may have hovered about the lawns of Seawood Abbey, engaged in that graceful sport; many may even have revisited the scene as mildly astonished ghosts in long whiskers and peg-top trousers or in cloudy crinolines swaying and floating like balloons. Many distinguished Victorian characters had doubtless honoured the amusement; but they did it within certain visible Victorian limitations. They shot their arrows correctly at targets and not (unaccountably) at top-hats. They used but few of those giant gestures that have belonged in the past to the great bows of the heroes. Sir Robert Peel, if prudent as Ulysses, did not turn, saying, "Now I will shoot at another mark," and transfix with his shaft the highly decorated waistcoat of Mr. Disraeli. It is nowhere recorded that Lord Derby balanced an apple on the top of the top-hat of Lord Stanley, and then grimly informed the Prime Minister (let us say Lord Aberdeen) that he was keeping another arrow for higher political uses. Lord Palmerston, though actually known by the nick-name of Cupid, did not attract the attention of such ladies as he favoured by transfixing their Victorian bonnets in this airy fashion. Lord Shaftesbury seldom appeared in the character and costume of the archer on the Shaftesbury Fountain; and it is an error to suppose that he is there represented. Above all, it certainly never occurred to the celebrated Rowland Hill that shooting arrows about in all directions might be made a substitute for the Penny Post. There was, therefore, no real historical precedent for the state of affairs that began to develop rapidly at Seawood Abbey, under the influence of the escaped librarian.

This last idea, of conveying casual communications to persons at some little distance, by sending a winged missile singing past their heads or crashing into their windows, seemed especially to have taken Mr. Herne's fancy; and it was by this means that he and his misguided group of sympathisers (who were beginning to enter into the fun of the thing) delivered to a large number of persons their proclamation of the New Régime. To describe at length all the details involved in the New Régime would involve the transcription of a considerable number of scrolls or strips of paper, which were conveyed to the neighbours in this rapid if not efficient manner. They all bore the title of The League of the Lion; and were apparently an appeal to all persons to imitate the better qualities of King Richard the First and the Crusaders, under conditions that could not be considered favourable to the enterprise. The astonished citizen was informed that England had now reached a crisis in which moral courage alone could save her; if it were only the moral courage required to aim a bow at a venture when engaged in dropping a line to a friend. But there was a great deal more of a more sincere sort, not without a certain juvenile eloquence, protesting against that suicidal pessimism of the great reactionary who declared that the age of chivalry was past.

Needless to say, most of the people who received these missives were amused; some were annoyed; and some, strangely enough perhaps, were rather relieved and revived, as if they had seen some game of their childhood or ideal of their boyhood rise suddenly from the dead. But it cannot be said that the appeal as it stood was adapted to the typical visitors to Lord Seawood's country seat. Noblemen and gentlemen who had come down to shoot were often quite vexed to be told by an ardent and enthusiastic person, dressed entirely in bright green, that this was the real definition of good shooting at a little place in the country. Venerable sportsmen, who considered themselves crack shots, were not soothed when the librarian patiently and kindly explained to them how cramped, how hunchbacked, how ungainly, was the crouching attitude of one holding a gun, compared with the god-like lift and leap in the figure that has just discharged an arrow, frozen as it is forever in the stillness of the Apollo Belvedere. In short, the further afield the arrows fared, the less likely it seemed that they would really have the softening effects of the arrows of the God of Love. And this seemed to reach to a remote extreme of improbability in the very last extent or extremity of their travels; when the flying herald of chivalry had actually reached so distant and impenetrable a mark as to arouse the attention of the master of the house.

As already noted, it is rather more than a metaphor to say that the news reached Lord Seawood as a bolt from the blue. The bolt came in a flash out of the blue sky of the summer into the black shadows of the summer-house. It fixed itself in the wall above the Prime Minister's head; and before Lord Seawood had taken it in, Lord Eden had taken it out. He found attached to it a curled-up document; which the two noblemen proceeded to stare at with somewhat differing degrees of patience.

It explained the necessity of a new order of voluntary nobility; and the two involuntary nobles found its exalted aristocratic tone almost terrifying. It stated the tests and trials by which a sterner conception of chivalry could be introduced into the world; though it is only justice to all concerned to say that it did not contain the word Samurai. It explained that an appeal to the ancient virtue of loyalty could alone rally mankind to the restoration of a worthy social order, such as was envisaged by the old orders of knighthood. It explained a great many other things; but from the point of view of the two elderly gentlemen in the summer-house, it did not altogether explain the arrow in the wall.

Lord Eden remained silent; indeed he seemed to be studying the document with more gravity or grim attention than might be expected. But Lord Seawood, after some abrupt ejaculations, turned by a sort of blind instinct to the doorway and the garden from which the thunderbolt had come. And there he saw, away in the middle distance, at the end of the long lawn, something that amazed him as much as a company of angels with haloes and golden wings.

They were a company of people fantastically clad in the garments of five centuries earlier; many of them were holding bows; but what hit Lord Seawood harder than any arrow was the fact that his daughter stood in the front of the whole group, in an outrageous form of attire terminating in two horns like a buffalo; and she wore a broad smile.

He had never even thought that things so close to him could go wrong—or rather go mad. He felt as if his own boots had kicked him, or as if his cravat had come to life and throttled him like a garotter.

"Good God!" he cried, "What has been happening here?"

His feelings were simply those of a connoisseur with a collection of precious china, who finds that a pack of school-boys have been letting off catapults within an inch of an incomparable blue Chinese vase. But prodigious porcelain vases of the Ming dynasty might have crashed on every side of him without arousing his attention as it was aroused now. The hobbies of men are many and strange and mysterious. And he did most deeply resent anyone damaging his collection of Prime Ministers. That summer-house in the garden was to him as sacred as any Chinese temple full of ancestors; for in it were the thin ghosts of many politicians. Many of these quiet conferences affecting the destinies of the Empire had been held in that toy hut. It was characteristic of Lord Seawood that what pleased him most was meeting public men in a private way; even a secret way. He was far too fine a gentleman himself to desire the Sunday papers to say that the Prime Minister had visited Seawood Abbey. But he went cold as death as he thought of the papers saying that the Prime Minister had visited Seawood Abbey and lost an eye.

The glance he gave at the gang of school-boys was, therefore, very cursory and, of course, entirely contemptuous. He did vaguely apprehend that one face stood out from its confused background, with a gravity that was almost ghastly. It was the high-featured and financial face of the librarian; and in comparison with it the rest were of a mixed and almost mocking sort. Some were smiling; a few were laughing; but that merely added a touch to the nobleman's natural annoyance and disdain. It was some silly rag, of course, among Rosamund's friends; she must have pretty rotten friends.

"I hope you are aware," he said coldly but in a clear and loud voice, "that you have just nearly killed the Prime Minister. Under these circumstances, I think you will see the propriety of choosing some other game."

He turned and walked back to the summer-house, having so far controlled himself with a conventional consideration for his unwelcome guests. But when he returned under the small thatched roof and saw in the shadow the pale and angular profile of the Prime Minister still poring over the scrap of paper with cold concentration, Lord Seawood's fury suddenly broke out again. He felt in that frozen face the unfathomable scorn which the great mind of the great statesman must be feeling for this dirty and yet deadly practical joke. The man's silence opened like an abyss of ice; an abyss into which apology after apology might be dropped without plumbing its depths, or awakening any answer.

"I simply don't know what to say," he said desperately. "I've half a mind to kick them all out of the house, the girl and all. . . . Anything whatever I can do. . . ."

Still the Prime Minister did not look up, but continued in a frigid manner to peruse the paper in his hand. Now and then he bent his brows a little; now and then he lifted them a little; but his tight lips never moved.

His host was suddenly struck with a sort of terror, the scope of which he could not himself follow. He thought he had offered an insult blood could not wipe out. The silence snapped his nerve and he said sharply: "For God's sake don't go on reading that rubbish! I know it's damned funny; but it's not so damned funny for me—happening in my own house. You can't imagine I like having a guest insulted, let alone you. Tell me what you want and I'll do it."

"Well," said the Prime Minister, and laid down the paper slowly on the little round table. "Well, we've got it at last."

"Got what?" demanded his distracted friend.

"Our last chance," said the Prime Minister.

There was a silence in the dark summer-house so sudden and complete that they could hear the buzzing of a fly and the distant murmur of the talk of the mutineers. The silence was merely accidental; yet something rose up in Seawood's soul to protest against it; as if silence were making destiny and must be stopped from doing it.

"What do you mean?" he demanded sharply. "What last chance?"

"The last chance we were talking about not ten minutes ago," replied the politician with a grim smile. "Wasn't I talking about this very thing before it flew in at the window, like the dove with the olive branch? Wasn't I actually saying that we must have something new because the poor old Empire has gone stale? Wasn't I saying we wanted a new positive thing to back up against Braintree and the New Democracy? Well, then."

"What on earth do you mean?" demanded Lord Seawood.

"I mean this thing has got to be backed up," cried the Prime Minister, slapping the little table with a vivacity almost shocking in one of his dry and dreary demeanour. "It's got to be backed up with horse, foot and artillery; or what's a damn sight more important, pounds, shillings, and pence. It's got to be backed up as we never backed anything in our lives. Lord, that a man of my age should live to see the break in the enemy's line and the chance for a cavalry charge! It's got to be rammed home for all it's worth and a lot more; and the sooner we begin the better. Where are these people?"

"But do you really mean," cried the staring Seawood, "that there's anything to be done with fools like—"

"Suppose they are," snapped Eden. "Am I a fool that I should fancy that anything could be done without fools?"

Lord Seawood pulled himself together; but he was still staring.

"I suppose you mean that a new policy—I can hardly say a popular policy—perhaps rather a successful anti-popular policy—"

"Both, if you like," said the other. "Why not?"

"I should hardly have thought," said Lord Seawood, "that the populace would be particularly interested in all this elaborate antiquarian theory about chivalry."

"Have you ever considered," asked the Prime Minister, looking over his shoulder, "the meaning of the word chivalry?"

"Do you mean in the derivative sense?" asked the other nobleman.

"I mean in the horse sense," replied Eden. "What people really like is a man on a horse—and they don't mind much if it's a high horse. Give the people plenty of sports—tournaments, horse races—*panem et circenses,* my boy—that will do for a popular side to the policy. If we could mobilise all that goes to make the Derby we could fight the Deluge."

"I begin," said Seawood, "to have some sort of wild notion of what you mean."

"I mean," answered his friend, "that the Democracy cares a damn sight more about the inequality of horses than about the equality of men."

And stepping across the threshold he strode across the garden with a step almost startlingly rejuvenated; and before his host had even moved he heard the Prime Minister's voice in the distance lifted like a trumpet, like the voice of the great orators of fifty years ago.

Thus did the librarian who refused to change his clothes contrive to change his country. For out of this small and grotesque incident came all that famous revolution, or reaction, which transformed the face of English society, and checked and changed the course of its history. Like all revolutions effected by Englishmen, and especially revolutions effected by Conservatives, it was very careful to preserve those powers that were already powerless. Some Conservatives of a rather senile sort were even heard still talking about the Constitutional characters of the complete subversal of the Constitution. It was allowed to retain, indeed it was supposed to support, the old monarchical pattern of this country. But in practice the new power was divided between three or four subordinate monarchs ruling over large provinces of England, like magnified Lords-Lieutenant; and called according to the romance or affectation of the movement Kings-at-Arms. They held indeed a position with something of the sanctity and symbolic immunity of a herald; but they also possessed not a few of the powers of a king. They were in command of the bands of young men called Orders of Chivalry, which served as a sort of yeomanry or militia. They held courts and administered high and low justice in accordance with Mr. Herne's researches into medieval law. It was something more than a pageant; yet there passed into it much of that popular passion which at one time filled half the towns and villages in England with pageants; the hunger of a populace which Puritanism and Industrialism had so long starved for the feast of the eyes and the fancy.

As it was more than a pageant, it was more than a fashion; but it had its stages and turning points like a fashion. Perhaps the chief turning point was the moment when Mr. Julian Archer (now Sir Julian Archer under the accolade of one of the new orders of knighthood) had seriously discovered that he must lead the fashion or be left behind it. All of us who have observed changes passing over a society know that indeterminate and yet determining instant. It applies to everything from women being allowed votes to women not being allowed hair. It was marked in the Suffragette movement, which many middle-class women had long supported, when great ladies began to take it up. It marks the transition from the time when it is the new fashion to the time when it is the fashion. Up to that moment examples may be numerous, but they are still notable; after that moment it is the neglect that is notable. That is the sort of moment, in every movement, at which Sir Julian Archer appears as he appeared now; a knight in shining armour, ready for every perilous emprise.

Yet Sir Julian Archer was too vain not to be in a sense simple, and too simple not to be in a sense sincere. Social changes of this sort are made possible among considerable masses of people, by two ironies of human nature. The first is that almost everyman's life has been sufficiently patchy and full of possibilities for him to remember *some* movement of his own mind towards what has become the movement of the time. The second is that he almost always makes a false picture of his past, and fosters a fictitious memory, whereby that detail seems in retrospect to dominate his career.

Julian Archer (as has already been faithfully recorded) had written a long time ago a very boyish sort of a boy's adventure story about the Battle of Agincourt. It was only one of the multifarious and highly modern activities of his successful career: and had not been even one of the most successful. But with the new talk all around him, Archer began to insist more and more on his initiative in the matter.

"They wouldn't listen to me," he said moodily shaking his head. "Doesn't do to be a bit too early in the field. . . . Of course, Herne's a well-read man; it's his business. . . . I suppose he sees practically every book that comes out. Seems as if he had sense enough to take a hint, eh, what?"

"Oh, I see," said Olive Ashley, raising her dark eyebrows in mild surprise. "I never thought of that."

And she reflected at once ruefully and whimsically upon her own concentrated passion of medieval things, which everybody had first derided and then imitated and then forgotten.

The case was the same with Sir Aubrey Wister, that gallant though somewhat elderly knight; for thus also had been transformed the figure of the old aesthete who pottered about drawing-rooms and praised the great Victorians who had praised the great Primitives. He talked rather more about the great Primitives and less about the great Victorians. But as he had so often in the past patronised Cimabue and said an encouraging word to Giotto and Botticelli, it was not difficult for him to persuade himself that he had been a prophet lifting up his voice in vain, and predicting the coming of Mr. Herne as the Medieval Messiah.

"My dear, sir," he would say confidentially, "the period was one of inconceivable vandalism and vulgarity. I really don't know how I lived through it. But I pegged away; and, as you see, my work has not been altogether fruitless . . . ahem . . . not altogether fruitless. The very patterns of their costumes would have perished; hardly a single picture from which they are taking their designs would have survived—but for my little protest. It shows what a word in time will do."

Lord Seawood himself was affected in much the same way. Insensibly, he shifted the centre of gravity between his two hobbies. He talked a little more about his private hobby of heraldry. He talked a little less about his public hobby of Parliament. He insisted less on the greatness of Lord Palmerston and more on the greatness of the Black Prince, from whom the Seawood family claimed descent. And in him also this touching belief grew silently in the shade; the sense that he had himself had a lot to do with the founding of the League of the Lion and the resurrection of Richard Coeur-de-Lion. He felt this all the more vividly because of the institution of the Shield of Honour, which was one of the latest and proudest additions to the scheme and had been inaugurated in his own park.

In all this change of climate, Herne was himself unchanged. Like many idealists, he was of a type that would have been content in complete obscurity, but could not measure or realise the scope of complete fame. If he could take one stride to the end of the park, he might as well take another stride to the end of the world. He did not see the world to scale. He had forced all his commonplace companions back into their masquerade clothes and compelled them to play the masque until they died. By hanging on himself to his Robin Hood bow and boar spear, he had come to find himself not left behind by the company but marching in front of it. The change from that loneliness to that leadership did seem to him a thrilling and triumphal thing. But the change from the leadership of that house-party to the leadership of all England hardly seemed to him a change at all. For indeed there was in that house-party one face that had fallen into the habit of watching for all changes, like the changes of sunset and dawn.

Chapter 14

# The Return of the Knight-Errant

In the great General Election, which had been produced by the big menace of Braintree and his new Syndicalism, and which had led up to the launching of the movement in opposition to it, it was reported that Mr. Michael Herne had gone into a polling-booth to record his vote; and had remained there for three-quarters of an hour, mysteriously occupied or possibly engaged in prayer. He had apparently never given a vote before; it not being a Palaeo-Hittite habit; but when it had been elaborately explained to him that he had only to make a cross on the piece of paper opposite the name of his favourite candidate, he seemed quite charmed and enchanted with the idea. By this time, of course, his Palaeo-Hittite period had long become prehistoric and stratified in the past; and his later medieval enthusiasm devoured his days and nights. Nevertheless he could apparently spare a somewhat abnormal time for the modern and rather mechanical process of voting; when he might have been engaged in drawing the long bow or tilting at a Saracen's head. Archer and his other colleagues became a little impatient, and not a little mystified, by his mysterious immersion in the ballot box; they kicked their legs restlessly outside and eventually went inside, to see his tall and motionless back still immovable in its separate cell, as of a modern confessional. They were at last goaded to the gross indelicacy of disturbing the Citizen when alone with his Duty, by going up behind him and pulling his coat-tails. As this had no particular effect, they committed the anarchical and anti-democratic outrage of actually looking over his shoulder. They found that he had set out on the little shelf, as on a table, all the illumination paints (presumably borrowed from Miss Ashley), paints of gold and silver and all the colours of the rainbow. With these he was engaged in doing his democratic duty with almost a painful care and patience. He had been told to make a cross and he was making a cross. He was doing it as it would have been done by a monk in the Dark Ages; that is in very gay and glorified colours. The cross was of gold, in one corner of it were three blue birds, in another corner were three red fishes, in another plants, in another planets and so on; it seemed to be planned upon the scheme of the Canticle of the Creature of St. Francis of Assisi. He was very much surprised to be told that this was not required by the provisions of the Ballot Act; but he controlled himself and only gave a faint sigh, when informed by the officials of the polling station that his vote was cancelled, because he had "spoilt" a ballot paper.

Outside in the street, however, there were a good many people who thought that even the usual hasty scratch on the ballot paper was almost as much of a waste of time as Mr. Herne's elaborate ritual. It was the paradox of that particular General Election that it was a great crisis because another thing was much greater; and it was intensely exciting because people were excited about something else. It was rather like one of the elections that take place during a great war. Indeed it might be said that it took place during a revolution.

The Great Strike that gathered all the workers in the dye and colour making trades, with sympathetic strikes among various bodies connected with Coal-Tar and Coal, had its headquarters in Milldyke and its leader in John Braintree. But it was much more than a strike of the local and limited sort that its description might imply. It was not the sort of strike at which men of the more comfortable classes had grown accustomed to grumble; being used to their discomforts as to their comforts. It was something entirely new, at which such men, not unnaturally and perhaps not unreasonably, ejaculated sharp and even shrill protests.

At the very moment when Herne was medievally occupied in the monastic cell of the polling-station, Braintree was filling the market-place of Milldyke with his thunderous voice in the most sensational speech of his career. It was sensational in substance as well as in style. He no longer, as in the first stages of this history, demanded what he called Recognition. He demanded Control.

"Your masters tell you," he said, "that you are greedy materialists grown accustomed to clamour for more wages. They are right. Your masters tell you that you lack ideals and do not understand ambition and the instinct to govern. They are right. They imply that you are slaves and beasts of burden, in so far as you would only eat up stores and escape responsibility. They are right. They are right so long as you are content to ask only for wages, only for food, only for well-paid service. But let us show our masters that we have profited by the moral lessons they are so good as to give us. Let us return to them penitent; let us tell them we mean to amend our faults of petty stipulation and merely materialistic demand. Let us tell them that we have an ambition; and it is to rule. That we have an ideal; and it is to rule equally. That we have a hunger and a high thirst for responsibility; for the glorious and joyous responsibility of ruling what they misrule, of managing what they have mismanaged, of sharing among ourselves as workers and comrades that direct and democratic government of our own industry which was hitherto served to keep a few parasites in luxury in their palaces and parks."

After that speech at Milldyke all communications were cut and a chasm yawned between Braintree and the parks and palaces to which he referred. The demand that the manual workers should become the managers of the works consolidated against him, indeed, a large mass of people who did not by any means live in palaces or parks. It was so manifestly and madly revolutionary that hardly anyone did agree with it who was not already prepared to call himself a revolutionist. And real revolutionists are rare. Rosamund's friend Harry Hanbury, a very kindly and reasonable squire, spoke for the rest. "Hang it all, I'm all for paying people good wages, as I try to pay my chauffeur and valet good wages. But Control means that the chauffeur can drive me to Margate when I want to go to Manchester. My valet brushes my clothes and has something to say about them. But Control means that I must wear yellow trousers and a pink waistcoat if he chooses to lay them out for me."

The next week brought the news of two great elections: the one a defiant answer to the other. On the Tuesday the news was brought to Herne that Braintree had been elected by a huge and howling Labour majority.

And on the Thursday was received by that abstracted mind, blind with inner light, the shout and scurry and acclamation which announced that he himself had been chosen by the Orders and Electoral Colleges, as King-at-Arms over the whole world of the West Country. It was in a sort of waking dream that he was escorted to a high throne set upon that green plateau of Seawood Park. On one side of the new King stood Rosamund Severne, Dame of some new degree and holding the Shield of Honour, shaped like a heart and blazoned with the lion, which was to be given to the best knight who had achieved the boldest adventure. She looked very statuesque; and few could have guessed how energetically she flew round in preparing the ceremony; or how very like it was to her way of preparing the theatricals. On the left stood her friend, the young squire and explorer, whom she had once introduced to Braintree, looking very serious indeed; for he had passed the point of self-consciousness and felt his heraldic uniform as natural as that of the Scots Grey. He held what was called the Sword of St. George, with the cross-hilt upwards; for Michael had said, in one of his mystical fragments, "A man never deserves a sword until he can hold it by the blade. His hand may bleed; but it is then that he sees the Cross." But Herne sat on his high throne above all the coloured crowd, and his eyes seemed to inhabit the horizons and the high places. So have many fanatics ridden high on clouds over scenes as preposterous; so Robespierre walked in his blue coat at the Feast of the Supreme Being. Lord Eden caught sight of those clear eyes, like still and shining pools, and muttered: "The man is mad. It is dangerous for unbalanced men when their dreams come true. But the madness of a man may be the sanity of a society."

"Well!" cried Julian Archer, slapping his sword-hilt with that air of answering for everybody that was so hearty and refreshing. "It's been a great day and the world will hear of it. The people round here will find we've really got to work. This is the sort of thing that will hunt out Braintree and all his rabble of ragamuffins and make them run like rats."

Rosamund was still rather like a smiling statue; but Olive standing behind her had seemed as dark as her shadow. Now Olive suddenly spoke and her clear voice rang like steel.

"He is not a ragamuffin," she said. "He is an engineer; and knows a lot more than you do. What are most of you, if it comes to that? An engineer is as good as a librarian. I should think."

There was a deathly silence; and Archer, with a helpless gesture, looked upwards, as if the sky would crack at the blasphemy; but most of the ladies and gentlemen looked downwards, at their pointed medieval shoes; for they realised that it was worse than blasphemy; it was certainly, under the circumstances, exceedingly bad taste.

But though the groups had begun to break up and mingle, the King-at-Arms had not yet left his throne; as they were soon to find, in more ways than one. He took no more notice of the woman who had just insulted him than if she had not been there; but he suddenly bent his brows upon Julian Archer; and a sort of subconscious thrill told everybody that in one mind at least the royalty was a reality.

"Sir Julian," said the King-at-Arms sternly, "I think you have read your books of venery very wrongly. You do not seem to know that we are back in braver and better days and have left behind the time when gentlemen could swagger about hunting vermin. Ours is the spirit of the ages when royal beasts could turn to bay and slay the hunters; the great boar and the noble stag. We are of the world that could respect its enemies; yes, even when they were beasts. I know John Braintree; and there never was a braver man walking this world. Shall we fight for our faith and sneer at him because he fights for his? Go and kill him if you dare; but if he should kill you, you will be as much honoured in your death as you are now dishonoured by your tongue."

For one instant the impression, or illusion, was stunning and complete. He had spoken spontaneously and simply out of himself; but it might have been a reincarnation. So exactly might Richard the Lion Heart have spoken to a courtier who imputed cowardice to Saladin.

But in that still crowd there was a change that might have been even more surprising if many had noticed it; for the pale face of Olive Ashley had turned to a red flame; and a sort of cry, that was half a gasp, was rent out of her.

"Ah, now I know it has really begun!"

And from that moment she moved lightly in the coloured procession, as if a load had been lifted off her. She seemed to wake up for the first time to all that decorative dance, that was so near to her old dreams and take her part in it without further doubt or distress. Her dark eyes were shining, as at a memory. A little later in the proceedings she found herself talking to Rosamund. She lowered her voice and said almost like one telling a secret:—"He really means it! He really understands. He isn't a snob or a swaggering bully or anything of the sort. He really believes in the good old days—and the good new days, too."

"Of course he means it!" cried Rosamund very indignantly. "Of course he really believes it and behaves like it too! If you only knew what it was for me to see anything *done,* after the eternal talking at large of Monkey and Julian and the rest. Besides, he's quite right to believe in it. What business has anybody to laugh at it? Beautiful dresses are not half so laughable as ugly dresses. We ought to have been doubled up with laughter day and night in the days when men wore trousers." And she continued to pour out her defence, with all the passion with which a practical young woman, repeats the opinions of somebody else.

But Olive was looking from the high lawn up the long white road that wandered away to the sunset and seemed to melt its silver in that copper and gold.

"They asked me once," she said, "whether I thought King Arthur would return. On an evening like this . . . can't you imagine the culmination coming, and our seeing some knight of the Round Table pricking along the road, ever so far away, bringing us a message from the King."

"Well, it's jolly queer you should say that," said the more practical Rosamund, "because there really is somebody coming along; and I believe he's on a horse, too."

"He seems to be behind a horse," said Olive in a low voice. "That low sun dazzles my eyes. . . . Can it be a Roman chariot? I suppose Arthur would *really* be a Roman?"

"It's a very queer shape," said Rosamund; and her voice also had altered.

The knight-errant from King Arthur's Court certainly was a very queer shape; for as the equipage came nearer and nearer, it took on to the amazed eyes of the medieval crowd the appearance of a dilapidated hansom cab, surmounted by a cabman in a dilapidated top-hat. He removed his battered headgear with a polite salutation and revealed the unpretentious features of Douglas Murrel.

Mr. Douglas Murrel, after thus saluting the company, replaced his remarkable hat, perhaps a little on one side, and proceeded to fall off the hansom cab. It is not easy to fall off a hansom cab with gravity and social ease; but Mr. Murrel accomplished it with the acrobatic accuracy of old. The hat fell off, but he caught it with great dexterity; and immediately walked across to Olive Ashley, observing without any embarrassment.

"I say; I've got that stuff you wanted."

The company looking at his collar and tie and trousers (which were specially conspicuous when he turned a cartwheel from the top of the cab), had the curious sensation of seeing somebody dressed in the quaint costume of a by-gone age. In fact, they had very much the same feelings which he himself had had when he first saw the hansom cab; though hansom cabs had only recently begun to dwindle and disappear in London. So rapidly does human fashion harden and people become accustomed to a new environment.

"Monkey!" gasped Olive. "Where on earth have you been all this time? Haven't you heard anything about anything?"

"I had to poke about a little bit to find the paints," said Murrel modestly, "and since I bought the cab I've been giving people rides on the road. But I've got it anyhow."

Then for the first time he seemed to think it necessary to notice the singular scene that surrounded him; though the contrast was as great as if he had fallen out of another world and appeared in the ancient setting like the Yankee at the Court of King Arthur; if anybody so very English as he was could ever be compared with a Yankee.

"I've got it in the cab," he explained. "I'm pretty sure it's what you wanted. . . . I say, Olive, is your play *still* going on? Back to Methuselah, eh? I know you have a fertile pen; but really a play that lasts a month—"

"It isn't a play," she answered, staring at him in a stony fashion. "It began as a play; but we aren't playing any longer."

"Sorry to hear that," he said. "I've had a good deal of fun myself; but there was a serious side to that, too. Is the Prime Minister here? They told me he was coming—and I'd rather like to see him."

"Oh, I can't tell it all in a minute," she exclaimed, almost impatiently. "Don't you know there isn't a Prime Minister now; not of that sort? The King-at-Arms is managing everything round here."

And she gestured rather desperately towards that potentate, who was still sitting on his high seat; probably because he had forgotten to come down. The same reason had once detained him on the top of the library shelf.

Douglas Murrel seemed to take it all in with more composure than might have been expected; perhaps he remembered the incident in the library. But his demeanour towards the medieval monarch was scrupulously correct. He bowed slightly, and then dived into the interior of the hansom cab; and re-emerged, holding a shapeless parcel in one hand and his hat in the other. He seemed to have a difficulty in unwrapping the parcel with one hand, and he turned towards the throne with a very proper air of apology.

"Pardon me, Your Majesty," he said. "May my family have the ancient and ancestral privilege of wearing its hat at Court? I feel sure something of that sort must have been given to us after we tried unsuccessfully to rescue the Princes in the Tower. You see, it's so awkward holding a hat; but I have a great affection for this hat."

If he expected to see any gleam of answering humour in the face of the fanatic above him, he was disappointed; but the King-at-Arms said with perfect gravity: "Most certainly be covered. It is only the intention in courtesy that counts. I doubt whether those who had such privileges really insisted on them; I seem to remember a King who said, very rightly, to such a privileged lord, 'You have the right to wear your hat before me, but not before the ladies.' In the same spirit, where (as in this case) the purpose is actually to oblige a lady, the form is obviously dispensed with."

And he looked round in a reasonable manner, as if his logic had surely satisfied everybody as it satisfied him, and Douglas Murrel solemnly put on his hat and proceeded to take a prodigious number of wrappings off the parcel.

When it eventually emerged, it was a cylindrical glass jar or bottle, extremely dirty, with indistinguishable inscriptions and ornaments; but when he handed it to Olive, he saw that his search had not been a futile one. There is no explaining how the mere shape and detail of things lost in childhood can startle and stab the emotions; but when she saw the shape of that obsolete pot of paint, with its large stopper and the faded trade mark of decorative fishes upon it, her eyes were stung with tears so that she herself was startled by them. It was as if she had suddenly heard the voice of her father.

"How on earth did you find this?" she cried, in a very contradictory fashion; since she had only intended him to look for it, at the most, in the nearest shop in the nearest town. But that cry alone revealed the subconscious pessimism that had underlain all her archeological affections; she had not believed that any of the dead things that she desired could return. When she saw this one, it crowned and completed that restoration of confidence which she had felt when Herne had rebuked Archer. Both these things somehow rang with reality. All the costumes and ceremonials that had been restored might after all be, as Murrel had suggested, a mere continuation of the play-acting. But Hendry's Illumination Paints were a real thing; as real as a wooden doll loved in the nursery or lost in the garden. After that moment she never had a doubt about her side in the great debate.

Few indeed, however, in that coloured crowd were likely to share Miss Ashley's emotions about the parcel. Nobody else could feel the contrast between Monkey being sent out rather like an errand-boy and his coming back like a knight-errant. To the others, now in the full swing of the statelier new fashions, poor Monkey did not look at all like a knight-errant. However much they might vary in the intellectual appreciation of the change, their limbs had grown used to the fall of freer draperies and their eyes to the colours of gayer crowds. They no longer thought so much that their own dress was picturesque; they merely thought that his dress was out of the picture. He was not only a blot on the landscape but a block in the traffic. He patted his horse in an affectionate manner, and that queer prehistoric monster seemed even to make uncouth movements as if returning his affection.

"Odd thing is," said Archer in his confidential, emphatic style to the young squire who carried the sword, "Odd thing is he can't *see* he's out of it. Always so difficult to manage fellows who can't *see* when they're out of it."

He relapsed into gloomy silence, and in company with all his associates, settled down to listen rather nervously to a dialogue that had already begun between the newcomer and the potentate on the throne. They had some cause for feeling nervous; sensible as they were of how this preposterous procession out of a three-act farce must have sprawled across the vision of the visionary king. It was all the more alarming when the incongruous Murrel insisted on addressing the throne with a somewhat burlesque civility, but with an apparent pertinacity of intention. He seemed to be appealing to the King-at-Arms, since that person now discharged the functions both of Prime Minister and Lord of the Manor, about the details of his own recent adventures; those wanderings on the borderland of things where he had come upon the ruins of a hansom cab. Archer heard his polite impertinencies gradually linking themselves up into a long soliloquy. He might really have been a traveller telling his travels at the court of some fabled king. But when Archer began to listen a little wearily to what the experiences were, he lost all such romantic illusions about them. Monkey was certainly telling a story; a long story; and a damned silly story, Archer thought.

At first he had gone to a shop. Then he had gone to another shop; or another part of the same shop. Then he had gone to a public-house. So like Monkey to turn up sooner or later at a public-house, and you bet sooner rather than later; as if a gentleman couldn't have anything he wanted sent quietly to his rooms. Then followed long confusing conversations at the public-house, including an imitation of a superior barmaid; most unsuitable on such an occasion. Then he seemed to have gone for a walk, lord knows where, and talked to a cabman, lord knows why. Then he went to some slum or other in a seaside town and got into trouble with the police. Everybody knew of course that Monkey was fond of practical jokes; but to do him justice, he hadn't generally bored you with them afterwards, let alone at this length. He seemed to have played a trick on some doctor in charge of some lunatic, so that they didn't lock up the lunatic but only the doctor. Pity they hadn't split the difference and locked up Monkey. But what in the world all this had to do with The Movement and the chances of beating Braintree and the Bolshies, Archer would very much like to know. . . . Oh lord, the story was still going on. There seemed to be a girl in it now; and of course that might explain it all, even with a chap like Monkey, who always played at being the wild bachelor. But why in the devil was he pouring it all out *now*, when they were just going to begin the regular formalities of the Shield and Sword? And why was the King-at-Arms listening in that style, so steady and almost stony? Perhaps he was frozen with rage. Perhaps he had gone to sleep.

Most of the company indeed, including the young man with the sword, were not quite so sensitive as Mr. Archer about the tone, the really right and very best tone, suitable to social occasions. They were not so vexed as was that artist in life at the discord or the Monkey monologue. But they were no more favourably, or at least no more seriously impressed. Some of them began to smile, a few to laugh; though they had a certain air of doing it decorously, as if they were laughing in church. Nobody had the least notion of what Murrel was talking about, or at any rate why he was talking about it. But those who knew him best were a little puzzled by the eager exactitude with which he was telling his long-winded story. And all the time the King-at-Arms sat as motionless as a statue and nobody knew whether he was mortally offended or merely stone deaf.

"You see," Murrel was concluding in an easy and confidential style, thought by some to lack certain elements of the noble prose of Malory, "you may say they were all a blasted lot of blighters; but there's blighters and blighters; some are born blighters, some achieve blightering and some have blightering thrust upon them, as the poet says. And it seemed to me that poor old Hendry had blightering thrust upon him pretty bad, by a run of the most putrid luck you ever heard of, and a lot of dirty scallywags doing him down. But the other doctor was a natural born blighter, and loved blightering for its own sake; so I really didn't give a damn whether they stuffed the stinker into a padded cell or not; but I don't believe they did, because I tipped them the wink afterwards. And then I did a bunk before the bobby could get a move on; and came away on the cab, which runs faster than a bobby does anyhow. And there you are. There, so to speak, you bally well are."

This peroration also fell into an abyss of silence; but after the silence had lasted for a few moments that seemed eternal, some of the more anxious and watchful of the crowd perceived that the statue upon the throne had moved. It was already almost as if a real statue had moved. But when the man spoke, it was not with any of the thunders of a god, but with a casual but decisive action like that of an ordinary magistrate making a decision.

"That is all right," he said, "give him the Shield."

It was at this moment that The Movement escaped from the imaginative grasp of Sir Julian Archer. Afterwards, when the great catastrophe had occurred, he was in the habit of saying, with moody sagacity, to his friends at the club that he had always realised that the whole thing was beginning to go wrong. But at the moment, in point of fact, his trouble was that he did not realise anything; the thing seemed to slip out of his hands like the smooth but enormous swelling of some small toy balloon growing big and breaking its string. He had adapted himself with agile grace to the change from fashionable morning dress to fantastic medieval dress. But there he had been supported by a movement in the whole social world around him; not to mention the daughter of a nobleman. He found considerably more difficulty in adapting his medieval dress yet more abruptly to the atmosphere of the hat and the hansom cab. But when Michael Herne suddenly stood up in his high place and began to talk, in a sort of stern and breathless style, he could not take the last leap of logical or illogical connection at all. He seemed to have come into a nonsense world in which events occurred without any sequence. It was impossible to understand anything, except that Herne was in a towering passion about something. Any fellow might be justified, of course, in being in a towering passion when confronted with a hat like that. But the hat had been blighting the landscape for quite a long time without the King-at-Arms taking any official notice of it; and now they seemed to have got on to something quite different. He could not in the least understand what Herne was talking about. He seemed to be telling a story. He was telling it in a strange sort of way; stiff and yet straightforward; somehow as if it were out of the Bible and all that sort of thing. Nobody could possibly have supposed that it was the same story that

Douglas Murrel had told. Anyhow, it was not the same story that Julian Archer had heard.

Herne had lost something of the normal slowness of his gesture and diction, and his words seemed to come quicker and quicker; his breathlessness was like that of a man who has received a blow. But Archer could make nothing out of it, except that it was a story about an old man who had a daughter; and how she followed him faithfully in his wanderings, when he had been robbed by thieves and fallen on evil days. Archer saw as in a vision the hard illustrations of an Early Victorian Sunday School story, with a very dowdy daughter and an old man with a long grey beard. They had nothing but each other; they were forgotten by the world: they stood in no man's way; they threatened nothing and provoked nobody. And even in their hole they were hunted out by strange men, with a cold and causeless malignity that had not the human decency of hate. They examined the man as if he were an animal and dragged him away as if he were already a corpse. They cared nothing for the tragic virtues on which they trampled; or that unbroken lily of loyalty which they stamped into the mire.

"You," cried the King-at-Arms indignantly to all his enemies who were not there, "You who talk of our rebuilding the ruins of tyranny or bringing back the barbarian crowns of gold! Is it written of kings that they did these things? Is it written even of tyrants? Was a tale like this told of King Richard? Was it told even of King John? You know the worst that can be said of the wildest that the feudal world could do; it is you who say it. You know what John Lackland is in all your popular history taken from Ivanhoe and penny dreadfuls. John is the traitor; John is the tyrant; John is the universal criminal; and what are the crimes of John? That he murdered a royal prince. That he broke faith with an aristocracy of nobles. That he took away a tooth from one wealthy Jewish banker; possibly it was stopped with gold, hence the outcry! That he attacked the King his father or supplanted the King his brother. Ah, it was dangerous to stand high in those days! It was dangerous to be a prince, to be a noble, to be near to the walking whirlwind of the wrath of the

King. He that went into the palace often carried his life in his hands; he was entering the cave of the lion, if it was the cave of the Lion Heart. It was unfortunate to be rich and rouse royal envy. It was unfortunate to be powerful. It was unfortunate to be fortunate.

"But when was it spoken of the tyrant, of the mighty hunter before the Lord or the Devil, that he stayed his hunting to turn over a stone to steal the eggs of insects or poked in a pool to separate the tadpole from the frog? When did he have that minute and microscopic malice that could leave nothing untormented, that could hate the helpless more than the proud, that could cover the land with spies to spoil the love-stories of serfs or mobilise an army to carry off an old beggar from his child? The kings rode by and hurled such beggars a curse or a coin; they did not stop laboriously to dismember their little families limb by limb; that the human heart that feeds on its sad affections might suffer the last and longest agony. There were good kings who waited upon the beggars like servants; yes, even when the beggars were lepers. There were bad kings who would have spurned the beggars and ridden on, and then probably remembered it with terror in the hour of death and left money for masses and charities. But they did not chain up a medieval old man merely for his blindness, as they chained up the modern old man merely for his theory about colour-blindness. And this is the sort of spider's web of worry and misery you have spread over all the unfortunate mass of mankind, because, heaven help us, you are too humane, you are too liberal, you are too philanthropic to endure human government and the name of a king.

"Do you blame us if we have dreamed of a return to simpler things? Do you blame us if we sometimes fancy that a man might not do what all this machinery is doing, if once he were a man and no longer a machine? And what is marching against us to-day except machinery? What has Braintree to tell us to-day except that we are sentimentalists ignorant of science, of social science, of economic science of hard and objective and logical science—of such science as dragged that old man like a leper from all he loved? Let us tell John Braintree that we are not ignorant of science. Let us tell John Braintree that we know too much about science already. Let us tell John Braintree to his teeth that we have had enough of science, enough of enlightenment, enough of education, enough of all his social order with its mantrap of machinery and its death-ray of knowledge. Take this message to John Braintree; all things come to an end and these things are ended. For us there can be no end but the beginning. In the morning of the world, in the Assembly of the Knights, in the house, among the greenwoods of Merry England, in Camelot of the Western Shires, I give the shield to the one man who has done the one deed of all our days worth doing; who has avenged one wrong upon at least one ruffian and saved a woman in distress."

He stooped from his throne with a swift movement and took the great sword from the man below; lifted and shook it so that it seemed to flame like the sword of St. Michael. And then there sounded over all that staring crowd the ancient words that accompany the Accollade and dedicate a man to God and the cause of the widow and orphan.

## Chapter 15

# The Parting of the Ways

Olive Ashley came away from the scene of the indignant oration looking even paler than usual; nor was she only pale with excitement, but also with a sort of self-inflicted pain. She seemed to have come suddenly to the end and edge of something; to a challenge and a choice. She was one of those women who cannot be stopped from hurting themselves, when once their moral sense is strongly moved. She needed a religion; and chiefly an altar on which to be a sacrifice. She also had in her own way a singular intellectual intensity; and ideas to her were not merely notions. And it seemed to her, with an abrupt and awful clearness, that she could not any longer maintain her merely romantic parley with the enemy, unless she was prepared honestly to go over to him. If she went over, she would go over for ever; and she had to consider what exactly she would leave behind. If it had been merely the whole world, or in other words society, she would not have hesitated; but it was England; it was patriotism; it was plain morals. If the new national cause had really been only an antiquarian antic, or a heraldic show, or even a sentimental reaction such as she might once have dreamed of, she could have brought herself easily to leave it. But now with her whole brain and conscience she was convinced that it would be like deserting the flag in a great war. Her conviction had been finally clinched by the denunciation of Hendry's oppressors in human and moving terms; the cause was the cause of her father's old friend and of her father. But it is an ironical fact that what had most convinced her of the justice of Braintree's great enemy had been the truth of his tribute to Braintree. Without a word to anyone, she went out of the main gateway and took the road to the town.

As Olive walked slowly through the dreary suburbs to the even darker central places of the town of the factories, she became conscious that she had crossed a frontier and was walking in a world she did not know. Of course she had been in such towns a thousand times, and even in that particular town often enough; as it was the nearest town to Seawood Abbey and the house of her friend. But the frontier she had passed was not so much of space as of time; or perhaps not of space but of spirit. Like somebody discovering a new dimension, she realised that there was, and had been all the time, another world beside her own world, a world of which she had heard nothing; nothing from the newspapers; nothing from the politicians, even when they were talking after dinner. The paradox was that the papers and politicians were never so silent about it as when they were supposed to be talking about it.

The great Strike that had begun far away in the mines had been going on for nearly a month. Olive and her friends regarded it as a Revolution; in which they agreed with the very small but determined group of Communists among the strikers. But it was not its being a revolution that surprised or puzzled her. It was rather that it was unlike anything she had ever associated with the word. She had seen silly films and melodramas about the French Revolution and imagined that a popular rising must be a mob, and that a mob must be a mob of half-naked and howling demons. She had known this thing in front of her described as much fiercer than it was and much milder than it was; described by one sort of party hack as a conspiracy of gory brigands against God and the Primrose League; and by another sort of party hack as a trivial though regrettable misunderstanding, which would soon be smoothed out by the sympathetic statesmanship of the Under Secretary to the Ministry of Capital. She had heard about politics all her life; thought she had never been interested in them. But she had never doubted that these were modern politics; and that being interested in modern politics meant being interested in them. The Prime Minister and Parliament and the Foreign Office and the Board of Trade and tiresome things of that sort—there were those things and everything else was Revolution. But as she passed first through the groups in the groups in the street, and then through the groups in the outer offices of official buildings, there dawned on her a truth quite different.

There was a Prime Minister she had never heard of; and he was a man she knew. There was a Parliament she had never heard of; and he had just swayed it with an historic speech that would never go down to history. There was a Board of Trade she had never heard of; a Board that really met and had a great deal more to say about Trade. There were Government Departments quite outside the Government; Government Departments quite against the Government. There was a bureaucracy; there was a hierarchy; there was an army. It had the qualities and defects of such systems; but it was not in the least like the frightful French mob on the film. She heard the people talking round her and mentioning names as her own class mentioned the names of politicians; and she found she knew none of them, except Braintree, and that of one other who had been capriciously picked out by the papers from all the rest and caricatured as a sort of raging buffoon. But the statesmen of this buried state were spoken of with an air of calm familiarity, that made her feel as if she had fallen from the moon. Jimson was right after all and though Hutchins had done good work in his time, he was wrong now. They mustn't always let Ned Bruce talk them round. Now and then Braintree was mentioned as the chief leader, and not unfrequently criticised, which annoyed her a good deal; she was a little thrilled when he was praised. Hatton, the man who had been caricatured so often in the papers as the fire-brand of Red Revolution, was a good deal blamed for his extreme caution and consideration for the employers. Some even said he was in the pay of the capitalists.

For never in any newspaper or book or magazine of modern England had anything remotely resembling a History of the

Trade Union Movement come the way of an intelligent and educated English lady like Olive Ashley. The whole of that huge historical change had happened, so far as she was concerned behind a curtain; and the curtain was literally a sheet of paper; a sheet of newspaper. She knew nothing of the differences between Trade Unionists; nothing of the real faults of Trade Unions; not even the very names of men who were directing masses as large as the army of Napoleon. The street seemed full of strange faces or faces all the stranger for being familiar. She caught a glimpse of the large lumbering form of the omnibus-driver that Monkey used to make such a friend of. He was talking, or rather listening, with the others; and his large, shiny, good-humoured face seemed to assent to all that was said. Had Miss Ashley accompanied Monkey on his disgraceful tour round the public-houses, she would even have recognised the celebrated Old George, who now received the challenge of political dispute as he had received the chaff of the tavern. Had she known more of popular life, she would have understood the menacing meaning of the presence of these very sleepy and amiable poor Englishmen amid those sullen groups in the streets. But the next moment she had forgotten all about them. She had only succeeded in penetrating into an outer court of the temple of officialism (it was very like waiting in a Government office) when she heard Braintree's voice outside in the corridor and he came rapidly into the room.

When John Braintree came into the room, Olive instantly and in a flash saw every detail about him; all that she liked in his appearance and all that she disliked in his clothes. He had not grown a beard again, whatever his reaction into revolution; he was always thin and it was partly an effect of energy that he looked haggard; he seemed as vigorous as ever. But when he saw her, he seemed to be simply stunned and stupefied by the mere fact of her presence. All the worries went out of his eyes; and showered beneath them rather a sort of shining sorrow. For worries are never anything but worries, however we turn them round. But a sorrow is always a joy reversed. Something in the situation made her stand up and speak with an unnatural simplicity.

"What can I say?" she said. "I believe now that we must part."

So, for the first time, it was really admitted between them that they had come together.

There is a great deal of fallacy and folly about the ordinary talk of confidential conversation; to say nothing of the loathsome American notion of a heart to heart talk. People are often very misleading when they talk about themselves; even when they are perfectly honest, and even modest, in talking about themselves. But people tell a great deal so long as they talk about everything except themselves. These two had talked so often and so long about all the things that they cared for so much less than for each other, that they had come to an almost uncanny omniscience, and could sometimes have deduced what one or the other thought about cookery from remarks about Confucius. And, therefore, at this unprepared and apparently pointless crisis, they talked in what would be called parables; and neither for one moment misunderstood the other.

"My God," said Braintree, out of his full understanding.

"You say it," she said, "but I mean it."

"I am not an atheist, if that is what you mean," he said with a somewhat sour smile. "But perhaps it is true that I only have the noun and you have the possessive adjective. I suppose God does belong to you, like so many other good things?"

"Do you think I would not give them all to you?" she said. "And yet I suppose there is something in one's mind one cannot give up to anybody."

"If I did not love you I could lie," he said; and again neither of them noticed that a word had been said for the first time. "God, what a gorgeous feast of lying I could have just now, explaining how much you mystified me by your incomprehensible attitude; and what had I done to forfeit our beautiful intellectual friendship; and had I not at least a right to an explanation; and all the rest. Lord, if I were only a real politician! It takes a real politician to say that politics do not matter. How lovely it would be to say all the ordinary and natural and newspaper things— widely as we differ upon many points—opposed as we are in politics. I for one am free to say that never—it is the proud boast of political life in this country that the wildest party differences do not necessarily destroy that essential good feeling—oh, hell and the devil and all the dung-heaps of the world! I know what we mean. You and I are people who cannot help caring about right and wrong."

Then after a long silence he said: "I suppose you believe in Herne and all his revival of chivalry? I suppose you really believe it is chivalrous; and even know what you mean by it?"

"I never believed in his chivalry," she said, "till he said he believed in yours."

"That was very good of him," said Braintree quite seriously. "He is a good man. But I am afraid his compliments would do me a good deal of harm in my own camp. Some of those words have already come to be symbols of something else with our people."

"I might answer your people," she said, "rather as you have answered me. I know I am called old-fashioned; and your people have all the new fashions. I feel cross with them; I feel inclined to insult them by calling them fashionable. But they really are. Don't they take up all this business about a woman living for herself and sex making no difference and all the rest of it; just like the intellectual duchesses? They would all say that I was behind the times, and talk of me as if I were a slave in a harem. And yet I will challenge them on that, out of the tragic and hateful tangle in which I am standing to-day. They talk about a woman thinking for herself! They talk about a woman standing alone! How many of the wives of your Socialists are out attacking Socialism? How many women engaged to Labour Members are voting against them at the polls or speaking against them on the platform? Nine-tenths of your revolutionary women are only going along with revolutionary men. But I *am* independent. I am thinking for myself. I am living my own life, as they call it; and a most miserable life it is. I am not going along with a revolutionary man."

There was again a long silence; the sort of silence which endures because it is unnecessary, or rather impossible, to ask questions; and then Braintree took a step nearer and said: "Well, I am miserable enough, if that is part of the logic of the case; and yet again it is just part of this infernal furnace of reality that I cannot attack logic. How easy it is to attack logic! How impossible to find anything else except lying! And then they say that women are not logical; because they never waste logic on things that do not matter. My God, is there any way *out* of logic?"

To anyone who had not known their knowledge of each other, this conversation would have seemed a series of riddles; but Braintree knew the answers before the riddles were asked. He knew that this woman had got hold of a religion and that a religion is often a renunciation. She would not go with him without helping him to the death. And she would not help him; she would resist him to the death. That antagonism between them, as it had arisen in silly remarks and random *repartees* in their first interview in the long room at Seawood, that antagonism, transfigured, enlightened, deepened but all the more defined by knowing all the best of each other, was risen again to a noble height of reason, which he was the last man in the world to despise. People laugh at these things when they find them in the old stories of Roman virtue. They are people who have never loved at the same time a truth and a friend.

"There are some things," she said at last, "that I do know more about than you. You used to make fun of my old stories about knights and ladies; I don't think you will stoop to laugh at them now you are fighting them; but you would laugh again if we were back in the old idle days. And yet those things are not altogether idle or laughable. Poetry sometimes talks plainer than prose, I think; and somebody said our souls are love and a perpetual farewell. Did you ever read that part in Malory—about the parting of Lancelot and Guinevere?"

"I can see it in your face," he said and kissed once, and they parted like the lovers of Camelot.

Outside in the dark streets the crowds had grown thicker and thicker; and there were murmurs about mystifications and delays. Like all men in the unnatural posture of revolt, they needed to be perpetually stimulated by something happening; whether it were favourable or hostile. A defiance on the other side would do; but a defiance on their own side was the best; and there had been promises of a great demagogic display that evening. There had been as yet no positive unpunctuality; but something told them that there was somewhere a little hitch. And it was five minutes later that Braintree amid a roar of cheers, appeared on the balcony.

He had hardly said a dozen words before it became apparent that he was talking in a tone that had been unusual in English politics. He had something to say that was of the final sort. He refused a tribunal; and in that there is something of the sort that always moves the deep element of epic poetry in a mob. For nothing can really be approved or applauded except finality. That is why all the ethics of evolution and expansive ideas of indefinite progress have never taken hold upon any human crowd.

The new seat of government had set up a seat of judgment, or chamber of inquiry, for the settlement of the strike which Braintree led. It was a strike now largely confined to the Trade Unions of his own district; which were engaged in the manufacturing of dyes and paints, originally derived from Coal-Tar. The very genuine energy that supported the new government had grappled immediately with the industrial problem in question. It was probable that it would be settled on somewhat saner and simpler lines than those of the complicated compromises of the old professional politician. But it would be settled. That was what the new rulers very legitimately claimed. And that was what Braintree and the strikers very legitimately objected to.

"For nearly a hundred, years," he said, "they have thundered at us about our duty to respect the Constitution: the King and the House of Lords—and even the House of Commons. We had to respect that too. (Laughter.) We were to be perfect Constitutionalists. Yes, my friends, we were to be the only Constitutionalists. We were the quiet people, the loyal subjects, the people who took the King and the lords seriously. But they were to be free enough. Whenever the fancy took them to upset the Constitution, they were to be indulged in all the pleasures of revolution. They could in twenty-four hours turn the government of England upside down; and tell us that we were all not to be ruled by a Constitutional monarchy but by a fancy dress ball. Where is the King? Who is the King? I have heard he is a librarian interested in the Hittites. (Laughter.) And we are summoned before this revolutionary tribunal—(cheers)—to explain why we have for forty years, under intolerable provocation, failed to resort to revolution. (Loud cheers.) We do not mind their listening to their lunatic librarian if they like. We will leave this ancient traditional order of chivalry that is ten weeks old; we will respect the profound Conservative principles of continuity that never existed until the other day. But we will not listen to its judgment. We would not submit to lawful Toryism. We will not now submit to lawless Toryism. And if this Wardour Street curiosity shop sends us a message that we must attend its Court—our answer is in four words, 'We will not come.'"

Braintree had described Herne as a librarian interested in Hittites but he never failed, in public or private to recognise him as a leader of men much more interested in the resurrection of the Middle Ages. And yet it would have surprised Braintree very much to know how Herne was actually occupied at the moment the words were spoken. There was between them indeed that eternal cross purposes which arises between the two opposite types of truthful man. There was all the contrast between the man who knows from the start exactly what he stands for, whose circle of vision whether narrow or no, is intensely clear, who sees all external things as agreeing or disagreeing with it—and that other type which is conscious of everything before it is conscious of itself, which can devour libraries before realising into what mind they have been absorbed, which can create fairy lands in which its own figure is invisible or at least transparent. Braintree had known from the first, almost from the first quarrel in the long room at Seawood, the irony of his own irritated admiration. He had felt the paradox of his impossible romance. The pale and vivid face of Olive Ashley with its lift and poise and pointed chin had entered his world like a wedge, like the spear of something external and antagonistic. He had hated all her world all the more for not hating her.

But with a man like Michael Herne the whole of this process worked backwards. He had hardly realised what personal romance was inspiring the impersonal romance of his historical revolution. He had had nothing but a sense of growing glory within; of a world that grew larger and loftier like an expanding sunrise or a rising tide; and which was yet of the same unconscious stuff as the day-dreams of his youth. He had had at first the feeling that a hobby had become a holiday. He had then had more and more feeling that the holiday had become a festival, in the sense of the solemn festival of a god. Only at the back of his mind did he assume that the god was a goddess. He was a man whose life had been almost wholly without personal relations. Therefore even when he was in fact growing from head to foot with a personal relation, he hardly knew that it was personal. He would have said in a sort of rapture that he was supported in his work by the most glorious friends that God had given to man. He would have spoken of them radiantly and collectively as if of a cloud of angels. And yet at any moment, even from the first, if Rosamund Severne had quarrelled with him and left that company, he would instantly have discovered his disease.

And yet it happened, as such coincidences do happen, hardly half an hour after those two that had met as enemies, and continued as friends, and had parted as lovers. So soon after they had said their farewell amid the incongruous clatter of industrial politics, the man who had in some sense divided them, if only symbolically, discovered that a man is meant in this world to be something more than a symbol. He saw Rosamund standing on the high terrace of the lawn, and the whole earth changed around her.

The news of Braintree's defiance brought a certain doubt and depression to the more romantic group at Seawood but nothing but rage and fury to Rosamund Severne. She was the sort of woman inevitably irritated by strikes if only because they are delays. Waste of time was more vivid to her than loss of principle. Many have imagined that feminine politics would be merely pacifist or humanitarian or sentimental. The real danger of feminine politics is too much love of a masculine policy. There are a good many Rosamund Severnes in the world.

She could get no relief from her impatience from the tone of the men around her, though most of them were in principle far more prejudiced against Braintree than she was. But they did not seem to react as one should react to a challenge. Her father told her at some length the real essentials of the situation, which he would have no difficulty in placing before the malcontents in due course. But as his remarks affected even his own daughter with a sensation of faint fatigue, she could hardly persuade herself that they would affect his mortal enemies to an emotional repentance. Lord Eden was more brief but not much more brisk in his comments. He said that time would show; and expressed doubt about the ultimate economic resources of the revolt. Whether designedly or no, he said nothing about the new organisation of society which he himself had helped to establish. For all of them it seemed as if a shadow had fallen across all that shining array. Beyond the park, beyond the gates of their chivalric paradise, the modern monster, the great black factory town, lay snorting up its smoke in defiance and derision.

"They're all so slack about it," Rosamund confided to Monkey, that universal confidant. "Can't you do something to get a move on? And after all our flag-waving and blowing of trumpets."

"Well," said Murrel dubiously, "all that has what they call a moral effect; only some people call it bluff. If it goes swinging along and everybody falls in with it, the thing works; and it often does. You can try your luck in rallying everybody to a flag. But you don't fight with a flag."

"Do you realise what this man Braintree has done," she cried indignantly. "He has dared us all. He has dared the King-at-Arms and the King."

"Well," replied Murrel in a detached manner, "I don't quite see what the devil else he could do. If I were in his place—"

"But you're not in his place," she cried vehemently, "you're not in the place of any rebel or rioter. Don't you ever think, Douglas, that it is time you were in your own place."

Murrel smiled rather wearily. "I admit," he said, "that I happen to be able to see two sides of a question. And I suppose you'd say its done by walking round and round it."

"I say," she said rising in wrath, "that I never met a man who saw both sides of a question without wanting to clout him on both sides of the head."

Presumably lest she should yield to this impulse, she departed in a storm, and swept up the long lawns and terraces towards the old raised garden in which the play of Blondel the Troubadour had once been performed. And the coincidence came back to her with something of a pang of memory; for in that green deserted theatre stood one green deserted figure in forester's costume, with a mane of light hair and a lifted leonine head, looking across the valley towards the smoking town.

For a moment she stood as if caught in a mesh of memories merely elfin and fantastic; as if she had loved and lost something unreal; the music and emotion of the theatricals revisited her and lulled her lust for action; but in a moment she had brushed it away like a cobweb and spoke in her own firm voice.

"You know your revolutionists have sent their reply. I hear they will not come to the Court."

He looked round slowly in his rather short-sighted fashion; only the pause before he spoke expressed the change in his feelings on hearing the voice that hailed him.

"Yes, I have received their message," he said mildly. "It was addressed to me. They certainly state their position clearly; but they will come to the Court all right."

"They will come!" she repeated in some excitement. "Do you mean that Braintree has yielded?"

"They will come, yes," he repeated, nodding. "Braintree has not yielded; indeed I did not expect him to do so. To tell the truth, I rather respect him for not doing so. He is a very courageous and consistent man; and it is always so much pleasanter to have an opponent of that kind."

"But I don't understand," she cried. "What do you mean by saying they won't yield but they will come?"

"The new constitution," he explained, "provides for the situation, as I suppose most constitutions do. It's rather like what we used to call a *subpoena*. I don't know how many men I shall want with me; but I suppose some of the Hundreds may have to turn out."

"What!" she cried. "You don't mean that you are going to *fetch* them to the Court!"

"Oh yes, the law is quite clear on that point," he answered. "And as the law makes me the executive officer, I have really no will in the matter."

"You seem to have more will than anybody else I've come across yet," she said. "You should hear Monkey!"

"Of course," he said in his pedantic way, "what I state is a purpose and not a prediction. I cannot answer for what anyone else will do or will succeed in doing. But they will come here or I shall not come."

His meticulous phraseology suddenly thrilled through her thoughts as she understood what he meant.

"You mean there will be fighting," she said.

"There certainly will be on our side if there is on theirs," he answered.

"You are the only man in this house," cried Rosamund and found herself suddenly trembling from head to foot.

It seemed as if his stiff attitude was staggered so that he lost control of himself quite unexpectedly. He uttered a sort of cry.

"You must not say that to me; I am weak; and weakest of all now, when I should try to be strong."

"You are not weak at all," she said, recovering her firm voice.

"I am mad," he said. "I love you."

She was dumb. He caught both her hands and his arms thrilled up to the shoulders as with an electric shock.

"What am I doing and saying?" he cried harshly. "I—to you to whom so many men must have said it. What will you say?"

She remained leaning forward and looking steadily into his face.

"I say what I said," she answered. "You are the only man."

"Your eyes blind me," he said.

They spoke no more; but the great land about them and above spoke for them as it rose in the mighty terraces towards the colossal corner-stones of the mountains; and the great wind of West England that rocked the tops of its royal trees; and all that vast valley of Avalon that has seen the muster of heroes and the meeting of immortal lovers, was full of a movement as of the trampling horses and the trumpets, when the kings go forth to battle and queens rule in their stead.

So they stood for a moment on the top of the world and in the highest place of our human fortune, almost at the moment when Olive and John Braintree in the dark and smoky town were taking their sad farewell. And no man could have guessed that the sad farewell was soon to be followed with fuller reconciliation and understanding; but that over the two coloured and shining figures, on the shoulder of the golden down, hung a dark cloud of sundering and division and doom.

Chapter 16

# The Judgment of the King

Lord Seawood and Lord Eden were seated in their favourite summer-house on the lawn, the same into which the arrow had once entered like the first shaft of a new sunrise; and to judge by their faces they were doubtful whether the sun were not in eclipse. Lord Eden's rigidity of expression might indeed have many meanings; but old Seawood was shaking his head in an openly disconsolate manner.

"If they had availed themselves of my intervention," he said. "I could I think have made clear the impossibility of their position; a position quite unparalleled in the whole of my public life. The restoration of our fine old historical forms must have the profound sympathy of every cultivated man; but it is against all precedent that they should use these forms for the practical suppression of material menace. What would Peel have said, had it been proposed to use only the antiquated halberds of a few Beefeaters in the Tower instead of the excellent and effective Constabulary which he had the genius and imagination to conceive? What would Palmerston have said, had anyone suggested to him that the Mace lying on the table of Parliament could be used as a club with which to quell a riot in Parliament Square? Impossible as it is for us to project upon the future the actions of the mighty dead of the past, I conceive it as likely that he would have made it the subject of a jest. But men in the present generation are devoid of humour."

"Our friend the King-at-Arms is devoid of humour all right," drawled Eden. "I sometimes wonder whether he is not the happier for it."

"There," said the other nobleman with firmness. "I cannot agree. Our English humour, such as that to be found in the best pages of *Punch* is—."

At this moment a footman appeared silently and abruptly in the entrance of the hut, murmured some ritual words and handed a note to his master. The reading of it changed his master's dolorous expression to one of unaffected astonishment.

"God bless my soul," said Lord Seawood; and remained gazing at the paper in his hand.

For upon that paper was scrawled in a large and bold hand a message destined in the next few days to change the whole face of England; as nothing for centuries had ever been changed by a battle upon English soil.

"Either our young friend is really suffering from delusions," he said at last, "or else—"

"Or else," said Lord Eden gazing at the roof of the summer-house, "he has surrounded and taken the town of Milldyke, captured the Bolshevist headquarters and is bringing the leaders here to the trial."

"This is most remarkable," said the other nobleman. "Were you informed of this before?"

"I was not informed of it at all," answered Eden, "but in any case I thought it highly probable."

"Curious," repeated Seawood, "and I thought it so highly improbable; so highly improbable as to merge itself in what we call the impossible. That a mere stage army of that description— why I thought all educated and enlightened people were aware that such weapons are quite obsolete."

"That," answered Eden, "is because educated and enlightened people never think. Your enlightened man is always taking away the number he first thought of. It seems to be a sign of education first to take a thing for granted and then to forget to see if it is still there. Weapons are a very good working example. The man says he won't go on wearing a sword because it is no longer any good against a gun. Then he throws away all the guns as relics of barbarism; and then he is surprised when a barbarian sticks him through with a sword. You say that pikes and halberds are not weapons against modern conditions. I say pikes are excellent weapons against no pikes. You say it is all antiquated medieval armament. But I put my money on men who make medieval armament against men who only disapprove of modern armament. And what have any of these political parties ever done about armament except profess to disapprove of it? They renounce it and neglect it and never think of the part it played in political history; and yet they go about with a vague security as if they were girt about with invisible guns that would go off at the first hint of danger. They're doing what they always do; mixing up their Utopia that never comes with their old Victorian security that's already gone. I for one am not at all surprised that a pack of pantomime halberdiers can poke them off the stage. I've always thought a *coup d'état* could be effected with very small forces against people who won't learn to use the force they've got. But I never had the moral courage to do it myself; it needs somebody very different from our sort."

"Perhaps," remarked the other aristocrat, "it was due to our being, to quite a very recent political formula, too proud to fight."

"Yes," replied the old statesman. "It is the humble who fight."

"I am not sure that I quite follow your meaning," said Lord Seawood.

"I mean I am too wicked to fight," said Lord Eden. "It is the innocent who kill and burn and break the peace. It is children who rush and smash and knock each other about and of such is the kingdom of heaven."

It is not certain that even then his venerable Victorian companion was wholly and lucidly of one mind with him; but there was no more to be got out of him on the subject; and he remained with a face of flint looking up the long path towards the gates of the park. And indeed that road and that entrance were already shaken with the tumult and triumph of which he spoke; and the songs of young men who come back from battle.

"I apologise to Herne," said Julian Archer with hearty generosity. "He is a strong man. I've always said that what we wanted to see was a Strong Man in England."

"I once saw a Strong Man at Olympia," said Murrel reminiscently. "I believe people often apologised to him."

"You know what I mean," answered the other good-humouredly. "A statesman. A man who knows his own mind."

"Well, I suppose a madman knows his own mind," answered Murrel. "I rather fancy a statesman ought to know a little about other people's minds."

"My dear Monkey, what's the matter with you," demanded Archer. "You seem to be quite sulky when everybody else is pleased."

"It's not so offensive as being pleased when everybody else is sulky," answered Murrel. "But if you mean am I satisfied, I will admit your penetration in perceiving that I'm not. You said just now that we wanted a strong man in England. Now I should say that the one place where we never have wanted a strong man is England. I can only remember one person who went into the profession, poor old Cromwell; and the consequence was that we dug him up to hang him after he was dead and went mad with joy for a month because the throne was going back to a weak man—or one we thought was a weak man. These high-handed ways don't suit us a bit, either revolutionary or reactionary. The French and the Italians have frontiers and they all feel like soldiers. So the word of command doesn't seem humiliating to them; the man is only a man but he commands because he is the commander. But we are not democratic enough to have a dictator. Our people like to be ruled by gentlemen, in a general sort of way. But nobody could stand being ruled by one gentleman. The idea is too horrible."

"I don't know what you mean exactly," said Archer discontentedly, "but I am glad to say that I think Herne knows what he means all right. And he'll jolly well make these fellows understand what he means as well."

"My dear fellow," said Murrel, "it takes all sorts to make a world. I don't gush about gentlemen, as you know; they're a stuffy lot, often enough. But gentlemen have managed to rule this island pretty successfully for about three hundred years; and they've done it because nobody ever did understand what they meant. They could make a mistake to-day and undo it to-morrow, without anybody knowing anything about it. But they never went too far in any direction to make it quite impossible to go back. They were always yielding here and modifying there; and patching things up somehow. Now it may be a jolly fine sight to see old Herne charging with all his chivalry. But if he will charge, he can't retreat. If he figures as a hero to you, he will figure as a tyrant to the other fellows. Now it was the very soul of our old aristocratic policy that even a tyrant must never figure as a tyrant. He may break down everybody's fences and steal everybody's land, but he must do it by Act of Parliament and not with a great two-handed sword. And if he meets the people he's disposed, he must be very polite to them and enquire after their rheumatism. That's what kept the British Constitution going— enquiring after the rheumatism. If he begins giving people black eyes or bloody scars, those things will be remembered in quite another way, whether he was right or wrong in the quarrel. And Herne isn't by a hell of a long way so right in this quarrel as he thinks he is; being a simple-minded sort."

"Well," remarked Archer, "You're not a very enthusiastic comrade-in-arms."

"As to that," said Murrel gloomily, "I don't know whether I'm a comrade-in-arms; but I'm not an infant in arms. And Herne is."

"There you go again," remarked the aggravated Archer. "You were always defending him so long as he was futile."

"And you were always abusing him so long as he was harmless," replied Murrel. "You were always calling him a lunatic. Well, that may be; personally I rather like lunatics. What I complain of is that you have swung clean round to his side, merely because he is a dangerous lunatic."

"Pretty successful for a lunatic," said the other.

"That is the only dangerous sort," said Murrel. "That's what I mean by his being an infant; and an infant that shouldn't be allowed to bear arms. Everything is too simple to him. Even his success is too simple. He sees everything in black and white; with the need of restoring holy order and a hierarchy of chivalry on the one side and nothing but howling barbarians and blind anarchy on the other. He will succeed; he has already succeeded. He will hold his court and impose his judgment and bring the mutiny to an end; and you will not see that a new sort of history will have begun. Our party leaders have always been reconciled by history; and Pitt and Fox had statues side by side. But you are starting two histories, one told by the conquerors and the other by the conquered. Herne will deliver his judgment, which will be praised by all organs of the State like a judgment of Mansfield; but Braintree will make a defence or defiance that will be remembered by all rebels like the dying speech of Emmett. You are making something new; at once a sword that divides and a shield with two sides to it. It is not England; it is not ourselves. It is Alva a hero for Catholics and a hobgoblin for Protestants; it is Frederick the father of Prussia and the murderer of Poland. When you see Braintree condemned by this tribunal, you won't understand how much is being condemned with him; how much that you like as much as I do."

"Are you a Bolshevist?" enquired his friend, staring at him in a puzzled fashion.

"I am the last Liberal," said Murrel. "In fact I've escaped from Madame Tussand's."

. . . . . . . .

Michael Herne took all his duties seriously, but it was soon apparent to some that he took one of them sadly. It was apparent at least to Rosamund Severne, and she guessed quickly at the cause. She was a woman of the sort that is very much of a mother; that sort of lady is often found attached to that sort of lunatic. She knew that he took the other and more external functions seriously, and strangely without a smile. She knew that he could lead his men as Commander of the Hundreds and then give judgment as President of the Court of Arbitrament, without ever once thinking of Pooh-Bah. She knew that he could lay aside the red cape and crest he wore as a Commander and put on over his green suit dark purple robes and a high cap of strange shape, like that of Doge before ascending the judgment seat, and never for a moment remember the hundred uniforms of the German Emperor. But in this later case of the Court of Arbitrament she could see there was something a little graver than gravity. To begin with, there seemed to be an immense load of labour. Herne worked all day and sat up nearly all night over mountains of books and bales of papers; and grew pale with wakefulness and concentration. She knew in a general way that it was his business to lay down the law, the old feudal law or whatever it was that was now being reconstituted, and apply it to the crushing of all this industrial anarchy and delay. She heartily approved of that; indeed it had been almost the basis of her approval. But she had not realised that it would mean so much research and codification out of the queer old codes and charters. Nor indeed were the queer old codes alone involved; there were things she thought queerer still. New documents on what seemed the most irrelevant subjects, chiefly scientific subjects, were handed in to swell the pile; one was endorsed on the back with the signature of Douglas Murrel. What in the world Monkey could have to do with it she could not conceive. But though there were all these things to weary and even worry the Arbiter, she knew well enough that something else made his duty somewhat distressing to him.

"I know what you are feeling like, Michael," she said. "It is hateful to have to triumph over people we like. And I know you like John Braintree."

He looked at her for a moment over his shoulder and she was quite startled by the expression of his face.

"I didn't know you liked him so much as that," she said.

He turned his head away abruptly; indeed there was something strangely abrupt in his whole manner.

"But I know the other part of you as well," she said. "You will do justice."

"Yes," he answered. "I shall do justice." And he put his head on his hands.

She felt a fine reverence for his broken friendship and silently left the library.

A minute or two after he picked up his pen again and continued to annotate documents and turn over reports; but before doing so he looked for a moment at the vast roof of the library where he had laboured so long; and especially at that high corner of the bookcase to which he had climbed in the beginning of this story.

John Braintree, who had never preferred any particular reverence for the romantic pageantry of the hour, even when it was praised by the person for whom he cared most, was not likely to admire it when it came arrayed with all the terrors of judgment against him, and adorned with the purple robes and golden sword-hilts of all the people he cared about least. His demeanour was openly contemptuous; but contempt is never contemptible in those who are defeated and defiant. When asked whether he wished to add any preliminary statement to the documents placed before the Court, he had appeared as defiantly detached as Charles the First.

"I see no Court," he said. "I only see a lot of people who seem to be dressed up as court cards. I know of no reason why I should recognise the brute force of the brigands, merely because they are stage brigands. I suppose I shall have to listen while the mummery proceeds; but I do not propose to say anything until you bring out the racks and the thumb-screws and the faggots to burn us alive. For I presume you have revived these also with all the vanished beauties of the Middle Ages. You are a scholar of admitted learning and I suppose you will give us a complete historical reconstruction of medievalism."

"Yes," replied Herne with complete gravity. "Not in detail perhaps, for no one would defend every detail of any system, but in general plan we do desire to reconstruct the medieval scheme. You are not, however, charged with any conduct which could in any case involve the punishment of burning; and that question therefore does not arise."

"Oh thank you," said Braintree agreeably. "But is not this favouritism?"

"Order, order," cried Julian Archer indignantly. "How can we proceed if the Court is not respected?"

"But for these things," continued the Arbiter, "for which you can be shown to be responsible, in relation to any public peril, for these you and any other persons will be judged by this Court and this Court alone. It is not I who speak: it is the Law."

Michael Herne cut short in midair, with a gesture sharp as the slash of a sword, the cry of acclaim and applause that greeted his words. The men who applauded him, anticipating his words with radiant faces, had always hitherto found those words like the words of a leader ringing and rousing and militant and even flamboyant. But he had too serious a sense of all the new parts he played to be flamboyant on the seat of judgment. Whatever condemnations he had to deliver against the enemies of his new realm, must be weighted with the composure and even coldness of impersonal justice. The applause simmered down into silence; but it was still an eager and even an enthusiastic silence. He proceeded in a voice singularly level and even monotonous.

"It has been our task," he said, "to recover an ancient order. We would remake an old law, but in this we cannot wholly escape the duty of making a new one. The great ages from which we draw our life were rich in variety and even in exception; and we must abstract from them general principles apart from contradictory details. In the case before us of the quarrels arising out of what are called the products of Coal, especially the work necessary for the production of dyes and colours from Coal-Tar, we must begin by recurring to certain general principles that once governed the necessary labour of the world. Those principles were very different from those of which we hear most in the more modern times, and in the movements of a restless and often lawless epoch. They were marked by order and, I will add, by obedience."

A murmur of approval broke out among his followers; and Braintree, on the other side, uttered a harsh laugh.

"In the old guild organisation," continued Herne, "this obedience was expected from apprentices and from journeymen towards a class that may broadly be called, as in our modern system, the Masters. A Master was one who produced a Masterpiece. That is, he had passed an examination by the guild in a complete piece of work of the craft; and the guild insisted on a serious standard of craftsmanship. It was normally with this Master's tools and shop and private capital that the work was done; the apprentice was one to whom this craft was being taught and the journeyman one who had not completely learnt it, but was finishing his education by hiring himself out to different masters, often in the course of a journey through different places. Men could eventually become Masters by producing Masterpieces in due course. That is, in general outline, the ancient organization of Labour. Applying it to the present case, we find the following situation. There are, in the large field covered by this work, practically three Masters; in the sense of men with whose tools and capital the craft is conducted. I have ascertained their names and I find that between them they practically share that ownership. One is Sir Howard Pryce, formerly a Master in the manufacture of soap, but having in some rapid fashion become in turn a Master in the matter of Paints and Dyes. The second is Hubert Arthur Severne, now Baron Seawood. The third is John Henry Heriot Eames, now known as the Earl of Eden. But I have no note of the date or occasion of their presenting Masterpieces in the manufacture of dyes or pigments. And I have been unable to obtain any evidence of their labouring personally in the craft, or of their educating their apprentices to do so."

The face of Douglas Murrel had worn for some time a lively and alert expression; but by this time an expression of an entirely new kind began to flicker upon some of the faces around him. Indeed the look of blank mystification, which had been fixed for a moment on the fine features of Julian Archer, had already given place to that smouldering protest which always lay so near the surface of his social self-expression; and he had already reached the point of ejaculating, "Oh! I say—."

"In this matter," went on the Arbiter, "we must be careful to distinguish the intellectual principle involved from any emotional differences about the tone and terms of discussion. I will not refer to the language used here by the Leader of the Labour organisation, especially in its reference to myself. But if he states that the Craft should be controlled by those who completely and competently practise it, I have no hesitation in saying that he states the ancient medieval ideal and states it correctly."

For the first time in the proceedings Braintree himself seemed to be brought to a standstill; staring and having nothing to say. If it was a compliment to be called a correct medievalist, it was one that he seemed to have a difficulty in receiving with proper grace. But among the changed and restless groups on the other side murmurs had already grown louder and more articulate; and Julian Archer, not yet prepared to interrupt the speaker, was conducting an indignant conversation with Murrel in very resounding whispers.

"Of course," continued Herne, "it is open to Lord Eden and Lord Seawood to take advantage of this system and present a Masterpiece of this form of manual labour. I do not know whether they would be resuming a craft, with which they were occupied at some time of which I have no record; or whether it would be necessary for them to be entered under articles; and act as two apprentices to some existing labourer. . . ."

"Pardon me," said the sturdy and sensible Mr. Hanbury suddenly standing up, "but are we all having a joke? I only ask for information; because I like jokes."

Herne looked at him and he sat down; and the former went on as steadily as ever.

"In the third case, that of the gentleman once interested in the making of Soap, I confess I can see my way less clearly. I do not quite understand by what process he passed from one Craft and Mystery to another; a proceeding by no means easy under the old order and organisation we are trying to restore. But that in its turn brings me to another matter; also immediately connected with the cause we are trying; about which I am compelled to speak more severely. Upon this first point, however, let the decision be clear. It is the judgment of the Arbiter and the Court of Arbitrament that the contention of John Braintree, that the Craft should be governed solely by Master Craftsmen, is in accordance with our tradition, is just and is approved."

"I'm damned if it is," said Hanbury, continuing to look quite stolid after uttering the remark.

"Hang it all, it's the whole question," cried Archer, in a highly reasonable voice that rose to something like a shriek. "Why, a decision like that—"

"The decision is given," said the Arbiter steadily.

"No, but—" began Sir Julian Archer not at all steadily, "you simply can't—"

"Order, order," said Braintree sardonically. "How can we get on if the Court is not respected?"

The Court appeared to take no notice of the interruption or the rebuke; but anyone looking closely at the man delivering its decision would have seen that his gravity grew more and more severe, like a strain, and that he was pale with the effort to be thus concentrated and cold.

Chapter 17

# The Departure of Don Quixote

And all this first hubbub, the two noblemen who had been named sat as still and stiff as mummies; though the reason of the rigidity might differ. Lord Seawood was simply gaping; he wore such an expression as the human head might wear if the body were suddenly blown away from under it and it were left hanging in midair. The judge might be joking; but it was not so that a judge should joke. And if he was not joking . . . where was earth and air and sky? But Lord Eden, curiously enough, sat quite unmoved and his archaic smile if anything deepened. He seemed, in his grim way, quite gratified. It was almost as if he had guessed what was coming. For the next moment the Arbiter went on.

"The principle is approved, that is, so far as that statement of it goes. Here again it is essential to understand such statements with a certain logical precision. If we are defining or describing a Craft or Trade, as it originally was and as it reasonably should be, that is the statement and we ask no other. The government of such a craft or trade rests of right with the master craftsmen and master traders. But the old order recognised other rights as well; and among them the right of private property. The craftsman worked and the trader traded with his own private property. In a case like the present, we must admit that even if the abstract right of management ought to belong to the workers, the materials do still in fact belong to the three men I have named."

"That's better," came the Archerian aside like a sort of explosive sigh; and old Seawood's head began to nod tremulously and doubtfully like that of a Chinese doll. But the hard head of Eden remained motionless, with its hard and confident smile.

"Broadly speaking," continued the expositor, "medieval ethics and jurisprudence affirmed the principle of private property with rather more elaboration and modification than most modern systems, till we come to the system called Socialism. It was generally admitted, for example, that a man might be actually or apparently in possession of property to which he had no right, because it had been acquired by methods condemned by Christian morals; as, for example, by usury. There were also laws against what was called forestalling and other methods for securing the whole of any particular material in the market. Outside such crimes, however, which were often severely punished by the pillory and even by the gallows, the personal possession of wealth was accepted as normal; and I cannot see any reasonable doubt that the personal wealth of these three persons is what is actually being employed in this industry. It is, I may remark, the greater part of their personal wealth. Two of them are the titular owners of large landed estates; but these have grown less and less profitable and are partly mortgaged. The wealth which makes them all wealthy men comes from the successful operations of the Coal-Tar Colour and Dye Company, in which they own most of the shares. Those operations are so successful that over the whole of this country, and practically over the whole of the industrialised world, the only type of artists' colours, crayons, pastels and so on that are sold and used come from the chemical works where these by-products are used. It only remains to ask by what form of commercial enterprise such a superiority has been achieved."

A curious change had come over the audience by this time. Most of them, lulled by the familiar phrases of the magnificent prospectus or commercial report, had nodded themselves almost into a slumber of agreement. But, what was much more remarkable, for the first time Lord Seawood was smiling; and Lord Eden was not.

"It so happens that an accident, or rather an adventure (one of the most honourable adventures of the new Comrades of this Realm) has revealed the facts about a typical test case. We actually have before us the history of a master Craftsman of the older sort; one who undoubtedly compounded his own pigments with his own hands and in accordance with his own taste and judgment; and who produced thereby a particular article which the best artists of his time regarded as unique and which later artists have tried in vain to replace. The article is not sold by the Coal-Tar Colour and Dye Company. The man is not in any way profited, or even employed, by the Coal-Tar Colour and Dye Company. What has happened to that Masterpiece? What has happened to that Master?

"From information laid before me by the gallant gentlemen I have mentioned, I am in a position to say what happened to them. The man was beaten down to a condition of beggary, was so much broken by despair as to be accused of insanity; and it is perfectly clear that the methods employed to drive him from his shop and his livelihood were the methods of which I have spoken; the buying up of materials before they could reach him, the cutting off of his supplies, the cutting down of his prices by a conspiracy to undersell and all the rest. I need not describe them more generally than I have done already; by saying that among our fathers the men who did these things could be pilloried or hanged. The men who have done these things to-day are the three shareholders of this Company; the three Masters of this Trade."

Then he named the three again formally and at length in a hard voice; but upon the name of Lord Seawood his voice seemed for an instant to break. He did not look at any face in the crowd.

"On this second point, therefore, the Court of Arbitrament decides that the private property employed in this business is not lawfully acquired; and cannot plead, as it normally would, the privilege of just possession. To sum up, it is decreed, first that the craft should be ruled by its fully enfranchised members, subject to any just claim of property; and second, that the claim of property made in this case is not just. We shall adjudge to the Guild—."

Old Seawood sprang up as if galvanised; and a simple sort of vainglory deeper than all Victorian vanities came gasping to the surface like a drowning thing. He forgot even the snobbish fear of snobbishness.

"I had imagined," he said, stammering with emphasis, "that this movement was to restore a true respect for Nobility. I am not aware that any of these workshop regulations applied to Nobility."

"Ah," said Herne in a low voice like an aside; "it has come at last."

It seemed as if he spoke for the first time in a human voice, and the effect was all the stranger because of the strange words in which he spoke again. "I am not a man," he said. "I am here only a mouthpiece to make clear the law; the law that knows nothing of men or women. But I ask you this before it is too late. Do not appeal to rank and title; do not make your claim as nobles and peers."

"Why not?" cried the boisterous Archer.

"Because about that also," replied Herne, who was deadly pale, "you have been fools enough to bid me find out the truth."

"Oh what the devil does all this mean," cried Archer in his agony.

"Damned if I know," replied the stolid Mr. Hanbury.

"Ah yes, I had forgotten," said the Arbiter in a vibrating voice, "you are not common craftsmen; you have not learnt to make paints; you have not dipped your hands in dyes. You have passed through loftier ordeals; you have watched your armour; you have won your spurs. But your crests and titles come to you from remote antiquity; and you have not forgotten the names you bear."

"Naturally we haven't forgotten our own names," said Eden testily.

"Strangely enough," said the Arbiter, "that is exactly what you have done."

There was another enigmatic silence, that seemed to be filled with the staring eyes of Archer and Hanbury; and then the voice of the Arbiter was heard once more; but it gave them a new sort of start, for it had taken on again the leaden weight of legal exposition.

"In the course of applying serious historical methods to these questions of heraldry and heredity, to which my attention had been directed, I have discovered a singular state of things. It would appear to be precisely the opposite state of things to that which prevails in the general popular impression. To put it briefly, I have found very few people possessing any pedigrees that would be recognised in the heraldic or feudal sense of medieval aristocracy. But those there are are quite poor and obscure persons, not even of the rank which we should call middle class. But in all the three counties coming under my consideration, the men who seem to have no claim whatever to noble birth are the noblemen."

He said it in a lifeless and impersonal tone, as if he were lecturing to students on the Hittites. But perhaps it was a little overdone; the words with which he went on were rather too dead and distinct. "Their estates have generally been obtained quite recently and often by methods of doubtful morality, let alone chivalry; by small solicitors and speculators employing various forms of mortgage, of foreclosing and the rest. In assuming the estates, these ingenious persons generally assumed not only the titles but the names of older families. The name of the Eden family is not Eames but Evans. The name of the Seawood family is not Severne but Smith."

And with that Murrel, who had been painfully watching the pale face and rigid attitude of the speaker, suddenly muttered an exclamation and understood.

All around there was a hubbub now altogether broken up and uncontrolled; but it was still not a concerted cry but a noise as of everybody talking at once; and high above it all the hard voice of the Arbiter could still be heard.

"The only two men in this section of the county who can claim the nobility, to which appeal has been made, are a man now driving an omnibus between here and the town of Milldyke and a small green-grocer in the same town. No other person can call himself *Armiger Generosus* except William Pond and George Carter."

"O Lor lumme, Old George!" cried Murrel, startled into throwing back his head with a shout of laughter. The laughter was infectious; it broke the strain and received them all into a roaring gulf; the true refuge of the English. Even Braintree, suddenly remembering the solid smile of Old George in the Green Dragon, could not control his amusement.

But, as Lord Seawood had accurately remarked, the Arbiter of the Court of Arbitrament was deficient in a sense of humour. He had never properly studied the back volumes of *Punch*.

"I do not know," he said, "why this man's lineage should be ridiculous. He has not, so far as I know, done anything to stain his coat of arms. He has not plotted with thieves and forestallers to ruin honest men. He has not taken money at usury and laid field to field by chicane, served the ruling families like a dog and then fed on the dying families like a vulture. But you— you who come here to grind the faces of the poor with your pomposities of property and gentility, and your grand final flourish of chivalry—what about you? You sit in another man's house; you bear another man's name; the blazon of another is on your shield; the crest of another is on your gate-posts; your whole story is the story of new men in old clothes, and you come here to me to plead against justice in the name of your noble ancestry."

The laughter had died down but the noise was even louder; there was now no disguise or hesitation about its nature; all the broken cries had come together; there was a new noise of the mob when it changes to the pack in cry. Archer and Hanbury and ten or twelve other men were standing up and shouting; and yet high above all the other noises the one voice still managed to soar unsilenced; the voice of the fanatic on the judgment seat.

"Let it be enrolled therefore for the third judgment and the answer to the third plea. These three men have claimed the mastery of a craft and the obedience of all their workmen; and their cause is judged. They make the claim of mastery and they are not masters. They make the claim of property and they are not the proprietors. They make the claim of nobility and they are not nobles. The three pleas are disallowed."

"Well," gasped Archer, "and how long is this to be allowed."

The noise had somewhat subsided as in weariness; and each man looked at the other as if really wondering what would come next.

Lord Eden had risen slowly and lazily to his feet, with his hands thrust in his trousers' pockets.

"Mention has been made," he said, "of somebody being charged with insanity. I am sorry that a painful scene of the sort should have occurred in this place; but isn't it time some humane person interfered?"

"Somebody send for a doctor," cried Archer in a crowing and excited voice.

"You appointed him yourself, Eden," said Murrel, looking sharply over his shoulder.

"We all make mistakes," said Eden soberly. "I'll never deny that the lunatic has the laugh of me. But it's a rather unpleasant scene for the ladies."

"Yes," said Braintree. "The ladies have an opportunity of admiring the grand finale of all your loyalty and your vows."

"If," said the Arbiter calmly, "it be an end of your loyalty to me, it is not an end of my loyalty to you; or to the law that I have sworn to expound. It is nothing for me to stand down from this seat; but it is everything to speak the truth while I stand here; and it is less than nothing whether you hate the truth or no."

"You were always a play-actor," called out Julian Archer angrily.

A strange smile passed over the pale face of the judge.

"There," he said, "you are singularly wrong. I was not always a play-actor; I was a very humble and humdrum person until you wanted me and made me a play-actor. But I found the play you acted was something much more real than the life you led. The rhymes we spoke in mummery on that lawn were so much

*193*

more like life than any life that you were living then. And how very like what we are living now." His voice did not change but seemed to roll on more rapidly, as if verse were more natural than prose.

"The evil kings sit easy on their thrones
Shame healed with habit; but what panic aloft
What wild white terror if a king were good
What staggering of the stars; what prodigy!
Men easily endure an unjust master
But a just master no men will endure
His nobles shall rise up, his knights betray him,
And he go forth, as I go forth, alone."

He stood down suddenly from the dais; and seemed to look taller for the fall.

"If I cease to be king or judge," he cried, "I shall still be a knight; though it be, as in the play, a knight-errant. But you will all be play-actors. Rogues and vagabonds, where did you steal your spurs?"

A spasm of something indescribable, like a twitch of involuntary humiliation, crossed the crabbed face of old Eden and he said testily, "I wish this scene would end."

It could only have one ending. Braintree was glowing with a dark exultation; but the men about him understood almost as little of the decision in their favour as the men in front; and in any case the latter were long past letting them intervene. And all that chivalric company answered with murmurs or sombre silence the appeal of their late leader for support. In answer to that call only two of them moved. From the outer skirts of the crowd Olive Ashley came slowly forward with the movement of a princess and, casting one darkly radiant look at the leader of the labourers, took her station by the judgment-seat. She did not dare to look at the white and stony face of the woman who was her friend. A moment after Douglas Murrel lounged to his feet with a singular grimace and went to stand on the opposite side of the Arbiter. They seemed like strange repetitions, and even parodies, of the lady and the squire who had held the shield and sword on either side of him, on the day when he was crowned.

Standing before his judgment-seat, the judge made one last ritual gesture like the rending of the robes of old. He rent from him the long dark robe of black and purple which was his judicial vestment, and letting it fall stood up in the complete suit of close fitting green which he had always worn since the dramatic day after the drama.

"I will go forth as a real outlaw," he said, "and as men do robbery on the highway I will do right on the highway; and it will be counted a wilder crime."

He turned his back on them and for a moment his wild glance seemed to stray hither and thither round the empty throne.

"Have you lost anything?" asked Murrel.

"I have lost everything," replied Herne and Murrel looked for a moment into his ghastly eyes.

Then he saw what he was seeking and picked up the great spear that had gone with his forester's garb and strode away towards the gateways of the park.

Murrel remained staring after him for a moment and then, as if propelled by a new impulse, ran after him down the path, hailing him by name. The man in green turned and looked at him with a pale and patient face.

"I say," said Murrel, "may I come with you?"

"Why should you come with me?" asked Herne, not rudely but rather as if he were addressing a stranger.

"Don't you know me?" asked Murrel. "Don't you know my name? Well, perhaps you don't know my real name."

"What do you mean?" asked Herne.

"My name," said the other, "is Sancho Panza."

Twenty minutes later there passed from the lands of Lord Seawood a *cortege* eminently calculated to show how the grotesque dogs the footprints of the fantastic. For Mr. Douglas Murrel had by no means the intention of losing his faculty of enjoying the absurd with a complete gravity. The last stage of that exit was worth seeing, though only a few of the strayed revellers or rioters were there to see it. As soon as Murrel had obtained the post of squire for which he petitioned, he vanished behind an adjoining outhouse and reappeared perched on the top of his celebrated hansom cab and driving its crazy cab-horse. Bowing from his perch with the deference of a polished servant, he appeared to be inviting his new master to get into the cab. But there was to be one more crescendo or bathos and medley of the sublime and the ridiculous; for with one last impulse of outrageous solemnity, the knight-errant in green sprang astride of the cab-horse and signalled with his lifted spear.

Like a revelation of lightning, in the instant before annihilating laughter came down like night, those who saw it saw a vision and a memory, bright and brittle as an instant's resurrection of the dead. The bones of the gaunt, high-featured face, the flame-like fork of the beard, the hollow and almost frantic eyes, were in a setting that startled with recognition; rigid above the saddle of Rosinante, tall and in tattered arms he lifted that vain lance that for three hundred years has taught us nothing but to laugh at the shaking of the spear. And behind him rose a vast yawning shadow like the very vision of that leviathan of laughter; the grotesque cab like the jaws of a derisive dragon pursuing him for ever, as the vast shadow of caricature pursues our desperate dignity and beauty, hanging above him for ever threatening like the wave of the world; and over all, the lesser and lighter human spirit, not unkindly, looking down on all that is most high.

And yet, though that towering and toppling appendage of absurdity was dragged behind him like an overwhelming load, for that instant of time it was erased and forgotten, in the force and appalling passion of his face.

Chapter 18

# The Secret of Seawood

It had been a day of amazement for many, in which their prophet who had come to bless had remained to curse and had at last gone away cursing. But of all those who were shocked at the judgment which had condemned them, perhaps not one had been more amazed than the man whom the judgment had justified. John Braintree stood staring throughout the whole process by which what seemed to him like laws of the Stone Age were dug up like stone hatchets and offered to him as weapons. Whatever else he had expected, whether feudal vindictiveness or chivalrous magnanimity, he had never dreamed of hearing his own cause supported as a piece of pure medievalism. So far as he could make out, he himself was much the most medieval person present. It made him feel very uncomfortable.

Then, as he stood rolling his eyes round the dissolution of that queer transformation scene, they alit on a special object; he stiffened, pulled himself together, gave a short laugh and strode across to where Olive was standing beside the empty throne. He put his hands on her shoulders and said: "It seems dear we are reconciled after all."

She looked at him without moving and with a slow smile. "It is dreadful," she said, "to think I should be glad of the quarrel that makes the—the reconciliation."

"You will forgive me for feeling only the gladness and not the dreadfulness," he answered. "People must be on my side if they are on his side—I mean if they are really on his side, like you."

"I shall not find it so very difficult to be on your side," she said. "I found it very difficult not to be. Especially when it was the losing side."

"We shall jolly well see now," he said, "whether it won't be the winning side. This has put heart into all my people, I can tell you. I feel as if I'd renewed my youth like the eagle's; only it isn't Mr. Herne that has done that."

She looked slightly embarrassed and then said doubtfully, "I suppose somebody else will inherit the organisation.

"Organisation be blowed," said Braintree. "You don't suppose we were beaten by an organisation, do you? We were beaten by a man and by men who were ready to follow him. Do you think I care anything about the men who were ready to desert him? I said I wasn't afraid of fourteenth century bows and battle-axes; I wasn't; and I'm certainly not afraid of a fourteenth century battle-axe brandished by old Seawood. Oh yes, I suppose they'll go on with the theatricals. We shall have the pleasure of hearing all about Sir Julian Archer, the brilliant Lord High Arbiter and universally popular King-at-Arms. But don't you give us credit for being able to go smash through all that sort of thing like coloured paper? The soul is gone out of it; the soul is riding down the road a mile away."

"Yes, I think you are right," she said after a pause, "and not only because Michael Herne has been something like a great man. It's more than that. Their pride has gone out of them; their youth and their innocence have gone out of them. They have heard the truth and they know it is true. And there's one of them about whom I am very unhappy."

He looked at her earnestly and said, "Well, of course I'm sorry for a lot of them in a way; but do you mean—"

"I mean Rosamund," she answered lowering her voice. "I think it's the most grim and grand and dreadful thing that ever happened to anybody; much worse than anything that ever happened to us."

"I'm not sure I understand," he said.

"Of course you don't," she replied.

198

He looked at her in a puzzled way; and she broke out with a kind of passion.

"Of course you don't understand! I know it has been hard for you; and it has been hard enough for me. But we haven't gone through what they have gone through—what *she* is going through. We parted because each of us believed the other was attacking something good; but we didn't, thank God, ever have to attack each other. You didn't have to stand up and abuse my father; and I didn't have to sit silent and hear it. It wasn't *you* who were directly individually cursing me and mine; it wasn't you, of all men, whom I had to hear saying hateful things about my own home. I don't know what I should have done. I think I should have simply died. What do you suppose she is doing?"

"I'm awfully sorry," he answered, "but I really do not know exactly what you are talking about. Who is *she?* Do you mean Rosamund Severne?"

"Of course I mean Rosamund Severne," she cried angrily, "and he would not even leave her name. How do you suppose I should have liked that? What are you staring at? Do you really mean that you don't know that Rosamund and Michael Herne are in love with each other?"

"I don't seem to know much," he said, "but if that's true of course I see what you mean."

"I must go to see her," said Olive, "and yet I hardly know even how to do that."

She crossed the now deserted garden towards the house; and as she did so, something made her stand and gaze for a moment at the monument that stood on the lawn; the broken image standing on the dragon. And as she looked at it strange and new things came into her soul and her eyes. In the clear exalted intensity of her happiness and unhappiness, she seemed to be seeing it for the first time.

Then she looked about her, as if almost scared of the stillness, the abrupt and utter stillness that had succeeded to all the hubbub of that horrible afternoon. The great lawn, enclosed on three sides by the front and two wings of the Abbey buildings, had been not an hour ago tossing with angry crowds and now it was as empty as the Courts of a city of the dead. Evening was wheeling towards darkness and the round moon rose and brightened steadily until the faint shadows of the new wan light began to change on the gargoyles and Gothic ornaments as they lost the last shadow of the sun. And as the face of all that ancient building flickered and changed under the changing light, it seemed to come more fully into the foreground of her mind and take on a meaning she had never understood before; though she should have been the first, she might have fancied, to understand it from the beginning. That pointed and tapering tracery, of which she had talked lightly to Monkey long ago, the dark glass of the windows, dense with colours that could only be discovered from within—suddenly told her something; a paradox. Inside there was light and outside there was only lead. But who was really inside? . . . Those three walls with all their hooded windows, seemed to be watching; seemed to have watched from the beginning of all their follies and to be still watching—and waiting.

Suddenly and silently, as with a sort of soft shock, she came upon Rosamund herself standing in the great gateway. She did not need to look at that perfect mask of tragedy; she avoided looking at it; but she caught her friend by the arm and said incoherently: "Oh I do not know what to say to you . . . and I have so much to say."

There was no answer and she broke forth again, "It's a shame that it should happen to you, who have never been anything but good to all the world. It's a shame that anybody should tell such tales."

Then Rosamund Severne said in a dreadful dead voice; "He always tells the truth."

"I think you are the noblest woman in the world," said Olive.

"Only the most unlucky," said the other. "It is nobody's fault. It's as if there were a curse on this place."

And in that instant of time Olive received a revelation like a blinding light; and understood her own trembling in the shadow of those watching walls.

"Rosamund, there is a curse on the place," she said. "There's a curse because there is a blessing. But it's nothing to do with anything we have ever talked about. It has nothing to do with anything that man said. It's not a curse on your name or anybody else's name, whatever your name is or whether it's old or new. The curse is in the name of this house."

"The name of this house," repeated the other in a dull voice.

"You've seen it at the top of your note-paper a thousand times and taken it for granted; and you have never seen that *that* is the falsehood. It doesn't matter whether your father's position is false or not: it doesn't matter whether it's old or new. This place doesn't belong to the old families any more than the new families. It belongs to God."

Rosamund seemed to stiffen suddenly like a literal statue and yet one could swear the statue had ears to hear.

Olive burst out again with her broken soliloquy; "Why have all our toppling fancies about kings and knights come with a crash; why is all our Round Table ruined? Because we never began at the beginning. Because we never went back to the Thing itself. The Thing that produced everything else; the love of the Thing where it really lives. On this spot long ago two hundred men lived and loved It."

She stopped and seemed to realise that her words were tumbling out in a tail foremost fashion; and that she was herself, hardly setting a good example of beginning at the beginning. She made a desperate effort at clarity.

"Don't you see—the modern people may be right to be modern; there may be people who ask for nothing better than banks and brokers; there may be people who think Milldyke a nice place. Your father and his friends may have been right in their way; I'm sure they weren't so wrong as they looked when he was abusing them . . . it was hateful, and anyhow he had no business to spring it on you like that, without telling you beforehand."

The statue spoke again; it seemed as if it never spoke except to utter one sort of stony defence.

"He did tell me beforehand. And I think that was more terrible."

"Let me say what I am trying to say," said Olive pathetically. "I feel as if it didn't belong to me, and I must give it away. There may be people to whom it's senseless to talk about a flower of chivalry; it sounds like a blossom of butchery. But *if* we want the flower of chivalry, we must go right away back to the root of chivalry. We must go back if we find it in a thorny place people call theology. We must think differently about death and free will and loneliness and the last appeal. It's just the same with the popular things we can turn into fashionable things; folk-dances and pageants and calling everything a Guild. Our fathers did these things by the thousand; quite common people; not cranks. We are always asking how they did it. What we've got to ask is why they did it. . . . Rosamund, *this* is why they did it. Something lived here. Something they loved. Some of them loved it so much. . . . Oh don't you and I know what is the only test? They wanted to be alone with it."

The statue moved ever so faintly as if turning away; and Olive clutched the arm again in a sort of remorse.

"You must think me mad to be talking so when you suffer; but it's as if I were bursting with news—with something bigger than all the universe of sorrow. Rosamund, there really is joy. Not rejoicing but joy; not rejoicing at this or that; but the thing itself, we only see reflected in mirrors—which sometimes break. And it lived here. That's why they didn't want anything else; not even what we want; not even the best we know. . . . And that's what's gone—the good itself. Now we have only evils to hate, and thank God we hate them."

She pointed suddenly at the monument in the middle of which the wrinkles and convolutions were traced elaborately by the silver-point of the moon-light, like the phosphorescence that outlines some goggling sea-monster.

"We have only the dragon left. A hundred times I've looked at that dragon and hated it and never understood it. Upright and high above that horror stood St. Michael or St. Margaret, subduing and conquering it; but it is the conqueror that has vanished. We have no notion of what it would be really like; we haven't tried to imagine what image really stood there. We danced round it and thought of everything else except that. There burned in this court a great bonfire of visionary passion which in the spirit could be seen for miles and men lived in the warmth of it; the positive passion and possession, the thing worth having in itself. But now the very best of them are negative; attacking the absence of it in the world. They fight for truth where it isn't. They fight for honour where it isn't. They are a thousand times right; but it ends in truth and honour fighting each other, as poor Jack and Michael fought. We haven't any sense or any place where these virtues are happy, where these virtues are simply themselves. I love Jack and Jack loves justice; but he loves justice where it isn't. There ought to be a way of loving it where it is."

"And where is that, I wonder?" said Rosamund in a low voice.

"How should we know," cried Olive, "who have driven away the men who knew?"

A deep chasm of silence opened between them; and at last Rosamund said in her simple way; "I am very stupid. I shall have to try to think about what you mean. I'm sure you won't mind if we don't talk any more now."

Olive went back slowly across the green courts and out of the shadow of the grey walls and found John Braintree waiting for her. They went away together, but were rather silent for the first part of the walk; then Olive said suddenly; "What a strange story all this is . . . I mean ever since I started poor Monkey running after red paint. What a rage I was in with you and your red tie; and yet in a queer sort of way it turns out to have been the same sort of red. I didn't know it and you didn't know it; and yet it was you who were working back blindly for the colour that I was after, like a child after a sunset cloud. It was you who were really trying to avenge my father's friend."

"I should have tried to get him his rights, I hope," replied Braintree.

"Oh you are always so rabid about rights," she said laughing with a faint impatience. "And poor Rosamund . . . you must admit you do talk a terrible lot about rights. Are you quite sure about them?"

"I hope to do a terrible lot about them before I've done," replied the implacable politician.

"But do you," she asked, "think anybody has really a right to be so happy?"

He laughed shortly and they went out along the grey road toward Milldyke.

# Chapter 19

# The Return of Don Quixote

Someday perhaps the story will be told of the adventures of the new Don Quixote and the new Sancho Panza, as they wandered about the winding roads of England. From the standpoint of the cold and satiric populace the story was rather that of the progress of the hansom cab, through scenes where hansom cabs very rarely figure. It was perhaps an unprecedented progress through forest glades and across desolate uplands; and as a method of travel chosen by a knight and his squire new even in the annals of chivalry. But some riotously romantic chronicler may yet give some account of how they attempted in various ways to use the vehicle for the defence and consolation of the oppressed. Of how they gave lifts to tramps and rides to children; of how they turned the cab into a coffee stall at Reading and into a tent on Salisbury Plain. Of how the cab figured as a bathing-machine in the dreadful affair at Worthing. Of how it was regarded by simple Calvinists of the Border as a perambulating pulpit, with a place below for the Precentor to sing and a place above for the minister to preach, which Mr. Douglas Murrel proceeded to do with great unction and edification. Of how Mr. Douglas Murrel organised a series of historical lectures by Mr. Herne from the top of the cab, and seconded them with comments and explanations, making the lecturing tour quite a financial success by methods perhaps not invariably respectful to the lecturer. But though there may have been moments when the squire fell short of a complete seriousness, it is probable on the whole that they did a great deal of good. They got into trouble with the police, in itself almost a sign of sanctity; they fought a number of people in private life, but mostly people who badly wanted fighting. And Herne at least was completely convinced of the serious social utility of this line of attack. A sadder and conceivably even a wiser man, he had many long talks with his friend, in which he never ceased to elaborate the Defence of Don Quixote and the necessity of his real return. One was especially memorable: which took place as they sat under a hedge in the high lanes of Sussex.

"They say I am behind the times," said Herne, "and living in the days that Don Quixote dreamed of. They seemed to forget that they themselves are at least three hundred years behind the times and living in the days when Cervantes dreamed of Don Quixote. They are still living in the Renaissance; in what Cervantes naturally regarded as the New Birth. But I say that a baby that is three hundred years old is already getting on in life. It is time he was born again."

"Is he to be born again," asked Murrel, "as a medieval knight-errant?"

"Why not?" asked the other, "if the Renaissance man was born again as an Ancient Greek? Cervantes thought that Romance was dying and that Reason might reasonably take its place. But I say that in our time Reason is dying, in that sense; and it is old age is really less respectable than the old romance. We want to recur to the more simple and direct attack. What we want now is somebody who does believe in tilting at giants."

"And who succeeds in tilting at windmills," answered Murrel.

"Have you ever reflected," said his friend, "what a good thing it would have been if he had smashed the windmills? From what I know now of medieval history, I should say his only mistake was in tilting at the mills instead of the millers. The miller was the middleman of the middle ages. He was the beginning of all the middlemen of the modern ages. His mills were the beginning of all the mills and manufactures that have darkened and degraded modern life. So that even Cervantes, in a way, chose an example against himself. And it's more so with the other examples. Don Quixote set free a lot of captives who were only convicts. Nowadays it's mostly those who have been beggared who are jailed and those who have robbed them who are free. I'm not sure the mistake would be quite so mistaken."

"Don't you think," asked Murrel, "that modern things are too complicated to be dealt with in such a simple way?"

"I think," replied Herne, "that modern things are too complicated to be dealt with except in a simple way."

He rose from his feet and strode to and fro on the road with all the dreamy energy of his prototype. He seemed trying to tear his real meaning out of himself.

"Don't you see," he cried, "that is the moral of the whole thing. All your machinery has become so inhuman that it has become natural. In becoming a second nature, it has become as remote and indifferent and cruel as nature. The Knight is once more riding in the forest. Only he is lost in the wheels instead of in the woods. You have made your dead system on so large a scale that you do not yourselves know how or where it will hit. That's the paradox! Things have grown incalculable by being calculated. You have tied men to tools so gigantic that they do not know on whom the strokes descend. You have justified the nightmare of Don Quixote. The mills really *are* giants."

"Is there any method in that case," demanded the other.

"Yes; and you found it," replied Herne. "You did not bother about systems, when you saw a mad doctor was madder than the madman. It is you who lead and I who follow. You are not Sancho Panza. You are the other."

He stretched out his hand with something of the old gesture.

"What I said on the judgment-seat I say again by the road-side. You are the only one of them born again. You are the knight that has returned."

Douglas Murrel was abruptly and horribly abashed.

That compliment was perhaps the only thing that could have stung him into speech upon certain matters; for under all this tomfoolery he had something more than the reticence of his breed. As it was, he looked uncomfortable and said: "Look here, you mustn't give me credit like that. I'm not on as Galahad in this scene. I hope I'd have done my best for the old Honkey; but I did like that girl; I liked her rather a lot."

"Did you tell her so?" asked Herne in his obvious manner.

"I couldn't very well," replied the other, "just when she was under sort of an obligation to me."

"My dear Murrel," cried Herne with impulsive simplicity, "this is quite quixotic!"

Murrel sprang to his feet and sent up a single shout of laughter.

"You have made the best joke in three hundred years," he said.

"I don't see it," said Herne thoughtfully. "Is it generally considered possible to make a joke and not to see it? But in the matter of what you said, don't you think there might be a statute of limitations allowing you a fresh start? Would you like to go down—down to the west again?"

Murrel's brow seemed knotted with a new embarrassment. "The truth is I rather avoided the neighbourhood—and the subject. I thought that you—"

"I know what you mean," said Herne. "For a long time I could hardly look out of a window facing that way. I wanted to turn my back on the west wind; and the sunsets burned me like red-hot irons. But a man gets calmer as the years go by, even if he doesn't get more cheerful. I don't think I could go to the house itself; but I would really be glad to hear the news about—anybody."

"Oh if we go there," said Murrel cheerfully, "I'll undertake to go in and enquire."

"Do you mean," asked Herne almost timidly, "go into—Seawood Abbey?"

"Yes," answered Murrel shortly. "I daresay we're in the same boat. I might find the other house a little harder."

They completed the rest of their programme by a tacit, not to say taciturn agreement; and so it fell out that, before they had exchanged many more words, they had actually come within sight of all that for so long they had not seen and had avoided seeing; the evening sun on the high lawns of Seawood and the steep Gothic roofs among the trees.

Certainly they needed no words of explanation when Michael Herne halted and looked across at his friend, as if bidding him go on. Murrel nodded and went quickly with his light and agile step up the steep woodland path and over the stile and dropped into the avenue leading up to the main gateway. The gardens seemed much as they were of old, but rather neater and in some nameless fashion quieter; but the great gate, that had always stood open, was shut.

Monkey was no mystic; but this fact affected him with a mournful thrill that had in it something of mysticism. That incongruous element increased upon him in some indescribable subconscious way as he approached the great doors and, for the first time in his life, knocked on them and rang a great iron bell. He felt rather as if he were in a dream; and yet as if he were near to some more strange awakening. But queer as were his unformed anticipations, they were not so queer as what he found.

About half an hour afterwards he came out of the great doorway, which was closed after him, climbed the stile and came quietly down the lane to his friend; but even while he was still approaching, his friend felt that there was something odd about his quietude. He sat down on the bank and ruminated for a moment; then he said: "An extraordinary thing has happened to Seawood Abbey. It has not been exactly burned to the ground, because somehow it seems to be still there, and looking rather more well-preserved than before. It has not been, in any material or meteorological sense struck by lightning from heaven. And yet I am not sure . . . anyhow a most stunning and crashing catastrophe has fallen on that Abbey."

"What do you mean? What has happened to the Abbey?"

"It has become an Abbey," said Murrel gravely.

"What do you mean?" cried the other, leaning forward with sudden eagerness.

"I mean what I say. It has become an Abbey. I have just been talking to the Abbot. He told me a good deal of the news, in spite of his monastic seclusion; for he knows a number of our old friends."

"You mean it is a monastery. What news did he give you?"

"He was full of Society Snippets," said Murrel in his melancholy voice. "It all began with Lord Seawood dying about a year ago. The property went to his—his heiress, who it seems has 'gone over' as the saying is. She's become a Catholic; and a very extraordinary sort of Catholic too. She has given up all this vast property to my friend the Abbot and his merry men; and gone down to work as a nurse in some Catholic settlement or other down in the Docks; Limehouse, I think, where Chinamen strangle their daughters according to the Twelve Immortal Principles."

The pale librarian had sprung up with all the energy of knight-errantry; but his look was turned away from the towers of Seawood.

"I hardly understand it yet," he said, "but it is all different. It is difficult but it is different. It is difficult because it seems strange to . . ."

"It seems strange," asserted Murrel, "to go down to Limehouse and ask a Chinese strangler for The Honourable Rosamund Severne. But I ought to tell you on the authority of the Abbot, that she declares that her name is not Rosamund Severne. I understand you may find her if you enquire for Miss Smith."

And at that once more did lunacy strike the librarian of Seawood like lightning out of heaven; and leaping over a hedge he went racing eastwards towards a pinewood that lay across his path, which might be presumed to be on the outskirts of Limehouse and offer opportunities for enquiring after Miss Smith.

It was rather more than three months later that the lunatics' progress came to its appointed end, and this story with it. Its pace had changed from capering to something more like plodding and to threading the labyrinths of the lowest quarters of Limehouse. But it ended one night when a sort of green fog of dusk hung like the fumes of some drug of witchcraft, as he turned down a crack of narrow street, at the corner of which hung a painted paper lantern. A little further down the dim defile glowed another lantern; which looked less Chinese; and when he came close to it he saw it was a leaden cage fitted with large fragments of coloured glass, the rude outline showing a figure of St. Francis with a burning red angel behind him. Somehow this childish transparency seemed like a password and a signal of all that he had once sought to do on a great scale or Olive Ashley on a small one; and yet with some secret and vivid difference; that the lamp was lit from within.

So much was that great thirst for colour, which had filled his life, fed as from a goblet of flame, by that trivial sign and in this sordid place, that it scarcely surprised him to find himself in her presence, who stood crowned in his dreams as in the melodrama and the tragedy of other days. A straight dark dress hung on her from neck to heel, but it was of a normal pattern; and her red hair still looked like a crown.

With that queer awkward promptitude, that belonged to him alone, he said his simplest thought in plain words, "You are a nurse and not a nun."

She smiled. "You don't know much about nuns if you think that is the natural ending of a story—a story like ours. Believe me, there's nothing in that sentimental notion that being a nun is a second best."

"Do you really mean," he said and then stopped.

"I mean," she said, "that I never quite left off thinking that I might have the luck to be the second best. I suppose it's the sort of thing that has been said a good many times. . . . I think I have always thought you would find me."

After a momentary pause she went on: "We need not re-member about that old quarrel; I think it was always something much better and much worse than a quarrel. My father was less to blame than you thought him; more to blame than I thought him; but it is neither you nor I that are to judge. But it was not he who did the real wrong of which all these wrongs have sprung."

"I know what you mean," he replied. "I had rather begun to think so myself, the more I read of history. But in all that history there is nothing so noble as you and what you have done. You are the greatest of historical characters; and the learned may come to call you a legend."

"It was Olive who understood it first," she said gravely. "She is so much quicker than I am and saw it all in a flash; a flash of moonlight, as she said. I could only go away and think things out slowly and stupidly by myself; but I got there at last."

"Do you mean," asked Michael slowly, "that Olive Ashley also has—got there?"

"Yes," she replied, "and the odd thing is that John Braintree doesn't seem to mind a bit. At least a good many people would think it odd; they are married now and they seem to agree about almost everything. I wonder how much there really was for good people to disagree about in those quarrelsome old times."

"I know," he answered. "Everybody seems to be married. And it has made me feel pretty lost and lonely in the last month or so."

"Even Monkey is married, I hear," she said. "It seems like the end of the world. But perhaps its the beginning of the world. One thing you may be sure of, though lots of people would laugh at it. Whenever Monks come back, marriages will come back."

"He went back to that seaside town and married Dr. Hendry's daughter," explained Michael Herne rather vaguely. "We parted by a sort of silent consent at Seawood Abbey and he went west and I east. I had to go and look for you alone: and I was very much alone."

"You say 'was,'" she said with a smile; and they suddenly moved towards each other and met as they had met in the garden long ago—in a silence full of many things; a silence which he broke by saying suddenly, in his abrupt and awkward way: "I suppose I am a heretic."

"We will see about all that," she said with a serene magnificence.

Herne's thoughts abruptly and absently went back to the old tangled talk between himself and Archer about the Albigensian heresy and what need to follow conversion from it; he stood a moment with his wits wool gathering. Then in that narrow street of the coloured lantern a new and astonishing thing happened; something that never had happened in all the topsy turvey happenings of his historical career. Michael Herne laughed. For the first time in his life he seriously saw a joke and deliberately made it. It is typical of him that his one joke was one which nobody else could see, or would probably ever understand.

"I say . . . *iit in matrimonium.*"

Lightning Source UK Ltd.
Milton Keynes UK
UKHW011803311019
352615UK00001B/55/P